Penguin Book 2777
The Watchers on the Shore

Stan Barstow, the only son of a coal-miner, was
born in 1928 in the West Riding of Yorkshire.
He was educated at the local council school and
Ossett Grammar School, and began his working
life in the drawing office of a local engineering
firm. It was the success of *A Kind of Loving*, his
first published novel, which was a Book Society
Choice in 1960 and later filmed, that allowed him
to become a full-time writer in 1962. His later
books are a collection of short stories, *The
Desperadoes* (1961), and the novels *Ask Me
Tomorrow* (1962), and *Joby* (1964). All four books
are now available in Penguins. *The Watchers on
the Shore* is a sequel to *A Kind of Loving*.

Stan Barstow, who is married and has a son and
a daughter, has also written for radio, television
and the theatre.

D1514310

Stan Barstow

The Watchers on the Shore

Penguin Books

Penguin Books Ltd, Harmondsworth,
Middlesex, England
Penguin Books Australia Ltd, Ringwood,
Victoria, Australia

First published by Michael Joseph 1966
Published in Penguin Books 1968
Copyright © Stan Barstow, 1966

Made and printed in Great Britain by
Cox & Wyman Ltd
London, Reading and Fakenham
Set in Monotype Times

For Alfred Bradley

Nobody heard him, the dead man,
But still he lay moaning:
I was much further out than you thought
And not waving but drowning.

Poor chap, he always loved larking
And now he's dead
It must have been too cold for him his heart
    gave way,
They said.

Oh, no no no, it was too cold always
(Still the dead one lay moaning)
I was much too far out all my life
And not waving but drowning.

    Stevie Smith
    Not Waving but Drowning
    (by permission of André Deutsch Ltd)

Part One

Lying back in the chair I swing young Bobby off my knee and high over my head, holding him at the end of my stiff arms, my hands round his deep little chest and shaking him. He giggles with helpless delight and a great blob of dribble rolls out of his wet open mouth and falls into my left eye.

'Aagh, you mucky little tyke!' I lower him on to my lap again and fish my hanky out. 'You've spit in me face. What d'you mean by that, eh? Come on, speak up. What d'you mean by that?'

'You'll frighten the life out of him, talking to him like that,' Ingrid says from her chair across the room, and my sister Chris, on her knees warming nightclothes at the electric fire, turns her head and laughs. 'No, I don't think he will.'

''Course I won't. He knows me, don't you, Bobby? Don't you, old lad?'

And he's already up again, feet kneading into my thighs, his wide-open eyes – Chris's eyes *and* my eyes, people say – close on my face.

'Do dat 'gen. Do dat 'gen. Do dat 'gen.'

'Do it again? All right, but no more spitting. Understand? Here we go, then.'

Up he goes again, giggling like before, happy to go on as long as I'm willing, nearly everything he does under command, no decisions, no worries, switching from happy to sad, sad to happy, laughter to tears and back again, life just a moment – now. A kid with good parents, and a future, as long as he doesn't get vaporized before he has a chance to taste it. And I wonder if he'll grow up happy and content like his dad or make a mess of things, take a wrong turning somewhere, like his mixed-up, half-miserable Uncle Vic.

'I know who'll tire of that first,' Chris says.

'So do I. I'm puffed. I'm puffed, young Bob. Enough! Down you come. I think I'll have a piece of Bobby's bottom for me supper.'

He squeals and wriggles in my hands and as I reckon to take a bite out of his firm little behind I catch Ingrid, her head lifted from the woman's magazine on her knee, with her eyes on the two of us, her mind somewhere deep in thought. She comes out of it as she notices me looking at her, and speaks to Chris.

'Aren't you scared of him catching cold, playing about with nothing on?'

'No, it's warm enough in here. Anyway, he can have his pyjamas on now.'

She gets up and comes over with them. 'Want me to take him?'

'No,' I say, 'I'll put 'em on for him.'

'You are a glutton for punishment.'

'I don't mind as long as he doesn't pee on me,' I say, and Ingrid says 'Vic!' in that shocked prissy voice she uses when she thinks I'm being vulgar.

But Chris just laughs. 'Oh, he'll warn you if he wants to do it.'

'C'mon then, lad; let's have you into these.'

I get him into his nightclothes, pale-blue winceyette stuff with little nursery-rhyme characters parading over it, and he plucks at his jacket with his podgy fingers.

'Pajamas.'

'Yes, pyjamas. And very smart they are, too. I wish I'd a pair like 'em.'

'And a sight you'd look,' Ingrid says, smiling.

'Make a change from Marks and Spencer's.'

'I'll run you up a pair on the machine,' Chris offers.

'Aye, you do that. Only I'll have dancing girls instead of Little Jack Horner.'

'You're frisky enough without having dancing girls on your pyjamas,' Ingrid says, and I look at Bobby, pretending to be shocked.

'Did you hear that, young Bobby? Your Auntie Ingrid's telling tales out of school.'

'I think it's time he was going down,' Chris says. 'I hope you haven't got him too excited to sleep.'

'He'll go. Won't you, Bobby lad? Robert Victor Lester, Esquire, dead-horse and donkey buyer, will now retire to his room.'

Ingrid puts her magazine aside and swings her legs out from under her.

'Can I take him?'

'You can see if he'll go for you,' Chris says.

Ingrid holds out her arms to Bobby. 'Can I take you to bed, Bobby?'

He pulls himself up on my knee straight away.

'Oh, you're deserting your Uncle Vic now, are you? Give us a kiss, then, before you go.'

He turns round and makes a great business of giving me a sloppy kiss on the face before going to Ingrid, who stands with him in her arms, Chris and I watching and probably pretty much the same thing going through both our minds. Our first, the reason we got married, would have been older than Bobby if Ingrid hadn't fallen downstairs and brought on a miscarriage at six months. The second, started on a night when we weren't bothering to take care, would have been born just about now, except it didn't last even as long as the first and there was no accident to cause the trouble. We hardly knew Ingrid was pregnant before it was all over and the doctor was saying perhaps she ought to see a specialist at the infirmary. *He* said there was no real reason why she shouldn't carry a baby the full term, but the next time it happened she'd have to be on her guard from the beginning and take care not to do anything at all strenuous. Which made everybody sorry for Ingrid and brought another touch of frost into my cold war with Mrs Rothwell; though why me giving Ingrid the first baby before we were married should make me responsible for everything that's happened since is something only her mind can work out. And I've stopped trying to reason with it.

'Night night to everybody, then,' Ingrid says and Bobby, tiredness come over him all of a sudden, flops with his head against her shoulder and sucks sleepily at his thumb.

'Everything's ready, Ingrid,' Chris says. 'You can pop him straight in.'

For a minute it looks as though he's going; then he decides that things aren't as they should be and at the door to the bedroom he twists round in Ingrid's arms and looks for Chris.

'Mummy come.'

Chris smiles. 'Hard lines. I shall have to do it after all.'

She goes and takes him from Ingrid and carries him into the other room. Ingrid comes back and sits down again and reaches for her magazine without saying anything to me. We haven't a lot of small talk and what we have she usually starts. I light a fag and as Chris comes out of the bedroom saying, 'There, let's hope we hear no more from him for a while,' the door from the hall opens and David comes in carrying bottles from the off-licence in a leather shopping bag.

'It's taken you a long time, David,' Chris says.

'I was just wondering if you'd stopped off for a crafty pint,' I say.

'You know I wouldn't have done that without you, Vic,' he says.

'I should hope not.'

David takes his raincoat off and hangs it up then comes back in and takes half a dozen pint bottles of pale ale and a bottle of gin out of the bag and puts them on the sideboard.

'You should have let me come with you and pay for some of that,' I say to him.

'Nonsense. We'd run right out anyway, and I like to have a drop in the house . . . Would you like a drink now or later?'

'Later,' I tell him. 'It's a bit early yet.'

'As a matter of fact,' David says, 'I've been having a short discussion about the state of the world with my esteemed colleague J. C. Fothergill, Senior History and Lower School Maths.'

'Where was he?' Chris asks and David smiles.

'In the off-licence, buying a drop of the stuff that cheers.'

'But he doesn't live round here, does he?'

'No, he doesn't. But J.C. is a man with a devious mind and also a pillar of his local chapel. If he wants to buy his booze where he isn't known then presumably he has his reasons. He seemed a bit taken aback when I walked in and caught him stuffing the whisky and gin into his bag. Now I suppose he'll be wondering just when I'll let it drop in the staff room that I've seen him stocking up for the cold nights.'

'But it doesn't matter, does it?' Chris says.

'Oh no. Only in his own mind.'

'He always was a two-faced old hypocrite, Farthingale,' I say. 'I remember him of old.'

David gives me a little smile.

'He treated me to an analysis of Mr Khrushchev's motives in the Cuban affair which I thought was very subtle. The only thing is there's no foundation for believing it's true. By the way, let's not miss the News. We didn't hear it at six.'

'I can't bear to listen to it,' Ingrid says. 'It's been nothing but news all week and all the regular programmes either changed or pushed back.'

She's talking about television and I can't resist saying, 'She's thinking of writing to President Kennedy to tell him she nearly missed "Tell your Partners Quiz" because of him messing about with his blockade.'

'Oh, shut up, sarcy,' Ingrid says.

'I thought we might be over the hump,' David says, 'but I'm worried now that the Americans will go the whole hog and invade.'

Just for a second I feel fear squeezing my heart like a clammy hand, as I did earlier in the week when it all blew up, and this puts an extra savage edge to my voice when Ingrid says:

'I don't see why they can't settle it between them. What's it got to do with us?'

I turn on her and it's all there, the fear, the irritation at her stupidity and knowing I could laugh it off if I wasn't married to her.

'Don't you know anything about *any*thing?'

'I don't see what you've got to be clever about,' she says. 'I'm sure other people think like me. Mother was saying the other day –'

'Yes,' I butt in, 'tell us what she said. Let's hear what bloody world-shaking pronouncement *she's* been coming out with.'

Ingrid blushes scarlet and looks away and I see David shoot a quick glance at Chris and both of them start to act as though they haven't noticed anything amiss.

The radio warms up and the newsreader's voice comes through. It's better news. The Russians have offered to bargain: the Cuban bases for the American ones in Turkey.

'Well, that's an improvement,' David says. 'And I'm having a drink on the strength of it. Join me, Vic?'

I tell him all right, I'll have a glass of beer now.

'Ingrid?'

'Oh, I don't know. Have you got any orange squash?'

'I think so. Sure you wouldn't like a drop of gin to liven it up?'

'No, just squash, please.'

He gives Ingrid her squash, me my beer, passes a gin and tonic to Chris, then lifts his own glass of pale ale.

'Well, here's to the future. Now that it looks as if there might be one after all.'

Which sinks me in a bit more gloom, as talking about the future always does. I'm already a bit irritated with myself for snapping at Ingrid like I did. A bit of peevish bickering is nothing new to us, but doing it when we're by ourselves is one thing and it's only lately I've started letting it show through when other people are there. And I don't like it, because being stuck with something you don't like is bad enough without showing it off to everybody. It hurts the pride. Especially when I'm with Chris and David, or thinking about them. They never bicker. Not when anybody's there and I'm sure not when they're on their own either. You can tell. You can tell from the way one of them might now and again get a bit impatient and the other turn it away with a soft answer instead of feeling the need to strike back. The thing that's missing from their marriage is resentment and it's a thing every marriage is better off without. With some couples it's as though one or the other is always trying to show what he's got to put up with; what sacrifices he's making in being married at all. And it's all wrong, because resentment in a marriage is like a drop of water falling all the time on a stone, weakening and weakening it till some outside blow can crack it apart. Then you either leave it in pieces or try a cement job. And one thing Chris and David will never need is a cement job, because they seem happier now, if anything, than they did when they got married nearly five years ago.

'Has Chris said anything about the job I'm after?' David says as he settles in his chair.

'I didn't know you wanted anybody to know about it yet,' Chris says.

'It's all right in the family,' David says. 'I've applied for a headmastership at a secondary modern school in Leicestershire,' he tells us. 'I had a letter this week to say I'm on a short list.'

'So you might be moving away?'

'If it comes off, yes. I don't see much prospect of early advancement where I am and this could be a move in the right direction.'

'You'll have to go for an interview next?'

'Yes, in ten days' time.'

'When will you be moving, if you get the job?' Ingrid asks.

'Probably not till Easter. I should have to give a full term's notice here.'

'We shall miss you,' I say.

'Oh, I might not get it yet. I've a long way to go. I don't know what qualifications and experience the other runners have.'

'Well I don't know; but my money's on you.'

'Thank you very much. I hope your confidence is justified.'

'It will be. You're a bright lad.'

He throws his head back and laughs at my cheek. 'No, you're the bright lad. I'm the once-promising young man, and at nearly forty I should be showing something more than promise.'

So he says. But he seems to be doing all right to me. I envy him. I always have. He seems happy in his career and he's got a wife who can keep up in anything he does and spur him on to better things. I don't see my sister as the kind of fount of all wisdom that I used to – she gave me some answers when I left Ingrid that I didn't expect then, and I'm still wondering if they were right – but she still ranks high with me as a woman and the main thing is that she loves David and he loves her. There are odd times when you see them shoot a glance at each other across a room, the sort of glance that seems to say as clear as words: You and me, and then the rest; and it's a thing I know I'll never have with Ingrid if we live together for a thousand years.

We talk for some time and have a few more beers before Chris makes coffee and serves it with crackers and cheese. Then about eleven, after Bobby's wandered out of his room complaining that he can't sleep and been taken firmly back again, Ingrid and I go downstairs to our own place on the ground floor. Our flat is one of the four that this old Victorian house was converted into after the war, and Chris and David got it for us at the time we were living with Ingrid's mother and I got drunk one night, had a stand-up row with Mrs Rothwell – finishing with me being sick on her carpet – and walked out. By now we've got it pretty comfortable, though I always feel it somehow lacks character compared with Chris's and David's place, only I can't just put my finger on where it falls down.

'Don't forget to put your clocks back,' David says as we leave them.

'No, we won't. Good night.'

I've got a tune from Beethoven's Pastoral Symphony going through my head for no reason at all as we go down the stairs and once inside the living-room I go to the radiogram and lift the lid. Ingrid looks at me as I take the record out of its sleeve.

'You're not going to put that thing on at this time of night, are you?'

'I thought it'd be nice to go to bed on.'

'You'll have the neighbours complaining.'

'You mean you don't want to listen to it, don't you? Is there any time at all when you don't mind me playing the gramophone?'

'I just said it was too late and it is. You don't have to make a thing out of it. I think you've been clever enough for one night.'

I say 'Oh, how's that?' though I know very well what she means.

'The way you snapped at me earlier on. Trying to show me up in front of Chris and David. I didn't answer back then because I don't like rows in front of other people, but I hope you didn't think you were getting away with it. Didn't you notice how embarrassed they were?'

'Not particularly.'

'No, you don't when you're showing off. Well it might seem clever to you but it doesn't to people listening.'

'All right then, I'm sorry.'

'I wish I thought it'd stop you doing it the next time you feel like it.'

'Well, I shan't feel like it if you don't make stupid remarks, shall I?'

'It must be really awful for you having a wife who's always saying stupid things.'

'We've all got a cross to carry.'

'Oh, what a clever devil you are! Too clever to live.'

14

With this she begins to move out of the room.

'Are you going to bed?'

'I'm going to have a bath.'

I sit down for a minute or two and leaf through the new *Radio Times* as the light snaps on in the bathroom and the water begins to gurgle in the pipes. I smoke a cigarette all through, marking up a few concerts I wouldn't mind hearing but don't expect I will, before going to drop the latch on the door and turning the hands of the mantelshelf clock back one hour. The end of summertime. Officially. Remembering the dreary mixed weather we've had all through the middle months of the year it strikes me somebody should be sued for misrepresentation. I adjust my wrist-watch as I'm undressing in the bedroom and wonder if Ingrid's mad enough to have locked me out of the bathroom. But the door opens to my push and I walk into the thin steamy atmosphere and take brush and toothpaste out of the wall cabinet, my back to Ingrid, hearing the whoosh of the water as she finishes soaping herself and slips down to lie full length.

Knowing what she looks like and already wanting her, I deliberately stop myself from turning round till I've rinsed my mouth and spat into the basin. Then I sit down on the little cork-topped chest and cut my toenails, trying to judge from her expression if she's in the mood to get her own back for tonight in the best way she can. But she gives nothing away: her eyes are half closed, her thoughts, from the look of her, on nothing more important than the heat of the water round her body. Her breasts, buoyant in the water, are a lovely shape and I think no, she wouldn't have bathed like this, knowing I'd see her, if she was going to turn me down. She'd have locked the door.

As I'm sitting there, the scissors idle in my hand, her eyes flick up to my face for a second.

'Are you staring at me?'

'Well, I'm looking,' I tell her. 'I was just thinking you're better-looking now than when I first knew you.'

'Oh, it's compliments now, is it?' she says, but I know she's pleased.

I go back to cutting my toenails.

'Early night tonight.'

'What time is it?'

I look at my watch. 'Well, it's twenty to twelve now, but at three o'clock it'll be twenty to eleven.'

'What on earth are you talking about?'

'Summertime. It ends at three o'clock.'

'I'd like to spend the extra hour in here, but I don't think there's any more hot water. I just love warm baths.'

'I just love warm beds, and that's where I'm going now.'

'Pass me the towel, will you?'

I unfold the big blue bathtowel and hold it up as she cleans the tidemark off the sides of the bath, pulls the plug out and stands up. She steps out into the towel and I wrap it right round her, keeping her trapped against me in my arms.

'Thank you, James. That will be all.'

'Will it?' I plant a kiss on the damp curve of her neck and shoulder.

'Yes, it will,' she says. 'On your way, lover-boy. I want to get dry.'

'I'll dry you.'

'I can manage, thanks, I don't want covering with bruises.'

'Would you rather have kisses?'

'I'd rather you went away and let me get dry.'

'I can take a hint.'

I leave her and go into the bedroom. I open a new book but I've hardly got into my stride with it when I hear Ingrid coming out of the bathroom, so I put the book away, switch off the bedside light and lie in the dark. She comes into bed and lies quietly beside me for a while. Then she says:

'Do you wish Bobby was ours?'

'What? No. Why should I?'

'You seem to make such a fuss of him.'

'I think he's a grand little lad; but there's a difference between playing with a kid for half an hour and having to cope with him all day and every day.'

'You would like to have children, wouldn't you?'

''Course I would. But there's no hurry yet.'

This isn't a new conversation with us. Every now and again Ingrid's got to be reassured that I do want kids and at the same time

16

that I'm not over-worried that in her case it's going to be a bit trickier than normal to produce them. But when I say there's no hurry it's not the real reason I give her. The real reason is that a baby would put another chain round us, tie us a bit more firmly, and try as I might I can't help resisting this. There's a part of me under the daily routine, the settled surface of our marriage, that never accepts, that's always holding out against a final surrender to the facts.

And it's a bit later, when we've made love, that the feeling hits me strongest; and I lie in the dark with nothing now between me and the thought that comes to me time and time again; the question that's always hanging round waiting for an answer I can't give: Is this all?

'What I want to know,' Henry Thomas says, 'is where's the catch.'

'You would, Henry,' I tell him. 'Everybody else is taking their first easy breath for a week and you're nattering about catches.'

'Oh, I'm relieved,' Henry says, taking a dog-end from behind his ear and lighting up. 'But perhaps I'm a bit more far-sighted than some people. I don't take things on face value as easy as most.'

It's Monday morning, first thing, a grey October morning out in the streets, and we're in the shop together. I'm looking through the post and Henry's leaning on the other side of the counter, having a chat like he often does before organizing his day's work.

'You see,' Henry says, pulling his great thinker's face, 'I can't understand why the Russians should build missile bases in Cuba without trying to camouflage them, and then agree to dismantle them when the Americans cut up rough.'

'Perhaps they didn't expect the Yanks to get as tough as all that.'

'Aye, and perhaps they did expect just that. I don't know. It's a mystery.'

'It is to me an' all. But I'm not trying to analyse it; I'm just bloody glad it's all over . . . Here, listen to this: "Dear Sir, That television I bought from your shop two months ago is very good

17

on the BBC but there is too much advertisements on the other side which keeps breaking into the programmes and spoiling them. Would you please send your assistant to adjust and oblige yours faithfully . . ."'

'Do you fancy a bit of adjusting and obliging mine faithfully?'

Henry takes it very calmly. 'Who is it?'

'A woman in Greenford.' I pass him the letter.

'This one's worse than that woman who wanted to swap her seventeen-inch for a twenty-one because she thought she wasn't getting all the picture. You'd better drop her a line. I've too much on to mess about with her.'

'You could always send Walt,' I say with a grin.

'Walt!' Henry's eyebrows go up in disgust. 'You can't send him for a box of screws. D'you know he brought six sets in last week that could have been seen to on the spot? And why? Because he couldn't do 'em himself. He's supposed to be a skilled man but I'm doing his work for him. All he's good for is fetching and carrying. Summat'll have to be done about him, that's all. I can't go on like this for ever.'

'It beats me how he got set on in the first place.'

'Because I didn't interview him, that's how. I'd have seen through him in two minutes, but he told the Old Man a tale and he swallowed it, hook, line and sinker.'

'Where's Walt now?'

'Out with the van, picking some more stuff up for me to repair.'

Olive comes through the door from the washroom at the far end of the shop. Another of Mr Van Huyten's appointments, she's a thin, mousy girl, quiet and a bit vague, but not bad at her work as long as you keep telling her what to do. She hovers about at the end of the counter till I call out to her:

'Will you have a bit of a dust round, Olive love, if you've nothing else to do.'

She takes a yellow duster from under the counter and wanders off among the TV sets and radiograms.

'I wonder if Mr Van Huyten's coming in today,' Henry says. 'I really ought to have a word with him about Walt.'

'I want to see him as well,' I say, 'Though as far as coming in's concerned I wish he'd keep clear altogether, because he's sure to poke his finger into something whenever you see him. The trouble is, we run the place but he won't stop interfering and let go. All we need him for is to sign the cheques . . . Here's a perfect example.'

I flourish a letter I've just opened at Henry.

'The electricity bill. He wouldn't let me see to it. No, leave it with him, he said. Now it isn't paid and they're threatening to cut the supply off.'

'He knows he's past it physically but he won't admit he's losing his grip mentally as well. Ah, well, I suppose it comes to all of us if we live long enough.' He stirs himself. 'I suppose I'd better get some work done.'

'Here you are, Henry; take these.' I hand him four letters asking for service. 'A bit of rescue work for you to do.'

Henry ambles away down the shop to the workroom and I carry on with the post. It's mostly bills, invoices and circulars, apart from the customers' letters, but one envelope is addressed to me personally. When I open it I'm surprised to see that it's from Albert Conroy, a bloke I haven't seen in years, who was making plans to emigrate the last I heard of him.

'Dear Vic, I hope this reaches you care of the shop as I don't know your home address. How are married life and the pop-record fans treating you? Any family yet?

'The reason I'm writing is because I was wondering if you'd ever given any thought to the possibility of coming back into engineering. I moved down here eighteen months ago to a job with a small structural firm called Joyce and Walstock and now I'm the chief draughtsman (no less!), first of all boss of myself and now in charge of two more draughtsmen, one of them Jimmy Slade, your old pal from Whittaker's, who I persuaded to come down twelve months ago.

'As I say, this is a smallish firm yet, but it changed hands just before I joined it and the new management is set on building the business up. We shall be needing some more men and there's a nice little opening for a bright lad like yourself, if you fancy it. Money, conditions and prospects are all good and there's room for a bloke to use his initiative.

'For all I know you're happy doing what you're doing but I thought I'd write on the off-chance you fancied a change. If it sounds interesting to you, let me know and I'll send you more details or, better still, I can fix up an expenses-paid trip so that you can come down and look the job over for yourself.

'Jimmy sends his regards. He suggested writing to you at the shop. He seems to have settled down here nicely and he's fraternizing with the natives to the extent of doing a bit of courting in the town.'

There's a p.s.: 'It's good ale,' that makes me smile.

The address on the letter is 33 Tavistock Road, Longford, Essex. The grin stays on my face because I'm flattered that Conroy's written to me like this. Most of the time we worked together in the drawing office at Whittaker's we didn't get on all that well; and it was only just before Conroy left that I found out there was more to him than a big mouth and a cocky sense of his own importance that put everybody's back up at times. Now I see that I must have made a bigger impression on him than I ever guessed.

I let my mind run on for a minute, wondering what it would be like to go down south and work with Conroy and Jimmy again, then I fold the letter and put it away, thinking I'll reply when I've ten minutes to spare. I know now what the answer will have to be, but it still makes me feel good to have been asked.

The day goes by without anything unusual happening. Walt drifts in and out, saying nothing much to anybody, the usual blank look on his long face, a half-smoked fag drooping at the corner of his mouth as always. You never see Walt light a cigarette or put one out, but he always has one, partly burned away, stuck in his face. Olive dreams her way through to six o'clock. Henry grumbles a bit more. Mr Van Huyten doesn't show up, nor does he get in touch. So I decide I'll have to go up and see him after I've closed the shop.

I ring Chris first and ask her to tell Ingrid I'll be late, then when I've locked up I hop on a bus which goes up the hill past the end of Mr Van Huyten's street. I have heard him talk at times, but not lately, about buying a bungalow, which would be cosier for him on his own; but he's never made the move and he's still in the biggish gloomy stone-built place I've always known him to live in; though

20

now he seems to have retreated into just a couple of rooms on the ground floor and dragged most of his possessions in after him in the most fantastic overcrowded hotch-potch of furniture, junk and knick-knacks I've ever seen. I don't think there's anything in the place I'd give him more than ten bob for, though I don't know about these things and it could be there's something an antique dealer might rub his hands over.

He's a long time in answering the door. With his heavy curtains drawn it's hard to tell whether he's in or out. I ring the bell a few times before I hear the shuffle of his feet in the hall and his voice on the other side of the door.

'Who is it?'

'It's me: Victor.'

Then he lets me in.

It's really a terrible change the last three years have brought in Mr Van Huyten. He's been old and frail for as long as I remember him, but now he's all of a sudden a lot older, a lot frailer, and eccentric into the bargain. And it's the last bit he doesn't seem to see himself.

I go for him over the electricity bill as soon as we're sitting in the big wing-chairs by his great dark marble fireplace.

He says dear me, tut, tut, tut, he's quite sure he paid it. But he can't ignore the notice I've brought with me and he gets up and pokes about in the pigeon-holes of his roll-top desk, which look from where I'm sitting like a model of untidiness and inefficiency, and in a minute he finds the bill and looks at it in surprise.

'Well, bless my soul; here it is. I could have sworn I'd attended to that promptly.'

'We all make mistakes, Mr Van Huyten,' I tell him. 'I've brought the cheque book with me. If you tell me the amount I'll make it out for you to sign and post it on my way home.'

He passes the bill over and sits down again. The chair seems to swallow him and his hands on the arms are thin, big-knuckled and never quite still. He's like a ghost sitting there; you get the impression you can see right through him. But he manages to sign his name to the cheque with an old-fashioned flourish that touches me as I look at it and remember all the talks we've had, the concerts we used to go to when he was running his car, and the way he used to

21

infect me with his enthusiasm for music; getting on his feet to clap at the end of a concert if he felt like it, and talking all the way home from Leeds or Bradford about Beethoven and Brahms and Mozart, Tchaikovsky, Berlioz and Elgar. He showed me that they were men like other men, but they had this extra something that left a mark on the world; they left their music and it was mine to enjoy as much as anybody else's. And when he did this Mr Van Huyten somehow seemed to open up the world for me. He gave me a feeling of being part of something bigger than this minute and the latest passing fancy. It was a feeling I tried to pass on to Ingrid, but never could. Or was I not trying to pass it on so much as looking for some kind of response to what I felt? Looking for, how can I put it, a sense of things that could spread out wider and wider like ripples on a pond instead of being tied to a straight line of direct experience that grew longer, just longer, with age?

'I really don't know what I'd do without you, Victor,' Mr Van Huyten's saying. 'I'm very grateful for your efficiency in handling things.'

'I'm glad you think like that, Mr Van Huyten,' I say; 'only, I might as well tell you that I'm not happy about it at present.'

'Oh?'

'Well, this electricity bill, for instance. If you'd left it with me it would have been paid long since.'

'Yes, yes. I'm sorry about that. Perhaps I am a little forgetful at times. But then, you must make allowances for me.'

'That's the trouble. I can make allowances for you, but you won't make them for yourself.' I wonder if I'm rattling him by talking like this, but I have to go on. 'What I mean is that I'm more or less running the shop from day to day – '

'And you do it very well,' he puts in.

'Well, thanks very much. But, you see, you haven't got your finger on things like you used to have, and when you decide to come down to the shop there's times when you – ' I want to say 'interfere' but I soften it, ' – when you do things off your own bat and throw the work out of gear.'

He looks at me and in his eyes there's a flash of the old Mr Van Huyten, canny and understanding.

'You mean I interfere where I'm not wanted?'

'I can't say you're not wanted, can I? I mean, it is your business.'

He sighs. 'Yes, it's my business. But perhaps I've clung to it for too long. I've never subscribed to the view that a man should automatically withdraw from active life at sixty-five; but there comes a time when he must let go . . .'

His voice has sunk almost to a whisper and I have to lean forward to catch the last words. He gazes into the fire for a minute or two then lifts his hand and looks round.

'I can feel a draught on my feet. I wonder if you . . . There's a rug . . .'

I get up and find the thick tartan travelling-rug and wrap it round his legs.

'Yes, that's better . . .' His hands fuss with the rug for a bit. 'As a matter of fact, I could probably sell out immediately.'

'Sell out!'

'Yes. Fenwick Brothers have intimated that they'd be willing to make an offer if I'm interested.'

'Well that's all right, Mr Van Huyten; but where does it leave me?'

'Oh, they'd be sure to take you on. I could make it a condition of sale.'

'But it's not the same thing at all, is it?' My voice is loud now, upset. I'm as near being really annoyed with him as I've ever been. 'I didn't leave engineering to be a shop assistant for any Tom, Dick or Harry. I did it to work for you.'

'But I shan't last for ever, Victor. I'm an old man.'

'I know, but . . .' And I'm wondering, is he getting really gaga? Can't he remember what he said, or didn't he say what I thought he said? Have I had hold of the wrong end of the stick all the time? No, perhaps there were no promises, but there was a lot of talk I couldn't have got wrong. And what's more, the Old Man talked to Mr Van Huyten as well, and came away satisfied.

'I find your loyalty very touching,' Mr Van Huyten says.

'I don't think loyalty comes into it at this stage, Mr Van Huyten,' I say, giving it to him straight in my anger. 'At least, not on my side. When we had that long talk before I came to work full-time for you, you promised me there'd be better prospects than there are for an ordinary shop assistant.'

'I said that one day I should want you to manage the shop when I felt like taking things more easily. And now you're doing that.'

'But there's another thing I wanted to talk to you about. It's about salary. I seem to have dropped behind lately and now I'm about three pounds down on what I'd be getting in industry.'

'Oh, so much?'

'Yes. You did say I wouldn't lose by coming to you.'

I tell him what an engineering draughtsman my age can be earning and point out the difference between that and what he pays me. In a minute, without any hesitation, he's offered me a two-pound a week rise and taken some of the wind out of my sails, but not all of it.

'And while we're talking I ought to say that we need some more staff.'

'More staff? You mean the work is becoming too heavy for you? You've got the little girl I took on in the summer. Isn't she efficient?'

'Oh, she's all right for what she does. But a young lad with some savvy would be a big help. He could take care of the counter with Olive while I got on with the books and paperwork. That side of it doesn't get any less, you know, Mr Van Huyten. Business is good and if you think about it we're worse off for help than when you and I used to do it all.'

'Yes, yes. I can see that.'

'And there's the question of a replacement for Walt.'

'Walt?'

'Henry's assistant.'

'Oh yes. Is he leaving us?'

'Henry'd give him his cards tomorrow if he could. He doesn't know a thing.'

'I don't know. He seemed capable when I interviewed him.'

'But you don't know anything about servicing television sets, Mr Van Huyten; and neither does Walt, according to Henry.'

There's a minute or two of quiet while he thinks all this over.

'Dear me,' he says then, 'how out of touch I seem to be getting. It really does look as though I shall have to rely on you a great deal more, Victor.'

'I don't mind,' I tell him. 'But this talk about selling out has upset me a bit.'

'Don't worry about that, Victor,' he says, leaning back in his chair with the tips of his fingers together. 'I thought you'd be interested to know, though, that our friends had made an approach.'

'They've got record shops all over the north. I suppose they'd be glad to take over an old-established business in Cressley.'

'They won't get mine. It will stay as Van Huyten's Music Shop until I die. What happens after that . . .'

I lean forward again, eager to catch what he's going to say; but he just lets the sentence die. His eyes close and he seems suddenly short of breath. I don't like the look of him at all and I get up and take a step towards him.

'Are you all right, Mr Van Huyten? Is there anything I can do?'

His hands are fumbling under the rug and one of them comes up holding a little bottle of pills.

'Would you . . .' I can't catch what else he says except the one word 'water'.

I run out and down the hall to the kitchen. This is the neatest room because his daily woman keeps it in order. It takes me a little while, though, to find a glass, then I fill it and hurry back to him.

'Here you are, Mr Van Huyten.'

I can't see him for the back of the chair and I go round and look at him, still holding the glass.

'Mr Van Huyten . . .'

I reach out to touch him but my hand stops short.

'Oh, crikey!'

I dash to the phone in the hall. Nothing happens when I lift the receiver and I've jiggled the bar a few times, swearing at the operator, before I realize that the line's as dead as a doornail.

The next minute I'm out of the house and racing down the hill to where I vaguely remember seeing a phone box on the corner.

3

'But he never actually said he'd leave the shop to me, Mother,' I say, irritated by the way she's talking about something that's settled now and can't be altered.

She's got her mending-basket open by her chair and one of the Old Man's socks pulled over a darning-stool, the needle giving off an occasional flash of light as she pulls the grey wool across the hole.

'You know very well that's the impression he gave both you and your father,' she says.

'Oh, he gave that impression all right,' the Old Man says, fiddling with his pipe; 'but he never made any promises except them he kept.'

'Well all I know is he persuaded our Victor to give up a good trade – against my advice, I'll have you remember – and now he finds himself in a dead-end job, just another shop assistant.'

'I can always go back into engineering,' I point out; 'and I've got five hundred quid to take with me, so I can't see that I've lost much by it.'

'It's not what you were led to expect,' the Old Lady says, her mouth in a stubborn line. 'And it's all right thinking about going back to draughtsmanship, but look at the seniority you've lost at Whittaker's.'

'I haven't said I'm going back to Whittaker's. There's lots of other places. I might even make a break and move right away.'

'Right away? Have you talked it over with Ingrid? She mightn't take too kindly to that idea now her mother's on her own. There's not just yourself to think about now, y'know.'

'I do know.' Oh, but she makes me wild the way she goes on. I wonder now how I ever stuck it when I was at home. 'All I'm saying is what I *might* do. I wish you'd stop pouncing on every little thing I say and driving me into corners.'

'Well, it's a job if your own mother can't talk to you now.'

'It's funny, though, y'know,' the Old Feller says, half to himself, 'the way Mr Van Huyten talked abut how much he liked you and he had no relatives that he knew about. I mean, there was only one construction you could fairly put on it.'

'I know there was, and he probably meant that. But he had to see how I made out first, see if I was capable and all that. And though he was very fond of pointing out how old he was I don't think he thought he was going to die for some time. I'm certain he didn't expect to go as sudden as he did. And for all I know he might have intended changing his will any time. The fact is he didn't, and so we've got to make the best of it.'

I'm fed up with all this talk. Of course I was disappointed, and no mistake. But looking back at it now it seems fantastic to think there was any chance of Mr Van Huyten leaving the shop to me. And I don't like my mother and father to talk as if I've been led up the garden path and made a fool of. I'm ready to bet that Mr Van Huyten never did that to anybody in his life.

'You'll be stopping on at the shop for a bit anyway, I reckon?'

'Until the bank gets everything settled, yes. I expect Fenwick's are ready to make an offer. Mr Van Huyten told me they were interested.'

'I expect they'd take you on if you wanted it, eh?'

'They might, but I'm not interested. I'd be just another salaried employee to them, one of scores. I probably wouldn't even get the chance of the manager's job. They'll have a trained man ready to take over. I think Henry's hoping he can stay on, though. I mean, it's his trade.

'Y'know,' I say in a minute, 'the old chap didn't do so flippin' badly with us when you think about it. Five hundred for me and two-fifty for Henry. He was a grand old feller and he couldn't help it if he got a bit soft in the head towards the end.'

'No,' the Old Feller says, 'you're right. And he's gone now, so it's no use trying to fathom what was in his mind.' Which makes all three of us go quiet, as though we're trying to do just that.

There's a great fire piled up orange and glowing in the grate and the Old Man and I sit and look at it without saying anything, the Old Lady going on with her mending until she finally gathers it all up and puts it in the basket.

'I could do with a woman's work,' she says, 'but it never gets any less.'

'It ought to do,' I say, 'with our Jim out of the way now.'

'What do you think Jim does with his clothes,' she says, 'mends 'em and washes 'em himself? He sends 'em home to his mother. That's one thing she's useful for, anyway.'

I know this note in the Old Lady's voice; she's got her back up with Jim over something.

'What's up with Jim, then? Haven't you heard from him lately?'

27

'Oh aye, we've heard. We don't see much of him these days, though.'

'When was he over last?'

'Three weeks since; and we had a postcard yesterday to say he won't be home this week-end. He's going home with a friend who lives in Cheshire.'

'Well, he goes to university to meet people as well as study, you know. Mebbe he did come home every week-end at first, but you can't expect him to carry on like that.'

'As long as he doesn't start to think his own home isn't good enough for him.'

'Nay, you know our Jim's not that sort o' lad, Mother,' the Old Man chips in.

'He wouldn't be the first lad to go away to university and end up having no room for his parents,' the Old Lady says. There's a couple of spots of colour on her cheeks and I can tell she's spent some time brooding about this and building it up.

'You've been watching too many television plays,' I tell her. 'Jim's at Manchester, not Oxford or Cambridge. There'll be a lot of people there from ordinary homes like his. And they're all cutting their apron strings together.'

'Aye, and a sorry state most of 'em 'ud be in if it wasn't for their mothers and fathers.'

'Well Jim knows that, doesn't he? What do you want him to do, write you a letter every day saying how grateful he is?'

'There's no need for that kind o' clever talk.'

'I'm only trying to make you see that you can't hang on to him. You seem to want to send him off with one hand and hold him back with the other. That's just the way to make him resentful. He's got enough to think about without you being on at him. You'll have to face the facts, y'know. You've lost Jim. He's gone. You'll never have him at home like you had Chris and me. He's off early and he's seeing a lot and meeting people that I never did. I was in a drawing-office at sixteen and the next thing I know I'm married. I hope he sees a bit more of things than I did before he settles down.'

'Well neither you nor our Christine seems to have done so badly out of it,' the Old Lady says.

I say nothing to this. Chris, all right. Me? What does the Old

Lady know about me? What has she ever known? Does my marriage to Ingrid look no different to her than Chris's and David's? I wonder how blind you can get.

'Anyway,' she says, letting it drop, 'I'll put the kettle on for a cup of tea.'

'Aye, and I shall have to be pushing off home.'

'Aren't you stopping for your supper?'

'I hadn't planned to. I don't know what time Ingrid'll be home.'

'You say her mother's not so well?'

'Apparently not. That's why Ingrid's gone over tonight.'

'She doesn't seem to have been right on form since Ingrid's father died,' the Old Man says.

'Well, are you stopping or aren't you?' the Old Lady wants to know.

'I suppose I might as well. What have you got?'

'Nowt so much, unless you feel like popping round to t'fish shop.'

'I'll take pot luck. I don't want to be too late.'

But it is cosy sitting in my old chair with my feet stuck out across the hearth in front of that big fire. It's nearly possible to imagine I'm still at home and a free man. Nearly.

'Will some brown bread and butter and a piece of fruit cake suit you?'

'Yes, fine.'

The Old Lady goes out and leaves me and the Old Man ruminating in front of the fire. My heels sink into the new listing rug on the hearth. It seems looking back to when I was a kid that we nearly always had a listing rug on the go, the frame propped up with one end on the table and the other on a cupboard or a chest of drawers; my mother sitting up to it, right hand on top holding the skewer, left hand underneath taking the lists as she prodded them through. It was possible to buy material for lists but it was unheard of in our house; it kind of defeated the object. We always collected the family's old clothes for cutting up, plus what a neighbour or friends might be throwing out. The lists would be nearly always drab navy-blue or dark brown and occasionally we might have the brighter colour of a woman's costume to liven the mixture up. I wonder how many listing rugs my mother and father have run through in their married life. They look pretty shabby when they get trodden down but there's nothing to beat them for comfort when they're new.

'A pity,' the Old Man says, talking about Mr Rothwell; 'a fine young-looking feller like that cut off in his prime. How old did Ingrid say he was?'

'Forty-eight.'

'Aye.' The Old Man nods. 'Forty-eight. No age at all. Aye . . . I rather liked Mr Rothwell.'

'Yeh, so did I.'

'Worth three or four of Ingrid's mother, I allus thought.'

'Me too.'

The Old Man and I sit and think about Ingrid's father, dead eighteen months ago of lung cancer and I remember how he talked to me in that pub café in Bread Street after I'd left Ingrid, and made it possible for me to see her again. I've thought many a time since, going back over that conversation, how clever he was that day; how he got to grips with the situation, saying just what needed saying at just the right time. He and Chris; they never talked to each other about it but they did it between them while all the others were washing their hands of it: Mrs Rothwell glad, I think, that I'd finally shown myself to be an ill-mannered pig, not good enough for her daughter (as she'd always thought), and the Old Lady saying she didn't want to see me till I was back with Ingrid again.

So we got back together and decided to give it a try.

'How do you get on with her these days, Victor?' the Old Man says.

'Who, Ingrid's mother?'

'Aye.'

'Oh, well enough. We have a sort of armed truce. We don't see much of each other really, and we're polite and civil when we do meet. I don't know what she says about me when I'm not there and she doesn't know what I say about her.'

'Ingrid'll get both sides of it, I reckon?'

'I suppose she does.'

He grins. 'It's a common enough situation, I suppose.'

'I suppose it is.'

My mother comes in from the kitchen with the supper and she and the Old Man start telling me they're thinking of flitting. This place is too big for them now we're all away and there's only Jim to put up when he comes home. They bought it before the war, a solid, roomy family house, at the price ruling then, which is about a quarter of what it's worth now. The mortgage has been paid off for some time and the Old Man reckons he can sell for seventeen- or eighteen-hundred and buy a four-roomed terrace house for about nine; which will give him knocking on for a thousand to put in the bank: a nice tidy sum to add to his savings and pension when he retires, which won't be long now. It sounds to me like a first-rate plan, and I say so.

'Aye,' the Old Man says, 'your mother had her work cut out talking me into buying this place when things were unsettled and you could rent a house any day of the week. But it's turned out for the best. Money's dropped in value but property's gone up.' He nods. 'We had a bit o' luck.'

It's a satisfied little nod from a chap who's come through all right. A chap who's worked hard all his life, when the work was there to be done, in foul and dangerous conditions, and brought three kids up and seen them go out into the world with better chances than he ever had. I reckon he has a right to be content.

Ingrid's already back when I get home, and not in a very good mood. She hasn't been in long from the look of it: her coat's over the back of the settee and the fire, which I banked up earlier, hasn't burned up beyond a few pale cold-looking flames.

'Where've you been?' she asks me as I walk in.

'I've been home, like I said.'

'I didn't think you'd be this late,' she says, as though it's three in the morning and I've kept her out of bed.

'It's only eleven,' I tell her. 'And anyway, you never asked me what time I'd be back.'

'I just thought you'd be back before this.'

I take my coat off and start to go with it into the passage.

'I stopped for my supper.'

'You might as well hang mine up now,' she says.

'What do you mean "now"?' I say as I turn back for it. 'You weren't going out again, were you?'

'I wanted to go back and stay with Mother tonight.'

'Why?' I say from across the passage. 'Isn't she well?'

'You know very well she's not well.'

She's sitting on the edge of the chair as I go back into the room, looking at the fire, her hands held palms together between her knees.

'I meant is she worse?'

'She's not well,' Ingrid says and I start to open my mouth, then shut it again, thinking what damn' silly conversations people have sometimes.

'If you think you ought to go, then go,' I say in a minute. 'I'll walk you back round.'

'It's too late now. She'll already have gone to bed.'

'Well, I'm sorry if I spoilt anything, but I didn't know, did I?'

'I'll have to pop round first thing in the morning, that's all, and tidy up for her and see if she wants any shopping done. You can ring the office for me and tell them I shan't be in, can't you?'

'I suppose so.'

It's a bit chilly in the room and I get down and give the fire a good poking, breaking up the coal so that the flames begin to roar up the back.

'I wasn't going to disturb that,' Ingrid says.

'No good sitting shivering,' I say. 'I can bank it up again when we go to bed.'

'I shall be going in a minute.'

'I shan't be long meself.'

I sit down on the other side of the fireplace and light a fag.

'How are your mother and father?' Ingrid asks after a minute.

'As usual. They're thinking of flitting to a smaller house.'

'I suppose that one is a bit big for them now . . . Did you tell them why I hadn't gone with you?'

'Yes.'

'What did they say?'

'Nothing special. Why?'

'Oh, I don't know. I sometimes think your mother hasn't much sympathy for mine.'

32

'What makes you think that?'

'It's just a feeling I get sometimes.'

'You know my mother never makes a lot of fuss.'

'Mmm,' she says. 'She's no need to, has she?'

'What d'you mean?'

'Well, she hasn't lost anybody and she keeps in good health.'

'I didn't mean that. Anyway, her health isn't all that good, but she doesn't grumble. And if she did lose me dad she'd square up to it. Better than some, I reckon.'

'You never know till it happens.'

'No, I suppose not.'

'She does miss him, but she's got used to it in eighteen months. It's her health that's the trouble.'

'Yes.'

'I don't like to think of her being on her own when she's not well.'

'No, it's not pleasant. Still, you're not far away. You can see her nearly every day.'

'Mmm,' she murmurs. She gives a sigh and stands up.

'You going to bed now?'

'Yes.'

'I'll just mend the fire again and lock up.'

She stands at one side of the fireplace. 'Have you thought about what you're going to do when you've finished at the shop?'

'I keep thinking about it.'

'It won't be long now, will it?'

'No, I'll be out of work in a week or two, I reckon. Soon as all the books have been sorted out.'

'Well you can't count on living on that money Mr Van Huyten left you because you haven't got it yet.'

'No, and as far as I can see it could be six months before I do get it. If I get it at all.'

'You will get it eventually, won't you? There's no doubt about that, is there?'

'Well, I suppose it'll depend on whether there's so much left when all the accounts have been balanced and the debts paid. It'll be all right as far as I can see, but you never know.'

'Why don't you give Mr Hassop a ring at Whittaker's and see if he can take you back?'

I pull a face. 'No . . . I dunno. It looks like engineering again, but I don't fancy going back to Whittaker's. I should be fidgety again inside a month . . . I've been thinking about that letter I had from Albert Conroy. I haven't replied to it yet, what with Mr Van Huyten going so sudden, and all the messing about since.'

'But we can't just pack up and go all that way.'

'Why not? Other people do it. We don't have to stick around here all our lives, do we?'

'I don't see why not. I like it here. All my friends are here. And besides, there's Mother to think about. I couldn't leave her now.'

'You wouldn't have to leave her straight away. Suppose I did go: it'd mean me living in digs till I saw if I like the job and found a house.'

'That'd mean me staying here on my own.'

'Well, for a bit.'

'I don't see why we have to go to all that trouble. There's plenty of engineering firms round here.'

'Look, Ingrid, things haven't worked out like we expected. I've got to go back to engineering but I just don't feel I can do it here. I fancy a change, a new place, fresh faces, a new start, and a job with prospects.'

'But all that way . . .'

'God almighty, it's only two hundred miles. People are moving about to new jobs like that all the time.'

She stands thinking and looking down into the fire.

'Have you mentioned it to your mother and dad?'

'I did say I might fancy moving away.'

'What did they say?'

'What does it matter what they said?'

'I know what my mother will say.'

This brings me up on my feet, my face set as my mind's set; ready to lay the law down now before we go any further along that road.

'Now look here, Ingrid, I know your mother's not well and all that, but she's young enough and she'll get over it. This is between you and me. Nobody else. If you say you don't want to go, I want good reasons. But *your* reasons, not ideas your mother's put into your head.'

'I'm sure there's no need to talk like that – ' she begins.

'Ah, but there is,' I butt in. 'Plenty of need. We've had all this sort of thing before. Remember? Well this time I'm scotching it before it starts.'

'You've already made your mind up, haven't you?' she says in a minute. 'I can tell.'

'Well you're telling wrong.'

'You wouldn't be so worked up about it if you hadn't.'

'It's the principle I'm getting worked up about, not the job.'

'Well there's no need to shout.'

Maybe my voice has risen a bit. It sometimes does when I'm on the subject of Ingrid's mother.

'I'm sorry. I didn't know I was shouting.'

'You were. And I've got a headache.'

'You go on to bed. I'll be with you in a minute.'

'I'd like to get this business settled before I go. *Have* you made your mind up?'

'How can I have when I haven't seen the place?'

'Well what do you intend to do?'

'I'm going to write to Conroy tomorrow and tell him I'd like to go down and look it over.'

'It's no good me talking then, is it?'

'There's not much point in anybody talking till I've been and had a look.'

'There's no point in moving all that way just out of spite, either.'

'Look, don't talk so damn' silly, Ingrid. I was happy enough at the shop, but that's all gone now. It's my place to think about our future. What's best for us. It's my responsibility and nobody else's. And people should remember that before they start handing out advice.'

She turns away, not looking at me. 'I'm going to bed.'

'Okay, we'll talk about it another time.'

'I don't think there's any point in me talking about it again,' she throws over her shoulder, the door shutting behind her and cutting off my chance to reply.

In a minute I pick up the coal scuttle and take a swing at the fire which scatters lumps of coal all over the hearth. And then I'm down on my hands and knees, picking them all up, my cup brimming over with the joys of married life.

4

''Course, you're on a pretty good thing today,' Conroy says. 'You don't have to prove yourself – we've got to tempt you.' He hunches over the little fake rustic table, one big hand round his pint of bitter.

'Well for God's sake don't ask me how you stress a beam, Albert,' I say with a laugh, 'because I've forgotten.'

'Oh, that'll come back in no time. You know where to look for the information, anyway. The main thing is, do you really want to come back into engineering?'

'I've got no option. I need a job. I'm not carrying on as a shop assistant now Mr Van Huyten's dead, and engineering's the only other trade I know.'

'You know, I wondered if you weren't making a mistake going into that shop. I remember thinking so when I heard.'

'Oh, it's a long story, Albert. I had a pretty good relationship with old Mr Van Huyten; that was the main reason. Things didn't turn out quite like I expected, but I don't really regret it.'

The little dark-haired barmaid who's dealing with the lunches comes over to our table with a fistful of cutlery.

'Would you like to start now?'

'Er, yes,' Conroy says, glancing at his watch, 'may as well, Shirley.'

'Soup for both?' she asks as she sets out knives and forks and spoons.

Conroy looks at me and I nod.

'Yes, two soups ... You haven't been introduced to Shirley, have you, Vic? This is a friend of mine. Vic Brown, Shirley. I want you to look after him because he might be coming to work for us.'

'Is he from up there as well?' the girl asks, and Conroy laughs.

'Aye, he is that, luv,' he says, laying on the Yorkshire.

36

'There'll be nobody left in Bradford if it goes on like this,' Shirley says.

Conroy's still laughing as she goes away. 'Nice kid. Thinks all Yorkshiremen come from Bradford.'

'You seem to be able to chat her up,' I say. 'Is this your local?'

'I come in quite a bit. It's a decent lunch they put on. Bowl of soup, help yourself off the cold table, piece of apple pie, and coffee to finish. Seven and six. Not that I can afford that every day. I have to use the canteen sometimes, and that's a bit rough yet. Give us another five or six years of prosperity, though, and I expect we'll have a canteen for every two people, graded according to status.'

'The rewards of industry.'

'Aye. You don't want to give a bloke more money so you soften him up by giving him a fancy title and letting him eat his dinner in a posh canteen. Me, I'll take this set-up we've got here. The boss knows everybody by his first name and there's no bull-shit or hangers-on serving their time till retiring age. It can't last, though: we've too much work coming in and we're forced to expand. I was the only designer when I first came. Now we've got Jimmy and another bloke as well; and we need another man desperate, maybe two. And it's going on in every department. In fact, there weren't any departments eighteen months ago, just a few blokes doing their jobs . . . Would you like another drink?'

'No, I don't think so. Drinking at dinner-time puts me to sleep.'

'You'll have to learn to cope with it, lad. Entertaining customers, and all that. It's these places the business is done in nowadays.'

I reach for his glass. 'Let me get you filled up, anyway.'

'No, we're on the firm today. I'll put an expenses slip in later on. Have a short, if you fancy one.'

I shake my head. 'No, what's left of this pint will do me.'

Conroy gets up and fetches another pint for himself and as he comes back the soup arrives.

'Heard any good music lately?' he asks as we start.

'Not recently, no.'

'You used to frequent the old concerts, though, didn't you?'

'Yes, I used to go with Mr Van Huyten now and again. It's not in Ingrid's line, though. Do you get anything like that round here?'

'Not here in Longford. But London's only forty minutes away.

I sometimes go up to the Festival Hall. I spent a week of my holidays up there last spring. Had a proper orgy of it. Heard Klemperer do the whole cycle of Beethoven symphonies. Bloody marvellous.'

'I'm not too keen on him in all of them. I prefer Beecham in the Pastoral, for instance.'

Conroy nods. 'Yeh, maybe old Otto is a bit straight-faced in that one.' He starts to grin. 'Y'know, they did that and the Fifth in the same concert and the minute they struck up the Fifth I started thinking about old Rawly and his big culture thing.'

I smile at this, remembering Rawlinson, one of the draughtsmen at Whittaker's, with his fancy tie-clip and a pocketful of fountain pens. The sort of bloke, as Conroy once said about him, who'd go to a concert once a year and talk about it at the top of his voice on the bus next morning. But by the time he said this Conroy was giving me another side of himself that I'd never thought existed under the loud-mouthed, big-headed front he put up at the time. Now it seems to me he's mellowed a lot. He's got responsibility and he's loving it.

'I wonder what happened to him, Conroy says. 'Do you know?'

'No idea. I haven't laid eyes on him since I left.'

'What about the rest of them? Do you keep in touch?'

'Afraid not. I'd no idea Jimmy was down here, for instance. The only place you might run across 'em is in some pub, and I don't go drinking much nowadays.'

Conroy's looking at me. 'No concerts, no booze . . . You've settled for marriage in a big way . . .'

'Well, you can't carry on as if you're single.'

'What does Ingrid think about the possibility of you coming down here?'

I hesitate, pushing my empty soup dish away. 'Well, tell you the truth, Albert, she's not all that keen at the moment. But she'll come round if she has to.'

'They don't all,' Conroy says. 'Women have deeper roots than men, y'know. Some of 'em can't bear to move out of their own backyard.'

'Well, they've bloody well got to go where the living is, haven't they? And that's all there is to it.'

This comes out with a bit of force and I see Conroy's eyes narrow ever so slightly. I'm sorry then that I've let him see so much. Not that he takes me up on it, but it's something for him to remember in future.

'You'll have to see how you fancy it yourself, first,' he says. 'Come on, let's go help ourselves.'

I follow him across to the long bar, one end of which is set out with the cold buffet: plates of ham and tongue, a big pork pie, and dishes of lettuce, tomatoes, slices of hard-boiled egg in mayonnaise, red cabbage, sliced onion, and so on.

Looking round as we eat, I can't see anything that straight away tells me I'm two hundred miles from home. Lots of pubs in the North have been slicked up in this fashion, with imitation beams, stone fireplaces, and timber that's nailed to the plaster and doesn't support a thing. And then I think to myself – what did I expect? That people two hundred miles south of Cressley would have two heads or four eyes and talk a lingo I couldn't understand?

But still, the strangeness of being here does hit me as Conroy and I sit and tuck in without talking. Some people seem to settle down as soon as they leave school and spend the rest of their lives growing old. With other people things are always changing, or they're making them change. I'm kind of in between. I've got a strong feeling I'm going to take this job, though I know next to nothing about it yet. And it's not so much the job itself, but more as though it's a dividing line in my life. A crossroads, if you like. A few weeks ago I'd no more idea than flying that I'd be going back into engineering. I hadn't heard of Longford; as far as I knew Conroy was on the other side of the world; the shop was my future. Then Mr Van Huyten dies and everything's changed overnight. Just like it changed when Ingrid told me she was pregnant. Only then the world closed in on me and now it could be opening out a bit.

After lunch we go out to the red Morris 1100 that Conroy picked me up at the station in (not his own car but the firm's, which is better for him because it's paid for by them, serviced at their expense, and most of the petrol is chargeable to expenses) and he drives me through the town. It doesn't seem like much of a place to me. I like a place to be either country or mucky industrial and this seems to be somewhere in between. Still, I suppose I saw the worst of it when I arrived, like you always do from a train. The main street is long and wide and straight with a lot of the new anonymous-looking supermarket and department store buildings you get in every town since the war. I notice a Woolworth's and a Marks and Spencer's and a cinema plastered with Bingo notices and, down a crossroads as we come up to a red light, a theatre. It's a dingy-looking shack with an iron fire-escape on the side wall, and I have time to register that they're doing *An Inspector Calls*, by J. B. Priestley, before Conroy moves forward on the amber and begins talking to me about the firm and the chap I'm going to see, whose name is Franklyn.

'He's a bit of a ball of fire,' Conroy says. 'An engineer, not an accountant. Been all over the place and done all kinds of things. He's the nearest thing I've ever met to those tough engineers in American pictures. You know – building a dam across a canyon one year and a road through a jungle the next.'

'He sounds a bit scaring,' I say.

'I'm exaggerating a bit,' Conroy says, 'He doesn't walk about with a six-gun strapped round him, but . . . well, he's a bloke who's obviously taken his talent wherever it was needed and he's just the opposite of the family retainer types we had at Whittaker's.'

'Well, I can do with a change from them. The first horrible thought I had when Mr Van Huyten died was I might end up back there. Locked in again for life.'

Conroy shoots me a sidelong look. 'Yeh, I know just what you mean. It's so bloody dead easy to get yourself in a cage. You hardly know it's happening till it's too late. But it's funny how things happen. You didn't know what a favour you were doing me that day in the office at Whittaker's when you made that crack. What was it now?'

'Summat about a pig, wasn't it?'

'Yeh, that's right.' Conroy's grinning now and I've got a sudden sharp memory picture of him standing there in the drawing office at Whittaker's, his face red with fury in the second before he comes for me and we go down scrapping among the plan-presses.

'If we hadn't had that little punch-up,' he says now, 'Althorpe wouldn't have talked to us the way he did and got my dander up

40

enough to look for another job.' He touches the brake and does a quick change down as a middle-aged woman tries to end it all by stepping out in front of the car. We get a glimpse of her staring eyes and open mouth as she realizes how near she was to being clouted and Conroy says amiably, 'Blind bitch,' and picks up speed again.

'Still,' he says in a minute, 'I suppose something else would have happened to get me out eventually.'

'What happened after you left?' I ask him. 'I never got the right tale about it all. I thought you'd gone to Australia.'

'I nearly did. I'd practically got my bag packed. Then I saw this firm advertising and applied on a whim. There again, y'see, when I left Whittaker's the first job I tried was with a firm in Bradford. It was okay for a while, but they were nearly as bad as Whittaker's. Old retainers in nearly all the top jobs, too many other people in line before you for promotion. Accountants and clerks round your neck, knackering things up all the time, we do it this way because we've done it like this for the last fifty years. All the old stuff. You know. I'd got to a pitch where the only way out of it as far as I could see was to bugger off somewhere where everything was new. Though I didn't really want to leave England for ever.' He throws me a grin. 'I like the beer too much.'

The old Conroy, I'm thinking: full of bad language, a liking for beer and skittles all mixed up with one for books and music, and all sorts of sensitive spots occasionally showing through. I say the old Conroy, but actually the first Conroy I knew was a loud-mouthed, thick-headed, ignorant lout who shook me no end when he let me see his hidden depths. He doesn't seem to keep them as hidden now; but maybe that's because he's a few years older and in a happier position, and partly because I know him better and he doesn't have to put on an act with me. Though he still has his secrets. That marriage of his, for instance; mentioned just once when he was drunk and then tucked away again out of sight . . .

We're up to a big traffic island with a sign showing roads off to Colchester, Chelmsford and Southend, and this seems to mark the end of the town proper. Beyond it, on the road Conroy takes, are semi-detached and detached houses, modern and posh-looking, behind well-established lawns and trees. Conroy swings the car left up a side road with open fields beyond it and in a couple of minutes we're going through a gate in a wire fence on to a stretch of flat ground, and there are the factory bays in front of us with the thump of a cropping machine coming from one of them and carrying to us on the cold air. Conroy parks in front of a long single-storey pre-fabricated office building next to a blue Zephyr estate car and we get out.

'Here we are, then.' He walks towards a door with me following. 'There's nothing fancy about this set-up yet,' he says over his shoulder, 'so don't expect fitted carpets and uniformed commissionaires.'

There's no commissionaire at all as far as I can see, and nothing on the floors except brown lino. There's perhaps half a dozen people to be seen and one or two heads lift on the other side of the glass as we go along the corridor. Sizing up the new man? No, more likely the vague interest anybody feels in a strange face. A funny thing, that, the way human beings swim about in the same tank, lots of them never seeing one another, others crossing tracks, and some bumping in real contact. For instance, if I go away from here today for good there's nobody who's seen me will remember me. If I come to a job, though, I'll become part of their lives; even altering some of them a little bit. All of which deep thinking flashes through my powerful mind as we go into the biggest office at the end of the building.

Jimmy Slade grins at me from behind one of the four drafting machines and I wink and grin back as Conroy has a word with a smoky blonde piece in a dark green wool frock who's sitting at a desk by one of the doors leading out of the main office. She stops typing to answer Conroy.

'Yes, he's by himself. I should look in. He's expecting you.'

What is it about birds in wool? They seem to give off an extra body warmth that their perfume floats on.

'Oh, by the way,' Conroy says, 'this is Vic Brown . . . Cynthia Holness.'

We say hello and her eyes come up to my face for a second's acknowledgement, then away again.

'You have a natter with Jimmy for a minute, Vic,' Conroy says. He taps on the door behind Cynthia and goes through, closing it behind him.

Jimmy grins again and swivels half round on his stool as I walk over to him. We shake hands.

'Nice to have something decorative about the place,' I say.

'Who, Cynthia? Yes. But her sights are set high, old cock, and draughtsmen – married or single – don't come into the picture.'

'What did *I* say?'

He laughs. 'Anyway, how's the old married man?'

'Fair to middling.'

'And Ingrid?'

'The same. I hear you're doing a spot of courting these days.'

Jimmy shrugs. 'It comes to most of us sooner or later.'

'What's the set-up here, then?' I look at what's on his board as I talk to him.

'The money's good and the work's interesting.'

'Any snags?'

'Well, I don't think there's anything to be scared of in the work itself. The only thing with a firm like this is you never know how they stand on the financial side. You know, whether they're sound or not. We've got a fair amount of work on but I wouldn't say we're established yet, exactly. For all I know the people behind us could make a decision tomorrow that would put us all out of work.'

'Well, I shan't have a job in a week or two anyway.'

'No, and there are plenty more about, so I'm not particularly worried.'

'What about this Franklyn feller, the boss?'

'Oh, he's all right. One thing about him is he can't stand – '

But I don't get to know what it is Franklyn can't stand because just then Conroy sticks his head out of the other office and shouts me over:

'Vic. You can come in now.'

'I might see you later,' I say to Jimmy.

'Yup. And astonishing good luck, mate.'

The bird, Cynthia, doesn't even look up as I go past her and through the door Conroy's holding open for me. If it comes to that, why should she? But she's a real cool piece, all right. You can see that a mile off.

And so's Franklyn, it strikes me, in a way. Or maybe preoccupied is a better word, and not much sense of humour to go with it.

He scrapes his swivel chair back and leans across the desk to shake hands as I go into his office and Conroy makes with the introductions. Then he waves me over to one of the two straight chairs. There's a sheepskin-lined coat over the other chair so Conroy stays on his feet, leaning his shoulders against the asbestos board wall, his hands in his trousers pockets. Franklyn hasn't done himself proud either. All there is is this biggish square double-sided desk in the middle of the lino, these two chairs apart from his swivel, a bookcase with some fat technical tomes in it, and a coat stand with nothing on it. His hat's on his head, a trilby, stained a bit round the band and pushed back far enough for me to see the beginnings of sandy hair that I'll bet is going thin on top. He looks for all the world like a smallish independent builder and I guess he's a lot happier out on site than he is behind a desk.

'Albert tells me he's talked to you about the set-up here,' Franklyn says, 'and I can take his word for what you can do . . . So the main thing now is whether you feel like coming and giving it a try.' He takes a fag from the Senior Service twenty on the desk and then offers the packet to me. We light up from his Ronson gas lighter. 'You're not in engineering at present?'

'No, I left it to help a man I knew in his music shop. I thought there were some good prospects but he died a bit sudden.'

'You want to come back into engineering now, though? You must do,' he says, as though it's a silly question, 'or you wouldn't have come all this way to see us.'

'There's no future in being a shop assistant.'

'Not much, I shouldn't think.' He rocks back in his chair and puts his knee to the edge of the desk. 'What about money?'

'Well . . .' I wish now I'd brought this up with Conroy, but it's an awkward point sometimes because draughtsmanship can be a funny trade in that respect. We have a union and there are recognized minimum rates up to twenty-five; but some firms pay more and others a bit less and it can be the case in some offices that you're never sure how much the bloke on the next board is getting. Now

I don't want to ask for either too much or too little, so I have to trot out the old formula.

'I couldn't consider less than union rate,' I say, wondering if this is right or wrong and how he's going to take it.

You see, all kinds of firms employ draughtsmen, from those with hundreds of men in offices all over the country, where a bloke hardly knows the name of the bod three boards away, to little concerns like this one where the boss himself knows everybody. In a big office there'll be red tape and wage scales laid down at top level, and you need a strong union representation to protect your rights. In a small firm there's likely to be more give and take. They might pay you a bit more than the rate but expect you to keep your eyes off the clock and not put in a bill for every odd hour of overtime you work. Again, on their side, pay for a long sick leave might be extended according to whether they like you and think you're playing fair. In a big firm they'll have to work to the book. So generally speaking, and taking cases as they come, shouting the odds in a little firm with a friendly atmosphere does nothing but stiffen relationships all round and make everybody worse off. And I don't want Franklyn to start out thinking I'm the sort of bloke who'll be quoting the rule book at every verse end.

And then he asks me what the rate is and I have to say I'm not sure because I haven't been in the union since I left Whittaker's.

Conroy looks blank as well. He's in the union but he can't quote the rate. 'Jimmy might know,' he says, and goes out, leaving Franklyn and me on our own.

'I think Albert said you were married.'

'Yes.'

'But no children?'

'No. Not yet.'

'That makes you a bit more mobile, anyway.'

'Yes. I was wondering about housing and all that.'

'What sort of accommodation have you got now?'

I tell him, a flat.

'You'll find houses a bit more expensive than they are up north; but you shouldn't have any trouble getting rooms for the time being, with no children. Does your wife fancy moving down here?'

'Well, she ...' I begin, and let it die as the door opens and

Conroy comes in with a union vacancy list which he hands to Franklyn.

'Did we advertise in this?'

'I thought I'd get in touch with Vic first.'

Franklyn says 'Mmm,' and looks at the wages table quoted in the list. 'Oh well,' he says in a second, 'there shouldn't be any trouble there.' He mentions a figure. 'I was thinking of that for a start. It's what . . .? Fifteen bob above the rate for the London area.' He looks at me. 'If you'd start on that and see what happens after a few months.'

'That seems fair enough.'

Franklyn throws the list on to the desk. 'All I'm bothered about is keeping the job moving,' he says. 'Providing we can do that I'm ready to pay as much as my superiors will let me.'

I nod. I can see that it's the work that interests him and all this chat about money is a bind he's got himself landed with.

The phone rings and he reaches for the receiver.

'Franklyn . . . Yes . . . Well I thought I'd made that plain, John . . . Yes, he might do but I told him quite clearly this morning . . . Well I'm sorry I didn't tell you but how was I to know he didn't understand plain English? . . . Yes, well I'll be over in five minutes and he'd better have a good story. I won't have both ends played off against the middle . . . No, you did right to tell me . . . Look, if I have to pin a bloody notice up every time I tell somebody to do something it's time we all packed up . . . Yes, five minutes, John.'

He puts the phone down. 'I'll have to leave you, Albert. You give Vic any more information he needs to make up his mind.' He looks at me again. 'I don't want to rush you and I don't expect a decision now, but when can you let us know?'

'Well . . . inside a week. Will that do?'

'Yes, fine.' He gets up. 'If I don't see you again before you go, have a nice trip back.' He's struggling into his coat as he goes out.

'Is that it, then?' I stand up, surprised that it's over so quick and easy.

Conroy shrugs. 'What could he ask you, your twelve times tables? If I hadn't known you he'd have had to interview you a bit more, but what can you tell about any bloke really before you set him on?'

'And what can you tell about a firm before you work there?'

Conroy nods. 'It's a gamble on both sides.' He opens the door. 'Come on, we'll go and get a cup of tea and then I'll show you round the shops. What time train have you to catch?'

I tell him the time of the last one which will get me my connexions at the other end.

'Oh, we'll see you catch it.'

'All done and dusted; interviewed, classified and filed?' Jimmy asks when we're back in the main office.

'It's in the envelope,' I say, and I'm pleased when he laughs because it's an old joke of ours from way back and the way he picks it up so quickly makes me feel at home with him like in the old days, and takes away some of the strangeness of this place.

Running back through the town to the station with Conroy, the lights on now, the figures huddled in their coats against the cold (it seems colder here than at home), I wonder if these people and these streets will soon be as familiar as those in Cressley; and I try to project myself and Ingrid into this new life.

But it's something I can't do. Behind all my thinking is a wall that I come up against when I try to think too far ahead for Ingrid and me. The best thing to do is take things one at a time, as they come. And this job . . . well, it's not so much the job itself as a feeling somehow that I've got to take it to prove something to myself.

5

The trains north are pretty quick these days and with something to read the journey isn't bad. But Cressley isn't on the main line and the last bit, by diesel from Wakefield and a bus up through town, is what makes it all a bit of a drag.

Sitting in the bus, seeing the lights of the town centre and thinking back over today, I've all at once got a hollow scared feeling in the bottom of my stomach. And I know just what it's saying to me. 'What do you want to go all that way off for, among people you don't know? Why don't you stay here? You know these streets and these people. You've lived here all your life. You belong here. You're safe here.' Yes, safe. You big soft nit. When are you going to stop hanging on to your mother's apron strings? Because that's what it amounts to. This place, these people, the old familiar life; you get collywobbles at the thought of leaving them. 'Why not ring Whittaker's and ask for a job? They'll give you one. They liked you. They were sorry to see you leave. They'll be glad to have you back. Or if you don't want to go back there, have a change. There are plenty of other firms who'd take you on. Why trail two hundred miles for the sake of it? Ingrid doesn't want to go, does she? You're going to have to do a lot of talking to win her over. And is it worth it?'

Is it worth it?

I let myself into the flat with my key and find it dark and empty, the fire out and a note to say Ingrid's round at her mother's and will I go and fetch her. And there's me expecting my slippers warming by the fire and supper waiting for me.

The streets are cold and empty, the pubs shut now, and only a few late cars humming by on the main road. I never know what to expect from Ingrid's mother these days and I'm not too easy as I go up the path and ring the doorbell. Ingrid answers it.

'Oh,' she says, 'you're here. I thought you'd got lost.'

'I came straight round,' I tell her. 'I didn't even take me coat off.'

She walks away from me down the hall as I'm talking and I step inside and shut the door behind me, thinking as I always do when I see this hallway about the night I got drunk and Ma Rothwell let me in and we had our big bust-up.

I'm pleased to see she's in a good mood, sitting in an armchair by the fire in her thick dressing-gown, and amiable Joe that I am, I take this at its face value. One of my troubles is that I don't dislike people very well. What I mean is, I can dislike somebody without holding it against him, and I'm easily won round.

'Good evening, Victor,' she says, nice as you please. 'Have you had a successful day?'

'Yes, I think so.'

'If I'd known you were going to be so late,' Ingrid says, 'I'd have gone home and let Mother go to bed.'

'I came as fast as British Railways would let me,' I tell her.

'Wasn't there an earlier train?'

'Not that I could catch.'

'Don't nag Victor so much,' her mother says. 'He's had a long day and he must be tired.'

I have. Up at six to catch the early train from Wakefield, and on the move ever since. A lot of my time's been spent sitting in trains, but that's one of the most tiring ways of resting I know. I catch a yawn.

'Yeh, I am a bit tired. Be nice if I could lie in in the morning.'

'A few hours' sleep and you'll be as right as rain again. You've got your health and strength, that's the main thing.'

'How are you feeling today?' this reminds me to ask.

'Oh, not too bad. It comes and goes. Some days are worse than others.'

I look at her, wondering how much of it's kid or imagination. There's no doubt about it, she has aged in the last few years. Her face is thinner, sallower. Whether it really is bad health, or losing her husband, or me just really looking and noticing a few more years on her, I don't know.

'Your mother seems a bit better,' I say to Ingrid when we're walking home.

'It's like she says, she's better some days than others.'

(No, she said she was worse some days than others.)

'Can't anybody find out what's wrong with her?'

'She's going for an X-ray next week. Then p'raps they'll find out. You know what she thinks it is, don't you?'

I grunt. 'They might find out it's something they can cure without a lot of trouble.'

'Yes, but she's scared. She doesn't say a lot about it, but I can tell. And this other thing doesn't help.'

'What's that?'

'The idea that I might go away and leave her.'

'Have you been talking about it?'

'Of course we've been talking about it. I had to tell her where you'd gone today. And besides, she's a right to know, hasn't she?'

'Whatever happened you wouldn't have to move for a bit. Not until I'd settled in and could look for a house.'

'But it's all upsetting. People don't know where they are. I don't know why you had to start all this just now.'

'Look, I didn't know old Mr Van Huyten was going to snuff it, did I? And Conroy's job's going now, not in six months' time.'

'There'll be other jobs.'

'Mebbe not with good money and prospects like this one, and among friends.'

'You sound as if you liked what you saw.'

'I liked what I saw,' I admit.

'Did you tell them you'd go?'

'No, I said I'd think about it.'

'When do they want to know?'

'I said I'd write within the week.'

'That's no time at all.'

'I wouldn't have to *go* next week. If I said yes they'd mebbe give me a month to clear things up at the shop.'

'It's still quick, all in a rush. We've never even talked about wanting to move away from here before.'

'It's the way things happen. As far as I knew I was settled at the shop. Now I've got to do something else. Make a decision that could change our lives.'

'I like my life well enough as it is.'

'It's all right for you. You'll give up working sometime and stop at home. I've got a lifetime of it in front of me. I just want to make a proper start, that's all.'

She says nothing, pulling her collar up closer round her neck as we walk along. There's frost sparkling on the pavements in tiny flashes of crystal. They say we're in for a hard winter.

When we're in the flat Ingrid asks me if I want some supper.

'I'm not bothered. The fire's gone out and it's too late to get another one going.'

'When did you eat last?'

'I had a sandwich about six.'

'You ought to have something, then. You must be famished.'

'Oh, I'm past it now. I'm not bothered.'

'Why didn't you have a meal on the train?'

'What, at that price? I'll have a cup of cocoa and drink it while I'm getting undressed.'

'I suppose I should have had your supper waiting when you came home.'

'I'm not complaining.'

She makes the cocoa and I drink it in the bedroom, draining the last of it just before I click off the light and slide down under the bedclothes. Ingrid's quiet now, lying with her back to me. I move in close, fitting myself into the shape of her body, and put my arm over the front of her. She mutters something I don't catch.

'What?'

'I said, it's the wrong time.'

'Well I *know* it is. Oh Christ!'

I roll over on to my back and look up into the darkness. In a minute she speaks again.

'I've been hoping all day you'd come back and say it was no good.'

'I can't say that.'

'It still doesn't mean you're forced to take it.'

'No . . . I'm not forced to. But somehow I feel I've got to. It's a . . . it's a sort of challenge, somehow.'

She's quiet for a minute.

'Do you want to get away from me? Is that it?'

'What? Don't be daft.'

'I should have to stay here on my own.'

'But only for a while, till I get something fixed up.'

All at once I begin to see further than her mother's illness, to what might be the real thing that's bothering her. She's not sure of me, whether I want her or not.

'Is that what you're really bothered about?'

'I don't want to be on my own.'

'It wouldn't be for long. And I'd be able to get home.'

'You wouldn't be able to afford it every week.'

'I suppose you could move in with your mother for a while. Keep her company till she gets better.'

'Where would you stay then, when you came home?'

'Oh, we'd have to keep this place on.'

'It's all expense.'

'It will be till we get settled down.'

'I don't think it's worth it. I don't see any need for it.'

'I just don't want to go back into engineering round here. I don't think I can face it.'

'You've made up your mind, haven't you?'

'No, not yet. I want you to see it my way.'

'D'you think we could take my mother with us?'

'What?' This really shakes me. In that case it's out. But definitely. 'I can see that working. You know what happened last time.'

'But we're more settled now. Aren't we? It wouldn't be the same.'

'It'd be just the same. You know the only way your mother and I get on is to see each other as little as possible. That way we can be nice and polite.'

'I don't want to leave her on her own.'

'She's not an old woman.'

'But she's not well.'

'She will be, then she'll be all right.'

'She might never be well again.'

'Oh Christ! I'm only trying to do what's best for us. I can't think for everybody.'

'You've got to consider other people. She is my mother. And I'm all she's got.'

'And she's capable of looking after herself. You know, I thought we'd finished with all that long since, but here we are – up against it again.'

'Circumstances alter cases.'

'They've altered mine all right.'

'You sound very bitter.'

'Do I?'

'Are you?'

'What about?'

'You know what about.'

'I thought we'd put all that behind us.'

'I have.'

'You're still thinking about it, though.'

'I can't help it sometimes. You don't let me.'

'What have I said?'

She stirs beside me. 'You know what I mean.'

'No, I don't. If you're going to carry on all the time looking for hidden meanings in everything I say or do, we shan't get anywhere.'

She turns towards me now. 'Do you love me?'

Ah, dear God, words, words, words. I'm here, aren't I, married to her, living with her?

'If you weren't unwell I'd show you.'

'You know that's not the same thing. There was always that.'

'Yeh, but we've been married three years. It can make a difference.' I find her hand and guide it down to me. 'Look what still happens when I get near you.'

'And what happens when it's over?'

Oh, but she should know better than to start all this. We got off on the wrong foot and we've never really found the step; but we're here, together, after three years, still making the best of it. And talk like this won't do us any good at all. When all's said and done we're no worse off than thousands of couples who walked down the aisle with the idea that eternal paradise was waiting for them on the other side of the vestry door.

'Well that's a law of nature, love. You can't blame me for that.'

'I wish you'd be serious.'

'I thought we were being too serious.'

'Do you really and truly want to take this job?'

'I think it'll be best for us. A change always does us good.'

'I don't want to be a drag, Vic.'

'I know.'

'It's just that . . .'

'Look, why not forget it for a couple of days, then let's talk about it again?'

'What's the town like? Are there some good shops?'

'Lots of them. And London's only forty minutes away. You could go up there once a week if you wanted to.'

'I'll bet it costs more to live than it does up here.'

'Oh, I don't know. I think there's a lot of rubbish talked about that sort of thing. Anyway, I'd be getting more money.'

'What about houses?'

'We'd probably be better off in a flat to begin with. You know, till we need more room.'

'You mean, when we have a family?'

'Mmm.'

'Do you feel like trying for another baby now, Vic?'

'It's up to you, love, really.'

She moves closer till I can feel her breath on my face. 'I want your baby,' she whispers. 'I want a boy who'll look just like you.'

'Well, the solution's in your hands,' I say.

I feel her begin to shake, her body close to mine, and for a second I think she's crying. Then I realize she's laughing, giggling fit to burst. And I wonder why I don't make her laugh more often.

The next day she capitulates. It's up to me, she says. I'm the one who earns the main living and one day I'll have to earn it all. So I can make the decision. If I want to go all that badly she won't stand in my way. But I can't expect her to be happy about it. Not yet. We shall have to wait and see. And contrariwise, now the way's open, I'm more undecided than ever. I had to put up the arguments for it to Ingrid and make her think I was keener than I really am. But I hadn't decided. I still had the feelings I had on the bus. Why not stay where I know my way around?

It's my mother who does decide me. She comes her usual wet-blanket act when I tell her, doing what she's always done when there's a smell of change or something new in the air, and using all Ingrid's arguments and a few of my own on me again. It's got nothing to do with her, of course. Oh no. She doesn't want to influence me. I'm old enough to know my own mind. But . . .

And then I know why I *have* to go: to get out, once and for all, of this dead, dreary, do-as-you've-always-done atmosphere to somewhere where I can stand on my own two feet in some good free air. I want to escape and it would have been better if I'd done it years ago, before I met Ingrid. Am I saying I wish I'd never met her? In a way I suppose I am. It's not that I don't like being married to her now. I've settled down to it in a way. It's not a bad life. Better than being at home. And I'm fond of her. I could even say I love her in a way. Her life's tied up with mine and that's all there is to it. It wasn't the way I wanted it to happen but it's the way it did happen. And if I'd got it in the way I always wanted it, it might well have come to this by now. You can waste a lot of time brooding about happiness. Maybe it just means jogging along and doing your best and taking your pleasures as they come. And when you

54

add up all those pleasures that's where your happiness is. No, it's all right – I don't believe it; but it's all most of us have got.

The Old Man's on my side. He doesn't say much in the house but when I leave he comes out to the gate with me.

'Don't take any notice of your mother, Vic,' he says straight out. 'You weigh it all up for yourself then make up your own mind. You can't blame her, I suppose. There's Jim away at university and David after this job in Leicester. She just thinks she's losing all her family at once.'

'It's not just that, though, Dad. She's always full of sour grapes. She just resists any sort of change.'

'That might be her age and upbringing, you know, lad. There's safety in what you know. When you've been through hard times like your mother has you can't forget 'em. You've allus half a feeling they're waiting round the corner again.'

'It . . . it just sometimes gets you round the throat and stifles you.'

'Well you break clear of it, lad. You've your own way to make in t'world and there's nobody knows better than you what you want. If you and Ingrid can agree about it there's nowt else matters.'

The man from Fenwicks has fair, slightly wavy hair, prominent fish-eyes and not much chin. I'm stocktaking in the shop with the door locked when he appears against the glass and taps on it, his face floating up close like a trout in an aquarium. I go over and open the door, thinking he's just another to add to the number who can't read the notice stuck to the inside of the window: 'Closed due to bereavement.'

'I'm sorry, we're closed.'

'I know,' the chap says. 'I'm from Fenwicks. The bank said it was all right for me to come round.'

'Oh, come in, then.'

I let him by me and lock the door again.

'You'll be Mr Brown.'

'That's right.'

He sticks his hand out. 'My name's Harrap.' He moves up the shop, carrying a fat briefcase. 'Is it all right if I have a look round?'

'If the bank says so.'

'Yes, they do.'

'Then it's okay by me.'

'What are you doing?'

'Stocktaking.'

'I'll try not to get in your way.'

'That's all right. Anything I can do to help, just say so.'

He looks at some stuff on the floor at the end of the counter. 'Sheet music? Have you been selling this?'

'No, I found it tucked away upstairs. I thought of chucking it out but I expect it ought to be accounted for.'

He picks up the top sheet. ' "Lily of Laguna". Good grief!'

I grin. 'There is some a bit more recent than that. It was Mr Van Huyten's main line at one time. That and pianos.'

Harrap looks round at me. 'You didn't find any pianos upstairs?'

I shake my head. 'No, no pianos.'

'That's all right, then.'

He's a man of about thirty-five, medium height, nice build, dressed in a neatly cut brown suit with trouser bottoms just that little bit too wide. He's from head office, he tells me, here to look the business over and put in a report to his bosses. With his easy manner he gives the impression of knowing not all the answers but all he needs to know to get by. The rest he probably doesn't bother about. I'm always interested in people who seem to have it sorted out.

'Just records, television and radio, isn't it?'

'And a few electrical appliances.'

He nods.

'We did all right,' I say defensively.

He nods again. 'I know. I've seen the books ... The owner hadn't been very active for some time, I understand.'

'No, he was an old man.'

'And you really ran the place.'

'I used to talk over most things with him, and he signed all the cheques.'

He walks to the window and gazes into the street for a minute before turning to look down the length of the shop.

'It's a good position, and a nice roomy interior. A lot could be done with it.'

'There were things I wanted to do, but Mr Van Huyten was too old for expansion and change.'

'You can't stand still these days,' Harrap says, 'not with the competition there is. You either go forward or slip back.'

'Unless you know your time's short anyway,' I say; 'then you don't care.' And for no new reason I'm suddenly full of bitterness and resentment, and anger with myself for not seeing that Mr Van Huyten was too far gone to plan for a business that would carry on in the same way after he was dead; a business that would perpetuate his name instead of becoming one more link in a growing chain. I'd have done it for him, and been proud to do it. But who'll ever know what went on in his head towards the end, or what changed between me coming to work for him and him losing his grip? Or even what he actually meant when he offered me the job with all kinds of hints about the future? Perhaps I should have seen the signs myself and put the cards on the table in time; told him straight the understanding I'd been working on. And perhaps a man like Harrap would tell me I should never have come in the beginning on such a half-baked pie-in-the-sky basis.

'What would you have done?' he's asking me now.

'Well, I'd have had this counter out for a start and a shorter one put in over there. It takes up too much floor space.' He nods. 'Then I'd have knocked the door to the stockroom out and made a showroom through an archway so's people could move about and see what we'd got.'

'Yes, I think those things would be an improvement.'

'Not that it takes a brilliant mind to think of them.'

'No, but . . .'

He goes off on another tack and starts asking me about myself until, after a few minutes, I have to stop him.

'You're not interviewing me, are you?'

He looks a bit taken aback at this straight question.

'No, it's my job to report on the business.'

'Well I don't go with it, y'know.'

'You'll be out of a job before long, though, won't you?'

'I've got another one.'

'Oh, well then . . .'

'I'm going back into engineering.'

'You know your own affairs best. But if you'd wanted to talk to somebody at head office I could fix it. And I can make recommendations.'

'They wouldn't let me keep the shop, would they?'

'We usually promote from inside the organization.'

'And I'd either be working under somebody here or moved to another shop.'

'There's plenty of chance of promotion.'

I shake my head. 'No. I had a special relationship with Mr Van Huyten. It's the only reason I came.'

He seems to have taken a bit of a shine to me, I don't know why. 'Well think about it. You're the kind of man we want. I don't think you'd be just a shop assistant for long.'

For a second I'm tempted. No upheaval, no moving away, no adapting myself to the drawing board again. And it would suit Ingrid.

'No, sorry. All my plans are made.'

'A pity.' He looks at his watch. 'I make it lunchtime. Where do you usually eat?'

'I have a sandwich round the corner.'

'Is there a place where they serve lunch?'

'There's the Dolphin in Bread Street. That's not bad.'

'Perhaps you'd like to join me. I think the expenses will run to it.'

'Okay, thanks very much.'

We get our coats and go out. It's market day and the streets are very busy. We have to wait for a table so we have a pint in the bar before going into the dining-room. I've only ever been in there once before and I look round and locate the table where I sat with Ingrid's father, and remember bits of the conversation . . .

– I get the impression that you feel badly done to and have for some time. As though marriage itself was something that had been imposed on you.

– I've had a bellyful of being married.

– So now you're going to chuck it and get out.

– I haven't said that.

58

– I thought you had.

– I said I could if I wanted to. I said I wasn't going to wait around for any favours and I wasn't going to be pushed into doing anything I didn't want to do. You can tell Ingrid that from me, and her mother an' all . . . She doesn't like me, y'know.

– I know she doesn't. But I do, and I don't shy away from the idea of you as a son-in-law.

– Thank you very much.

Thanks for everything . . .

'Do you use this place much?' Harrap asks me.

'No, I haven't been in for a year or two now.'

On the way back we pass the pillar box at the corner of Bread Street and Market Street. I walk by, fingering the two envelopes in my pocket. Then I say wait a minute to Harrap and turn back and slip the letters in. One's to Franklyn, saying I'll take the job, and the other's to Conroy, telling him the same thing and asking him to look out for digs for me. Putting my hand up to the slot, holding the envelopes poised for a second, then letting them drop seals the decision. That's it.

Ingrid sees me off at the station, something I hadn't thought of. The little ceremony of her riding down on the bus and buying a platform ticket so's she can wait with me till the train comes in makes me feel like a leave-end soldier going away for half a year, when the fact is I plan to be home for the week-end in a fortnight's time.

'You're sure you've got everything?'

I look at the big suitcase I borrowed from the Old Man. The handle's bitten into my fingers and the flesh is red and puffy. From the weight of it you'd think the only thing I hadn't brought was the furniture.

'I'll drop you a line if there's anything I want.'

'You'll write to me anyway, won't you?'

'In a day or two, when I know how it's going.'

'What will you do about your washing?'

'Send it to the laundry.'

'You could bring it home and let me do it for you.'

'I don't see much point in lugging things backwards and

forwards every other week-end. When it gets down there it might as well stay.'

Stay. For good. The visits, the temporary things, will be back here. Has she grasped it yet? Has it sunk in?

Oh yes, she's got it all right. She's saying good-bye on a deeper level than I am. There's more for her in this than see you in a fortnight. It's the end of something and the beginning of something else that might never be any good. And she's scared to death of it. And holding it in, standing there, moving her feet in the cold, her gloved hands together. She always did look her best in winter, I think; though her heavy coats muffle her neat little body, they don't hide the colour in her cheeks, the soft cleanliness of her hair, and her white teeth with the breath whisping away from them. Nor the length and shape of her legs.

'You're an attractive little piece, you know. And there's a black man looking you over.'

The quick lowering of her eyelids and the sideways flick of her eyes is more than a sharp looksee at the West Indian standing a few yards away; it's the way she always takes a compliment. Ingrid hardly ever looks me in the face in times of either personal pleasure or anger. When we make love she'll offer her body and hide her eyes. It might give some people the impression she's sly; but I know it's a deep basic shyness and a lack of confidence in herself that over three years of being married to me have done nothing to cure. And why should it have? The way we started our marriage it would need continuous doting attention like I gave her when I first began taking her out to put her in the position she ought to be in. And it's an act I can't put on. Not that she wouldn't know it was an act anyway. There's too much water gone under our bridge. But at least I'm what she always wanted and I'm what she's got, for what I'm worth.

The diesel slides into the platform and stops. I pick up the case. The weight of it tugs at my tired shoulder muscles.

'This is it, then.'

'Yes, good-bye. You will write, won't you?'

'Yes, soon as I can.'

I give her a quick kiss and catch the shine of tears under her eyelids as I pull back. I can't suppress the irritation.

'Oh, for Pete's sake, Ingrid. I'll see you in a fortnight.'

'You'd better get on.'

I move to the train and turn again once I'm inside the door. She's already walking away, striding briskly along the platform to the gate.

'Well, what the hell!'

But I can read unhappiness all over her back and when I go into the carriage and find a seat I've got agitation, restlessness and frustration leaping about inside me. Shovelling coal, digging a ditch, smashing windows. There's any number of things I'd rather do than sit for hours in a train. But something violent.

6

Conroy's pad is in a tall narrow house up a street off the London Road, near the railway. Mrs Witherspoon, his landlady, is a small, nodding, bird-like woman who fixes you with her bright little eyes and never seems to hear a word you say, though her head nods and nods as though she's taking all in and hearing the gospels for the first time. Very putting off, because you find yourself raising your voice until you're all but shouting at her and her head nods faster and faster as though to say yes, yes, yes, I can hear you, you don't have to shout, and you wonder if it wouldn't be possible if you ever got really mad with her and told her off for her to nod herself right into a convulsion or something. Conroy tells me not to mind as there's not much I'll need to talk to her about, and if ever I want anything seeing to, the best thing is to do what he does – leave a note (a memo, Albert calls it) on the kitchen table. ('Conroy, Room Four, to Mrs Witherspoon, c.c. Sanitary Inspector, Longford Borough Corporation, Subject upstairs lavatory. The above-mentioned installation is now in such a condition that it showers the puller of the chain with water rather than flushing away the waste matter in the bowl. I can only conclude that it constitutes a danger to health in this house and I should be obliged if you would kindly arrange to have it rectified.')

It's Sunday when I go down there and Albert's arranged to pick me up at the station. 'Tell me what time your train arrives King's X,' his letter said, 'and I'll calculate what time you'll reach here.' And only two minutes after I've come out of the station building and I'm stamping about the forecourt trying to keep my feet warm the little red Morris comes round the corner and pulls to a halt in front of me. He winds the window down, grinning at me.

'How's that for service?'

'Perfect, Albert.'

He gets out and hoists my case into the boot himself, exclaiming at the weight of it. 'Jesus, what you got in here, Kilnsey Crag?'

'That's what I've been wondering. I think Ingrid must have slipped a few bricks in when I wasn't looking.'

He gives me one of his quick looks. 'Everything all right on the home front, is it?'

This is a bit direct and I wonder what I've said to give myself away to that extent. The crack about the bricks and the little outburst in the pub when I came down for my interview are no more than the kind of things lots of husbands come out with: lines in the battle-of-the-sexes routine they subscribe to all the time. And Conroy, as I recall it, can't know the exact circumstances in which I married Ingrid. Neither could Jimmy be sure because I'd left Whittaker's by that time and the evidence went when Ingrid fell downstairs and brought on her miscarriage.

I shrug it off. 'Not bad. Ingrid's mother's not well and that complicates things a bit for her. I expect it'll work itself out, though.'

Conroy just grunts as we get into the car and starts telling me more about him getting me fixed up in his digs for the time being. Maybe I'm too sensitive and reading more into his remark than he meant. But it'll bear watching and I shall have to remember that he's got a bust-up marriage somewhere in his past and he'll be sharp on the signs of strife.

Mrs Witherspoon nods her way through the introductions then nods me upstairs and into what's to be my room; a pretty cheerless hole to be sure, but what boarding-house room isn't when you've been used to home comforts all your life? A few books, a gramophone, perhaps; maybe even a picture: they'll make a difference. One feature I do like is a narrow french window which appears to open on to a little iron-railed balcony overlooking the railway; but when I go over and try the handle Mrs Witherspoon tells me she had it screwed up in 1942 after a maiden lady living in the room fell three floors into the backyard.

'Saturday night, it was. She was all right then as far as I know; but on Sunday morning I found her, all crumpled in her nightdress.'

'What a nasty thing to happen.'

'Oh yes, indeed, Mr Brown. Very nasty indeed. It upset me for a long time, I can tell you. Not a nice thing to find when you get up on a Sunday morning. Not a nice thing at all.' (Nod, nod, nod.)

I hold my neck rigid till the muscles start to ache to stop myself from joining in and making her think I'm sending her up.

'Was it accidental, then?'

'Oh yes, yes. Accidental death. Or was it misadventure? She would have the window open wide, summer and winter alike, no matter what the weather. *I* think she walked in her sleep.' (Nod, nod, nod, with a step nearer to me and a conspiratorial look as though the bird in question had been a junkie and stupid with drugs before she fell.)

I make tut-tutting noises with my tongue. 'I think you did the right thing, Mrs Witherspoon.'

'I'm sure I *did*, Mr Brown.'

'I'm *sure* you did, Mrs Witherspoon.'

'Yes indeed. I'm sure there are more people who walk in their sleep than is generally realized.'

'I'm sure. And it'd look very odd if it happened again, wouldn't it?'

'Well, of course. That's just what I thought.'

I'm about to tell her that I've been known to indulge in a spot of nocturnal perambulation in times past, but decide this might unsettle her, so I let it go.

'The little pane at the top opens for ventilation. I'm sure you'll find that quite sufficient.'

'I'm sure that will be ample.'

'They say we're in for a severe winter.'

'Yes, they do.'

'I expect you've had snow already.'

'Only in Scotland, I believe. I come from Yorkshire.'

'Yes, of course. You'll find it a pleasant change to live here after being cut off every year.'

'I live in an industrial town, Mrs Witherspoon. It's only the villages and farms on the moors that get cut off.'

'Oh, how strange. But I should have known. I had a sister who lived in Yorkshire for a time. I visited her once at her house in Manchester.'

I'm getting a feeling of going quietly out of my mind when Conroy appears in the doorway behind Mrs Witherspoon and leans against the jamb, his head going in perfect time with hers, his face blank. I struggle to keep from laughing as she prattles on a bit longer. Then as she turns to go she sees Conroy. His head stops moving in a flash and his face takes on an expression of friendly interest as he looks at her.

'But here's Mr Conway. He'll see that you make yourself at home.'

'Yes, I'll show him the ropes, Mrs Witherspoon.'

He stands aside to let her pass, but she turns in the doorway with another thought.

'Just one more thing, Mr Brown. I don't allow dogs or children. I hope it won't inconvenience you, but I have to make it a positive rule.'

She disappears and I collapse on to the bed.

'For Christ's sake, Albert. Why didn't you warn me?'

'I thought I'd let you find out for yourself. Did she tell you about the bird who fell out of the window?'

'Yeh. That's why it's fastened up.'

Conroy grins. 'She must have fallen out of every upstairs window in the house. If she ever fell at all. I think it was two other fellers.'

'She is harmless, I suppose?'

'Old Lady Witherspoon? 'Course she is.'

'No dogs or kids. Jesus! What is it about me that makes me run into weird old birds, I wonder . . . Do you remember me going to Hassop's house and meeting his sister?'

'No, I never knew that.'

'It was one time when he had the 'flu. Miller sent me up with a

64

note. She was the queerest one of all. Just like something you find locked up in a turret in a horror film.'

'No wonder he was an odd bod himself.'

'Yeh, that's what I thought afterwards.'

'Is he going strong up there, still?'

'As far as I know.'

Conroy grunts. 'And the best of British luck to him.'

'To him *and* Lady MacHassop.'

'Anyway, you think you'll manage here for a bit? It's not exactly three star.'

'I can't afford three star prices.' I shift round on the bed and lie with my hands behind my head. 'I shan't be here all that long. Just till I can get settled down to the job and have a look round. I think a little flat's the thing to go for. There's only the two of us. We can take our time about finding a house then. Look for something nice.'

And Mr Van Huyten's legacy will come in nicely for a deposit. Very comforting it is to have the promise of a bit of money.

I let my eyes run over as much of the room as I can see from where I'm lying: the faded green wallpaper, the mushroomy paint on the door and skirting, the curtained-off alcove with a rail for hanging clothes up, a washbasin and a gas fire. The shape of the room is odd, not a square or a rectangle but trapezoidal, with three good strides from door to window along the longest side and a slope in the ceiling over the alcove where the wall butts up to the pitch of the roof. It'll do for me for a while, though it is small and Conroy, by the window, broad-shouldered and burly, seems to shut out most of the light and fill the room with his bulk.

'You couldn't have many friends in for a chat, that's for sure.'

'No, it's not made for parties.'

'What's your room like?'

'A bit bigger than this. Want to look?'

I say yes, getting up off the bed. He takes me down to the next floor and into a room at the front of the house. Different wallpaper, same paint. Square. Not big, but more room to walk about in than in mine.

'You can tell somebody lives here, anyway,' I say, standing in the doorway.

'Yeh, it's due for a clean-up. You can get to be an untidy sod when you live on your own.'

'I didn't mean that, actually. It's comfortable, though, homely ... When did you take up the rich man's game?' I point to the heads of the golf clubs sticking up behind the fireside chair in the corner.

'What, golf? Come off it, mate. All kinds of people play nowadays. Haven't you seen the colliers on the courses up north?' He takes a club out of the bag, and a ball which he putts across the carpet.

'I play with Franklyn on Sunday mornings sometimes. He's a lot better than I am, though. My handicap's colossal. I've tried to get Jimmy interested but I can't. What about you? Why not take up a pastime beneficial to mind, body and spirit?'

'I've got one,' I tell him, grinning. 'Anyway, I wouldn't be any good.'

'How do you know till you try?'

'You can't just barge on to a golf course slamming balls all over the place. It'd spoil it for everybody else.'

'We could pick quiet times and I'd show you the ropes. Who knows, you might have a hidden talent. And it would do my ego good to play with somebody worse than myself for a change.'

'Playing the gramophone's more in my line.' I go over to Conroy's record-player and look at the rack of L.P.'s in their bright-coloured sleeves. Beethoven, Brahms, Mozart, Schubert's Great C-Major, the Verdi Requiem, Bach, Vivaldi, Purcell, Vaughan Williams – the serious stuff, with a strong classical and English streak running through it – and some jazz, Ellington and Basie among it but most of it by small pick-up groups.

'You've got some good stuff here.'

'Well, of course I have. You don't think I spend my hard-earned loot on crap, do you?'

'One man's crap is another man's caviare. You'd be surprised the amount of money the kids pass across the counter for stuff that won't be worth listening to a fortnight next Thursday.'

'I reckon it's fine. Let them buy all they want. It subsidises the stuff we want, doesn't it?'

'True enough. There's more of that being sold than ever before as well, though. We had a chap used to come into the shop. Mind you, he wasn't typical, but he used to come in Saturday mornings and spend a couple of hours or more poking about among the racks and playing records in the booths. He always bought something and usually it amounted to four or five quid. He was a bachelor, a working chap, without much to say for himself. He didn't drink or smoke and he lived on his own, him and his hi-fi. I think he must have had the standard repertory a couple of times over. One time he thought he'd have a real go at Mahler so I ordered him all the symphonies there were on record. A nice little packet that cost him.'

'I'm just coming round to Mahler meself,' Albert says. 'I suppose I'm a slave of fashion.'

'Yeh, he is on the up and up. And Sibelius is going down. To read some of the critics you'd think he was going for ever.'

'But you don't think so?'

'Well, honestly, Albert, all you need is a pair of ears to know that he's in a direct line that goes back to Mozart and Haydn. Carrying on the great symphonic tradition. I don't see how anybody can deny him his permanent place.'

'Aw they'll change their minds in a few years' time. When he's been dead long enough.'

'And then they'll realize what nits they are.'

'Oh, they won't do that. They'll say they told you so all the time, even though they're on record as saying something else. Human nature, Vic.'

'Have you got anything?'

'Only the Second.'

'Well, that's all right. Very exciting and all that, but you want the Fourth, Sixth and Seventh. They're the ones. Marvellous. Christ!'

Conroy's watching me with a little smile on his face.

'I must say it does my old heart good to hear somebody enthusiastic about summat worth-while. What does Ingrid say when you carry on like that?'

'Ingrid? Oh, I don't talk to her about music ... Can we have something on?'

'If you like. What do you fancy?'

'I dunno.' I have another look through the rack. 'You don't have any trouble playing the thing, then?'

'Oh, I've got to keep the volume down a bit, you know. And I never play it after ten at night unless I know I'm in on my own. It's a bit restricting.'

'I know what you mean. I like to belt it out meself. Here.' I pass him an L.P. of mixed overtures and short pieces. 'Let's have the *Roman Carnival*, eh?'

Albert puts the record on the turntable and drops the stylus on to the Berlioz track. The old Wizard's orchestration flashes into the room like a drawn sword. Then on it winds through that lovely cor anglais tune and climbs to a climax that's all snapping, snarling brass . . . *doo-ah rratatah dee doo doh dah, rrumdidumdidumdidum-didumdumdah Dooooh daaaAH*!

In the electric silence that follows, Conroy and I grin at each other like a couple of kids.

Part Two

7

Starting a new job is like any other big change in your life. It's a time when you begin thinking about turning over new leaves, chucking out the bad old habits and approaching life full of conscientiousness, vim and vigour. No more pushing it till the last minute in a morning: you'll be up with the sparrows and have time to spare. You'll see that your shoes are polished the night before and that your trousers are always pressed. There's a new orderliness and with it a fresh enthusiasm for little things. You decide to have your hair cut regularly and wash your feet before you go to bed; and perhaps this is a good time to cut down on smoking, or even pack it in altogether. The novelty of the whole situation means you can carry it through. For a while, at any rate. Then you probably slide back into the sort of sloppy ways you had before.

The first couple of weeks slip by quickly while I'm working my way into the new routine, finding my way about, sizing up the job, and generally taking things steady till I know who's who and what's what. Conroy and Jimmy are a great help. Knowing I've been off the board for a few years they do all they can to smooth the way back for me. And with the people they're in a position to show me that certain little bits of behaviour that might seem odd can be put down to our old friend factory politics – the petty intrigues, enmities and spites that no works (in fact, no collection of human beings) seems to be free of. Not that Joyce's is riddled with plots and backbiting and so on – or if it is it doesn't show all that much on the surface. By and large the people I come in contact with seem decent enough and ready to help the new boy, some of them to the extent of going out of their way to do it.

This goes for Martin, too, the other draughtsman in the office, who keeps himself to himself unless he's approached, when he's very careful and correct. He's been a soldier at some time or other and it shows in his appearance. He'll be in his middle forties, with greying hair and a neat moustache. His favourite dress seems to be a navy blue double-breasted blazer with an R.A.S.C. badge, dark grey slacks and an R.A.S.C. tie. He hasn't come very far in the engineering world, having taken some sort of crash course in draughtsmanship when he left the Service, and he sticks to detailing. That's to say, he breaks down into detail component drawings somebody else's design schemes. This is the kind of work I start on to get my hand in again.

When I go home at the end of the fortnight I find Ingrid very loving and glad to see me because she's missed me. She's also happier about things in general. Her mother's been examined by a specialist and booked for a hysterectomy. I don't know what this is till Ingrid explains and then I remember hearing my mother talk about women having it done, only she called it having everything taken away. It's no picnic and it'll knock Mrs Rothwell up for a bit; but as far as I can gather it's not usually something women die from, and once it's done it's done.

I find myself going out in the evenings a lot more than I did at home. There's no telly to gawp at and my room isn't really a suitable place to just put your feet up and read. It's possible to turn one room into a kind of home, but this place is somewhere to keep your clothes and sleep. What reading I do I do in bed, but this grows less and less because a couple of pints are a marvellous nightcap and as I'm having a couple nearly every night I find that two or three pages are all I can manage before my eyes are too heavy to take any more.

I begin to wonder how I spent my evenings at home. I never went out much except to take Ingrid to the pictures perhaps once a week; and I didn't often go into a pub. But I suppose that in your own home, even if it is only a flat, with all your things around you, you can always spend a pleasant evening pottering about doing nothing very much. Having somebody around helps as well. You couldn't exactly call Ingrid and me exponents of bright intelligent conversation, but idle chit-chat about nothing in particular takes up a fair bit of time and there's comfort in a matey silence.

Conroy being a lone wolf, and living in the same house, he and I go out a lot together. We never see much of Jimmy outside working hours. He's knocking this bird off, the daughter of the people he's lodging with on the other side of town. He's the only lodger they have, and treated like one of the family. In fact, he's as good as married and living with his in-laws, except that he doesn't sleep with the bird. I think it's a very funny situation for a bloke to get himself into. The maximum of temptation with the minimum of opportunity. You might say he's at least in a position to get the full inside story and know the worst before he commits himself; but for my money he's committed already and the only way out for him if he ever changes his mind is through the bedroom window at dead of night.

Conroy knows a lot of people to say he's been in the town less than a couple of years and made all his contacts from scratch. Whichever pub we go into (and I see the inside of quite a few different ones in the first few weeks) there'll be somebody he'll nod to or pass the time of day with. If he chats with anybody he'll introduce me, but as I'm not good at catching names and they're complete strangers to me, it's not till afterwards when I get Albert to fill me in that I can fit them into any kind of slot and get some standpoint for joining in the conversation the next time we meet. Publicans, businessmen, tradespeople, a councillor or two, a doctor, a bank manager, and a journalist on the local evening paper: all kinds of people.

But all men (except for wives), and all, it seems to me, casual acquaintances without a steady friend among them. I begin to wonder if he takes women out and if he's knocked about on his own before I arrived, because he seems happy enough with my company now and I can't see that I've pushed anybody out. He looks easy-going and self-sufficient but it strikes me that under it he might be a lonely bloke; and then I tell myself to stop trying to weigh him up according to my own character. There *are* people who are happy on their own, friendly with a lot of people and really intimate with nobody. And there are men who are born bachelors, who don't need women except as an occasional little bonus on top of everyday life. Perhaps Conroy's one of these, who's had a bite at the apple, got a bad dose of bellyache, and doesn't intend to go back for more.

One night we're having a pint in a pub called the Mitre, standing by the open bar, when a party of people come in. They're all young and dressed casually and there's something vaguely arty about them that I can't put my finger on. Conroy tells me they're part of the company from the Palace and I remember that the theatre is only just round the corner. A tall bloke in sweater and slacks and a cravat in his open-necked shirt is getting the drinks. They all drink bitter, pints for the men and halves for the women. There are four men and two girls and one of the birds is the most gorgeous thing I've ever clapped eyes on.

'That redhead's a stunner,' I say, and Conroy nods.

'Fleur Dunham. She is a bit of a knockout.'

As I'm looking at her she sees Conroy and lifts her hand and smiles. At the same time the tall bloke turns from the bar and spots Albert as well. He raises his arm in a mock salute.

'You know 'em, then?' I say.

'Yes, 'course I do. Want to go across?'

'I don't mind.'

'Come on, then.'

'Hang on a sec. What d'you say her name is?'

'Fleur,' Albert says. 'Flower to her friends.'

He winks. I don't know if he's kidding or not as he sets off across the carpet with me in tow and suddenly wondering if my flies are zipped up and whether there's any snot on my face from the last time I blew my nose. These things do happen, you know.

There's the usual round of introductions with me missing most of the names, then Conroy says:

'Vic wanted to touch Fleur to see if she was real.'

The men laugh and I say, 'Now just a minute, Albert,' and shoot a glance at the other bird in the party, wondering how she'll take what seems to me like a stupid and tactless remark. But she just stands there holding her glass with a faint smile on her face and it occurs to me that she's probably used to waiting in the shade while this Fleur dazzles every bloke within thirty feet.

Fleur isn't disappointing from close up, either. No rough complexion or lines you can't see from some way off. It would be surprising really if she did have lines because she can't be more than twenty-one or -two and absolutely at the peak of her condition. She might be one of those women who weather well and get really interesting in their thirties but this combination of looks and freshness is something that can't last for ever and I wonder if somebody's having it off with her, because if there isn't it's a rotten crying shame. I don't know if she takes Conroy's remarks seriously or she's just being polite but she holds out her hand and I take it for a second and say hello. Just then I remember reading somewhere about a country where a man compliments a woman by saying, 'You look so beautiful I want to take all my clothes off,' and I turn away to hide my grin.

Nobody seems to notice but the second bird, who lifts her eyebrows at me as the others start a conversation.

'That was an amusing little thought you just had,' she says, and I feel my grin widen. 'It was, but I can't share it with you. I don't know you well enough.'

'Oh,' she says, 'like that, is it?'

I shake my head. 'No, not really.'

Apart from not knowing her I can't offend her by repeating the thought in connexion with another bird. Because this one is something of a looker in her own right – small face with nicely modelled cheekbones and fair hair with paler blonde streaks that look as though it's been bleached in the sun – and it's only Fleur knocking your eye out that stops you from noticing straight away.

'Have you been, er, performing tonight?' I ask her, and she nods.

'Is this the pub you usually use?'

'Yes. It's the nearest. By the time we've got our make-up off it's too late for more than a quick one.'

'How do you come to know Albert?'

'He once did some work for us. We wanted a light metal structure for a play we were doing. A very symbolic piece with skeleton sets. Esther Franklyn is interested in the theatre so she spoke to her husband and he sent Albert to help us.'

'My mother-in-law's first name is Esther.'

'Oh?'

'Yes. It's not a common name, is it?'

'No, I suppose not. You're married, are you?'

'Yes, only my wife's still in Yorkshire. She'll be coming down here when I get us a place to live.'

'And you work with Albert?'

'Yes. I used to work with him once before, back home. I've only been here a few weeks, though. I'm just finding my way round. I've seen most of the pubs but not much else.'

'Oh, it's not a bad town, and it has the great advantage of being close to London.'

'Can I get you another drink?'

'Is there time?'

'Just, I think. Anyway, I want another one before he puts the towels on.' I look round at the others. 'What about your friends?'

'Oh, I shouldn't bother. Don't get a full round.'

'Why not?'

'We usually pay for our own.'

'Are you proud, or something?'

'No, just broke most of the time.'

'Don't let me be awkward.'

I go and get the glasses filled, hoping she won't get absorbed into the other conversation while my back's turned, because I want to talk to her some more.

'Here you are, then.'

'Thank you. Cheers.'

'Cheers . . . Isn't there much money in rep., then?'

'Not that you'd notice. Most of them run on a shoestring.'

'How many are there in the company?'

'About ten permanent and some who double acting with stage management.'

'Do you get a salary or are you paid on a kind of piecework basis?'

'Oh, a salary. So we have to be kept working or we're so much dead weight. But we're luckier than most, really. Where they do weekly rep. you could be doing a play at night, rehearsing another one during the day, and learning a third in your own time.'

'Crikey!'

'But we're on fortnightly, so it's not so bad. Sometimes you alternate a big part with a small one, and sometimes you have a fortnight off altogether.'

74

'But not too often because you have to earn your keep, eh?'

'No, not too often. They watch that.'

'I noticed when I came down for my interview that you were doing *An Inspector Calls*. Were you in that?'

'Mmm. I was a maid.'

'What part are you playing this week?'

She pulls a face and grins. 'A maid. But I have a different wig.'

'They seem to have you in a corner.'

'No, it's not as bad as that. I've had some big parts. Lady Macbeth, Hedda Gabler; really strong meat. Next week I'm doing Blanche Dubois in *Streetcar*.'

'All sweat and suggestive looks.'

'If that were all you needed . . . It's a big part, and a scaring one.'

'Phoney Deep South accent and all that.'

'That's the least of my worries, though that's bad enough.'

'I'd like to come and see you.'

'You know the procedure. You buy a ticket at the door and walk right in. But don't come this week. It's a ridiculous play.'

'Oh?'

'A thriller.'

'You never know, I might like it.'

'I don't see how you could.'

'Somebody must like it or they wouldn't have put it on.'

'If it comes to that, I suppose you can find audiences for almost anything.'

Her voice seems cool now. She looks sideways at the rest of the group as though dropping the conversation, and me with it. Perhaps I'm reading her wrong but at the same time I could kick myself for going out of my way to make her think I might be a moron when I was getting on so well with her and, in fact, wanted to impress her. I can't remember talking to many bright birds, and this one is attractive into the bargain.

I'm still standing there feeling slightly stupid and trying to think of something to say that might change the impression I'm sure she's got of me now when the landlord calls for the glasses and the tall bloke finishes his pint and looks at the others.

'Well, children, who's for home?'

We troop out into the car park where Conroy asks if anybody needs a lift; but they're all going the other way. One of the bods gets up behind the tall bloke on a scooter and the rest of them pile into an A40 that seems to belong to the bird I've been talking to because she climbs in behind the wheel.

But before she gets in she looks across at me.

'We might see you next week, then?'

'I'll see *you*, anyway,' I say, glad she hasn't gone off me altogether.

'Don't expect Vivien Leigh, though,' she says.

'I won't form any opinions till afterwards.'

'And not too many then,' she says.

The scooter leaves the yard with a roar and shoots off up the street. Under its noise the bird says something else that I don't catch before ducking out of sight on the other side of the car. I follow Conroy across the yard. When we're in the Morris I say:

'What did you say that bird's name was? The one I was talking to.'

'Donna Pennyman,' Albert says. 'She's nice, isn't she?'

'Yes, she is.'

I feel his glance fall on me for a second as he twists in his seat. But he says nothing else just now, concentrating on backing the car out into the busy road.

It isn't exactly the best time of year to swap a cosy job in a warm shop for the partly outdoor number I've got now. Although I'm feeling my way into things nice and steady and I'm not in charge of any contracts yet, there's always something coming up to fetch me out of the office and into the bays, apart from the fact that keeping an eye on what's going on out there is the best way of getting on top of it all.

Winter's settling in. Fog comes down with the dark most nights and the days are damp with the distances closed in by mist, and moisture lying on the banks of steel in the yard round the shops. Sometimes, to make a change, an east wind with a razor edge on it scythes in across the low fields. Then the labourers handling steel in the yard are better off in some ways than the workmen in the bays, because the big doors are always open and it's not as easy to keep warm standing in a draught at a machine or a bench as it is humping angle iron or tee section about; though there's always a bit of hanging about waiting for cranes involved in work of that kind and I don't envy the blokes who are doing it.

The men's nickname for Conroy is 'Yorky' and Jimmy is 'Yorky's mate'. I suppose I'd be Yorky's mate if I'd arrived second but as it is they don't seem to have thought of a name for me. Some of them call me Mr Brown and others soon get on to first-name terms. One or two take the mick in a friendly way about my accent, but they've been through all that with Jimmy, if not with Albert, and they soon get tired of it. There's nothing familiar about it. There hardly ever is between staff and shop-floor men unless somebody gets off on the wrong foot. Each side keeps its discreet distance and knows its place.

So that one day when I'm cutting through one of the bays and a voice hollers out over the thump and clatter of the machines, 'Hey, you!' I just keep on going, not thinking for a minute it's me who's being called to. Then it comes again – 'Hey, you . . . Mister!' – and I automatically check myself for a second and look round. There's Bill Chisholm, one of the foremen, looking straight at me and, now he's seen me glance round, lifting his arm to wave me over to where he's standing by a bench with some cleats and drilled sections of various lengths and sizes on top. On one side of him there's an elderly fitter in a flat cap and on the other, lounging against the bench as if he'll fall over if he stands up straight, Chisholm's son, Wally, a lad of nineteen or twenty with tight blue jeans and, like he always has, a smirk on his face. Everything and anything makes Wally smirk. When there's nothing going off to amuse him he smirks at his own thoughts. As for Chisholm himself – I've known quite a few Yorkshire loud-mouthed know-alls in my time and they're bad enough. But London know-alls are worse because they're gifted a bit more with the gab and there's a whine in the voice that grates on my nerves. Chisholm is a Londoner and a know-all and so far I've kept out of his way.

Now I walk over to them.

'D'you want me?'

'We do want you, yes indeed. I was just going to phone the office for you.'

'Well I'm here. What's up?'

'You know, Mr Chisholm –' the elderly bloke starts, and Chisholm cuts him off short.

'Just a minute, Charlie.' He picks up a grubby print by one corner and pushes it over to me. 'This is yours, I believe? I'm right in saying it's yours?'

'Yeh, that's mine. What's up, is something wrong?'

Chisholm waves his hand at the clutter of steel on the old boy's bench.

'All this is wrong, that's what's wrong.'

'Won't it fit together, then?'

'No, it won't.'

'Is it the drawing?'

'I've got my own ideas,' Chisholm says in a very superior manner and making a lovely meal of it, 'but you tell us.'

'We'd better have a look, then.' I take my steel tape out and begin to run it over the drilling in the various pieces while Chisholm stands back with his arms folded, obviously waiting for me to condemn myself out of my own mouth.

His attitude has put my back up from the start but for a minute I'm keeping my mouth shut. There's no use me making a great bluster about the drawing being right and what the hell is he talking about because it's quite on the cards that it is wrong. You can drop some funny clangers when your mind wanders for a minute. I've done it before and I shall do it again. They say the man who never made a mistake never made anything. And this is a job I did a couple of weeks ago. I want breathing space to cast my mind back to what I was thinking of at the time.

It's not a major job; just a steel structure for holding a water tank, with a pump underneath. But what made it a bit tricky was that it has to go into a tight corner and be bolted on to two stanchions and a wall-member that aren't regularly spaced. I remember how careful I was with the measuring-up and the preliminary sketches.

So I stand there with three pairs of eyes and Wally's smirk on me, checking the parts against the drawing and knowing that if they're right and the drawing's wrong at least some of the steel's scrap unless I can see a way of rectifying it.

Then suddenly the penny drops. I begin to grin inside, but keep my face straight.

'Who marked this lot out, then?'

'He did. Wally,' Chisholm says, still with the same laboured air of waiting patiently for me to admit I'm wrong, and not seeing at all that I'm home and dry. It's this now that gets me shirty in my turn and this time it's me who cuts the old feller off as he tries to say something again.

'Has he got his boots on the proper feet?'

'Eh? What are you talking about?'

'He doesn't seem to know his right hand from his left, that's all.'

Chisholm starts to bluster but I see that the smirk has slipped off Wally's mug and he's not looking too sure of himself now.

'Look.' I pull two of the uprights to the edge of the bench. 'These want to be right and left hand. They've both been drilled right hand. There's some extra drilling for the pump bracket in the deep flange on the left-hand member and it's been drilled in the wrong one. Besides that, if they're both the same hand the diagonal stays won't marry up.' I look at Chisholm. 'I should've thought you'd see that straight away, Mr Chisholm.'

Now the old boy gets his word in. 'That's what I was trying to say.' He touches one of the sections. 'It's this one that's wrong.'

I look at him and nod. 'That's it.'

I get no pleasure in gloating over a bloke I've bested, even if he has asked for it, so I just stand there and say nothing else while Chisholm peers at the print, muttering to himself, and sees what he should have seen at the beginning, except he spotted me and jumped the gun.

'One as drawn, one opposite hand. This drilling in opposite hand member only . . . Why can't you draw the bloody thing out properly instead of – '

'Oh, come on,' I say. 'If he can't read the drawing he shouldn't be marking out.'

He can't bluff any more. He turns on Wally.

'You're a bright little bugger, aren't you? Who's going to explain about all this wasted stuff?'

Wally shuffles his feet. He's the apple of his old man's eye, but not just at this minute.

'Well actually,' I say, 'it's not as bad as it looks. If you swap those two uprights round, make the right hand the left and the left the right, you should be able to mark out again and drill some extra holes. 'Course, you'll finish up with some holes to spare but mebbe Mr Franklyn won't notice them and wonder how they got there.'

I say it quick and just once before I turn my back and walk away. I could show him what I mean in a few seconds but he'll work it out for himself when he gets over being made to look silly. Chisholm's not dim, just a bit impetuous; and in this case he's been very quick off the mark in going for me. I wonder why.

'I think I can tell you that,' Conroy says.

It's a couple of days later and Franklyn has suggested I should go out for the experience with Albert when he goes to look at a job he's doing: two loading bays for a firm of frozen-food manu-facturers near Chelmsford. It's another damp grey day and I get chilled through from tramping about the site and doing nothing except listen to Conroy as he talks to our men and discusses things with the works engineer of the firm we're doing the job for. I decide I'll have to buy myself a thick donkey jacket that I won't mind getting dirty, and something tough to keep my feet warm in mud and wet grass. It's lovely to feel the warm air from the car heater wrap round my legs like an electric blanket as we drive back.

Conroy brings the subject up. I haven't mentioned it to anybody but it appears word's got round that I've had a bit of a barney with Chisholm and come off best. So I tell Albert the full tale.

'I mean, I don't like the clever sod, but he's not stupid, is he? If he'd done a quick check, or listened to what the old bloke was trying to say, instead of shouting me over . . . I got the impression he was out to make me look silly. I don't know why.'

'He's been after a job in the drawing office for Wally,' Conroy says.

'Oh, aye?'

'We interviewed him, Franklyn and I, and we agreed he wasn't up to it. He's doing his City and Guilds at night school and he might turn out to be a decent fitter one day; but he's not drawing office material. When you came down Chisholm got the idea I was filling the office with my mates and you were the one who'd got Wally's job.'

'That's the way he sees it?'

'So I understand.'

'Oh Christ, so I've got that sort of a caper to contend with.'

'I shouldn't let it bother you,' Conroy says. 'Every firm has 'em.'

He flicks the headlight switch. I slump in my seat, wriggling my toes with enjoyment as we press on home through the misty darkness.

'Anyway, as far as I'm concerned, it's finished and done with.'

And so it is. As far as I'm concerned.

8

British actors playing Americans usually make me squirm. (It's on the pictures and the telly I'm talking about: I've never been much to the theatre except to see variety shows and there aren't so many of them about now. They used to mix seasons of plays with the variety stuff at Cressley Alhambra, but there's a block of offices on that site now; and the little Tivoli hasn't had a big name on its stage in years.) It's not the accents sounding phoney so much as the whole atmosphere feeling somehow wrong. They do say, though, that Americans believe their own version of England and, funnily enough, it's often far enough away from my own life – with its country mansions and cottages in sleepy little villages and Mummerzet servants, or else foggy London and Cockney taxi drivers – for me to take it in too.

But with this production of *A Streetcar Named Desire* at the Palace all this doesn't bother me. I make my adjustments when I see the set: a door without a wall, a row of posts that lets you into the street outside the Kowalskis' apartment, and a bit of a bead curtain between the living-room and the bedroom that's supposed to stop anybody in either place hearing what's going off in the other.

Conroy and I go towards the end of the first week. 'Give 'em a day or two to play themselves in,' he says. 'They're always better then.'

He looks at me with a little smile. 'She'll keep.'

'Who?'

'Fleur.'

'Oh. Is she in it?'

'She's playing the young bloke's girl friend.'

'Oh,' I say again; then, 'Will she keep, though?'

'What d'you mean?'

'Well *she* might. She might even get better. But you sometimes do see birds of about twenty who are right bang in their prime. Another twelve months and they start going to seed.'

'What about it?'

'Well then you think it's a rotten shame if nobody's having the benefit of something that'll never be as good again.'

'What makes you think nobody is with Fleur?'

'I don't know. I'm just speculating. You're the one who knows that crowd.'

'D'you make any wonder mothers used to turn pale when their daughters suggested going on the stage? Here's a modern enlightened young feller like yourself thinking that theatrical circles are hotbeds of vice and depravity.'

'I never said any such thing. Only there's a bishop spouting in the paper this morning about the country's morals going to pot and I just wonder where it's happening.'

'All round you. Where've you been?'

'Leading my clean wholesome life.'

'Aye, in clean wholesome Cressley, where nobody ever has a bit on the side and there are no bairns born out of wedlock.'

Well this could be a pretty accurate shot at me if I thought he meant it like that. And it confirms that he doesn't know enough to mean it or he'd hardly be tactless enough to say it. So I decide to get it out of the way.

'You know Ingrid was pregnant when we got married.'

'I wasn't sure. I believe somebody once did say they thought so. I'm sorry, I shouldn't have made that crack.'

'That's all right.'

'What happened to the baby?'

'Ingrid fell downstairs and brought on a miscarriage.'

'Bad luck.'

Bad luck what? That she lost the kid or that I needn't have

married her after all? Though if I hadn't it might not have happened. Not that I'm saying I'd have been glad for it to happen and let me off the hook. What I can't get away from is knowing that I'd never have married her in the normal way. That's one clear thing among the rest of the circumstances, which are so mixed and entwined together that you can't say 'if only' about any of them because they all affect one another.

But Ingrid became a statistic: another bird pregnant on her wedding day; symptomatic of the breakdown in morality. Except she's never had it with anybody else before or since, and neither have I. So what's that symptomatic of? And what is morality anyway?

I want to ask Conroy about his marriage but though we're talking round this kind of topic I don't feel it's just the right time. He doesn't volunteer any information and I don't say anything else to him. So now he knows that Ingrid was having a kid when we got married; but that happens in a lot of cases and there's no more to it than simply the fact.

It's none of Albert's business that in my case a little bit of rank lousy luck led to something that wouldn't have happened otherwise, and that I've got something niggling me about my marriage. A sense of grievance, of knowing I've taken a wrong turning through force of circumstances and not through choice. A tendency to ask myself 'Is this all?' in the quiet moments of the night.

But still, I've accepted it on a practical level. This is it and make the best of it. (After all, I did walk out once for a few days and then come back.) And when I look outside it isn't for a cure. I'm not even looking seriously. Just with an academic interest in the tempting runners in the adultery stakes; of which there are plenty, but who's bothering and what the hell? You know this is no cure for anything anyway, because this is the last thing bothering you, the last thing you can't find at home, with satisfaction given on both sides.

But when you see somebody like Fleur you speculate in an idle sort of way, along with every other man who's ever seen her and is normal in his instincts. She's gorgeous. You reckon every man should have somebody like her just once in his life and it's a crying shame she isn't for you. Then you wonder if she couldn't just possibly be in certain circumstances – wondering all this without stress or strain, and that maybe you'd muff it if the chance did offer itself on a plate with no bill underneath. All this a favourite pastime of the male mind. And then something sneaks up from one side and gives you a one-two clout that knocks all idle speculation about bed right out of your mind and leaves you so dizzy you don't know whether it's Ash Wednesday or Pancake Tuesday . . .

The theatre's small and old-fashioned, like a music hall, with shabby red plush and peeling gilt. I reckon there isn't much money holding it together. Well, none to spare, anyway, though the audiences are apparently good enough to let them change their plays fortnightly instead of every week, and this night, although it's Thursday and not the week-end, the house is about three-quarters full.

It's on this night that I first get some idea of what people are on about when they talk about the excitement of the theatre. Oh, I've felt the little flutter in my stomach when a pit orchestra strikes up and the lights dim before the curtain rises; but that was variety. What few plays I've seen, though, were either full of french windows and people with terribly posh accents who had nothing at all to do with me, or else they were thrillers that I think come off much better on the pictures. I wouldn't have reckoned I'd find much common ground with a bunch of rum customers in New Orleans, come to that, but they seem to me like real people even if most of them are oddballs with more steam rattling the kettle-lids than in a season of chapel faith-teas.

I have to look again to see that the bloke playing Kowalski is our tall cravated friend from the Mitre, and playing him very well with an accent that doesn't turn me up and a performance that's his own and not a scratching, mumbling fourth carbon of Brando. I look him up in the programme and find he's called Leonard Reeve. I can't see him being a hit with a name like that, but maybe he loves his mother, and how was she to know her little lump of squealing, mewling baby flesh was going to strike out for fame and fortune on the stage. And if it comes to that I suppose a doubt or two must have crossed Albert Finney's mind in times past.

Fleur hasn't much to do but she does it well enough. Donna

comes on, looking smaller and frailer than I remember her in the pub, in a wispy flowered chiffon dress, all great dark eyes and high-strung movements of her hands and arms. The regulars know the actors and give them little rounds of applause as they appear for the first time. Donna wrings their hearts. Perhaps she brings out the fallen woman in all the women there. A lady next to me feels for her handkerchief and sniffs as she touches it to her nose. My pulse rate is up for some reason as Conroy and I make for the bar in the first interval.

Sitting on the aisle lets us be first in there. Albert passes me a bottle of beer and a glass and we edge into a corner out of the crowd that's followed us in.

'How're you liking it?'

'They're very good, aren't they?'

'You didn't think they were amateurs, did you?'

'No, but professional standards vary, don't they?'

Conroy nods. 'Yes . . . Yes, they are good. I can't see Donna being here for very long. She'll get her break or I'm a Dutchman.'

'Oh, but they're all good.'

Conroy quizzes me with his eyes.

'Don't let your new-found enthusiasm for the theatre run away with you. Donna's really exceptional.'

I don't get what he's driving at for a second, then the penny drops. I think of setting him straight, then decide that protests from me will only convince him more. He's so sure I've got a lech for Fleur and I can't think what I've done particularly to make him think so.

'What about Fleur?' I say, wondering if there's a tell-tale gleam in my eye.

He looks away from me and round the bar.

'Oh, with looks like hers she doesn't need to be able to act, does she?'

It's all just that bit too casual. Oh, but you're a deep boyo, Conroy, I think. How long have you been trying to climb in beside her yourself? Is that why you keep bringing her name up?

We're in the Mitre for twenty minutes before they come in, in a group, some I've seen before and some I haven't. Conroy turns to the bar to get some drinks and I join him.

'Let me help you with this lot, Albert.'

'You can hand some glasses round.'

'No, I mean share the round.'

'Go on with you.'

'Look there's only time for one and you don't want to be saddled with the lot.'

'Are you insisting?'

'Aye, I am.'

I've got two half-crowns in my hand and I plonk them down in front of him and pick up the first two glasses. I hand one to a bloke I've never seen before except on the stage tonight and the other one to Donna who's standing nearest. I reach for my own half-drunk pint as the bod lifts his glass.

'Cheers.'

'Astonishing good luck, mate, and thanks for a nice evening's entertainment.'

Donna turns her enormous eyes on me. Funny I didn't notice before how big they are.

'Have you been to the show tonight?'

'Yes, we have. I told you we'd come.'

She says nothing. I don't suppose she can ask how it was.

'I thought you were marvellous.'

'Oh, really!'

'Yes, really.'

'You'll have me suspecting your judgement.'

Somebody's started talking to the bloke on the other side and he's not listening to all this.

'No, honest, I'm relieved I can tell the truth.'

'You mean I might have been dreadful?'

'Well I didn't know, did I?'

She laughs suddenly, a really amused laugh that comes from deep in her throat.

'That's true.' She looks directly at me. 'And I don't think blarney would be one of your weapons.'

'Weapons? I'm just telling you I liked you in the play, love, that's all.'

'Luv,' she says, mimicking me; but there's good humour in her eyes and I suddenly know she likes me.

86

A middle-aged woman touches her on the elbow. I've noticed her and the man she's standing with eyeing Donna and obviously talking about her.

'Excuse me, Miss Pennyman.'

'Yes?'

'Forgive me interrupting your conversation but my husband and I enjoyed your performance so much I felt I had to tell you.'

Donna excuses herself with me and politely turns to talk to the woman.

I drink my beer and glance at the group. Albert's standing next to Fleur and saying something to her that makes her laugh in spasms, her hand to her mouth as though she's got bad teeth or expects her dentures to shoot out. The rest of them stand around grinning. I can't be bothered trying to catch what's going on and I turn away again, wishing the woman would let Donna go. I look at my watch. We've only two or three minutes left.

The woman is talking intently to Donna, her face flushed with pleasure while her husband stands by with a small smile round his pipe-stem. Donna listens seriously to what the woman's saying. She's holding her glass high in her right hand and one finger of her left hand traces circles underneath. I'm conscious of the length of her fingers and the thinness of her wrists with the blue veins showing faintly through the white skin. And just then, at that moment, all the evening concentrates itself into a feeling that's a tender yearning ache under my heart; a feeling I haven't had for a long, long time; a feeling I hardly expected ever to have again.

9

Home for Christmas. Your real home, the place where you came from. The place married people refer to when they stand in their own house and say, 'I'm going down home.' The family home. Where the heart is . . .

In the week before the birds have hung a few streamers and paper chains round the office with bits of mistletoe in strategic places, and on the afternoon we pack up for the holiday some

bottles are brought in and we all gather in the drawing office –
the one with most space – for a drink and a friendly laugh.
Franklyn provides a bottle each of whisky and gin and a box of
cigars and we stand about like lords, filling the place with the
smell of good living. There's a few half-hearted embarrassed tries
at getting friendly with the birds under the mistletoe but somehow
the atmosphere isn't right for it until somebody brings in a tape-
recorder with a reel of pop music on it and dancing starts.

Jimmy and I stand by the window watching the men who've had
their Christmas dinner and a free bottle of beer in the canteen
drifting home across the frosty yard. Franklyn puts his sheepskin
coat on and goes out to see that everything's all right. Things
loosen up a bit then and Conroy, dancing with Cynthia, pulls her
to a stop under the mistletoe hanging over the door and puts her
one on, her responding quite enthusiastically until somebody
cheers and she remembers her dignity and pulls away, smiling in a
funny way, her face a bit flushed from the whisky.

Jimmy tops my glass up from a half-empty bottle of beer.

'Steady on, Jimmy. I want to get home sometime today.'

'You can sleep it off on the train.'

'I want to find time to buy some things in London, though . . .
When are you coming up?'

'Monday. Spend Christmas Day with the old folks, then back
here Boxing Day ready for starting Thursday.'

'Taking your girl friend?'

'Uh uh!' Jimmy shakes his head. 'Not this trip. No, it's a case of
doing my duty as a loving son and getting it over with.'

'It's awful really, the way you grow away from your parents.'

Jimmy looks at me. 'You've never met my mother and father,
have you, Vic?'

I say no, I haven't.

'Younger than yours, I think. The old lady's a simple soul, a bit
vacant. The old man's dead ignorant. When he's had a couple of
pints he can solve all the troubles of the world with a few glib
simplifications. We shall have a row before Christmas Day's out,
that's for sure. He'll tell me I haven't brought Pamela home with
me because I'm ashamed of them. And he'll be dead bloody right.'

'You'll have to let them meet her sometime.'

He shrugs. 'Sometime.'

'What are her parents like?'

'Oh, just ordinary people. But nice, likeable. They haven't got this dreadful crafty guile that passes for intelligence among some working folk.'

Well, that's one problem I've never had to cope with. My parents aren't the brightest people in the world and there are times when the Old Lady drives me clean up the wall; but I was never afraid of taking Ingrid to meet them and I still like seeing them in short doses.

I shall have to come back on Boxing Day as well, so Jimmy and I start comparing notes about trains so's we can travel down together. And as I'm thinking if the party doesn't finish soon I shall have to leave Conroy and catch a bus into town, Franklyn comes stamping in out of the cold and suggests we start breaking it up.

We hide the empties in a cupboard and the girls take the glasses and cups and wash them up in the cloakroom. Then we leave, with shouts of 'Merry Christmas!' 'Have a good time,' 'Don't get drunk more than twice a day,' and so on. Albert runs me down to the digs. He seems a bit lit up for some reason, though it can't be the booze because he's hardly had enough. He keeps shaking his head in a resigned sort of way at the drivers of oncoming cars, until I ask him what he's doing.

'It doesn't half put them off,' he says. 'A feller once did it to me and I checked my lights and flickers and finally stopped the car and got out to look round before I realized he was probably lost in his own thoughts.' He laughs. 'Ah, that Cynthia; she didn't half come out of her shell for a minute there. Made me wonder if it wasn't worth pursuing.'

'Get pursuing, mate. There's nothing to stop you.'

'Naw, it's a waste of time. You know her trouble, don't you? She's mad about Franklyn.'

'It's news to me. What does he think about it?'

'I doubt if he knows. He's got a wife and four kids to keep him in line.'

'They don't have to keep him in line.'

'No, but as far as I know he's clean.'

We call in at the digs for my bag, give the compliments of the season to Mrs Witherspoon (nod, nod, nod), and then Conroy takes me to the station.

'Give my love to Yorkshire,' he says and I say, 'Aye, right.'

I have thought earlier that I ought to ask him home with me for Christmas, but then he mentioned he was spending the holiday with some friends in London so I didn't bring it up. Now he gives me a wave from the car.

'We'll wind it up with a jar on Wednesday/night, then.'

'Aye, right, Albert. See you then.'

Once in London I take the underground to Oxford Circus and make a quick sortie into Regent Street. It's dark now and the Christmas lights and decorations slung high above the road are all ablaze and the crowds looking at them and moving in and out of the shops are thick and hard to hurry through. I head into the first department store I come to and buy a nightdress and some perfume for Ingrid. They've got some nice costume jewellery that I could pick my Mother's and Chris's presents from, but there's altogether too many people and not enough time. So I make my way out into the street again and dive for the tube and King's Cross. A copy of *Esquire* and the *Evening Standard* and I'm on the train, in the warm, my feet on the opposite seat and heading for home. Home. All my roots are there and everybody I'm involved with. It's where you ought to be at Christmas and I *am* looking forward to it. But at the same time I've a feeling that I'm going away from something that's important to me too.

Christmas morning finds us all together: Ingrid and me, Chris and David, Jim, and Mrs Rothwell. The Old Lady sent Ingrid's mother an invitation, not wanting her to be on her own at Christmas but not knowing if she'd accept. They've always kept their distance, never mixing much; you don't have to become bosom pals because your kids are married to each other; and last year she was still in her shell after Mr Rothwell's death.

Today she's ensconced in an armchair by the fireside while the rest of us, except for the Old Lady and Chris, who are busy in the kitchen, are deployed round the living-room as comfortably as possible to say the table's opened out full and taking up most of the space. Ingrid, with my mother supervising and telling her where things are, is spreading the best white linen cloth – the big one that only comes out on special occasions – and laying places for all of us. On the hearthrug young Bobby is playing happily, surrounded by all kinds of Christmas paraphernalia, occasionally getting up to show something to Mrs Rothwell who he seems to have taken a shine to, and her to him. There's a sideboard full of standing Christmas cards that blow over every time somebody opens the door, more on the mantelshelf, sprigs of holly behind the mirror, and paper chains running from the centre light to the four corners of the room. Christmas Day Family Favourites comes through as background on the wireless.

The Old Man wriggles his toes inside his new slippers and takes his pipe out of his mouth to make a reflection:

'My, but that's a grand fire.'

We all mutter yes, aye, it is, and so on.

'There's nowt like a good fire. They can all have central heating 'at wants it.'

'There's a fire in the front room,' my mother says, coming through from the kitchen for a minute. 'And more room to sit. I don't know why you're all huddled up together in here.'

'I'll sit in there, if you like,' Mrs Rothwell says.

'Nay, you stop where you are, Mrs Rothwell,' the Old Feller says. 'You're all right there. That front room takes a bit o' warming through. We can sit in there after dinner.'

'D'you fancy a walk up the road before dinner, Dad?' I ask him, and he says, 'Eh?'

'To the pub, for a drink,' I say, wishing he'd catch on a bit quicker.

'I've got a bottle or two in the house, if you want one,' he says.

'I just thought we might stretch our legs; get out of the way for half an hour.'

'What does everybody else think? What about you, David?'

David says yes, he doesn't mind a walk.

I catch Jim's eye and he gives me a wink and a little grin.

'I suppose it'll give our appetites an edge,' the Old Man says. 'Though I must say I don't like to leave that fire.'

He puffs at his pipe for another minute or two, then gets up and goes to the kitchen doorway to call to my mother.

'What time will it be ready, Mother?'

'It's coming as fast as we can manage it.'

Jim and I look at each other again, both of us thinking the same thing: why is it so hard to get a straight answer to a straight question in this house?

'Our Victor's talking about going out for a drink,' the Old Man says, and I could kick him for putting the responsibility on me when he hadn't the sense to suggest it himself.

'Oh, is he?' the Old Lady says. 'Well it'll be on the table at half-past one whether you're here for it or not.'

I feel a great spasm of irritation. Why does everybody have to be so short and disapproving about everything? It's Christmas, for God's sake. I get up and go for my coat, hiding my temper.

'We've got an hour, anyway,' I say.

The Old Man looks at me. 'Are you getting fond of your pint?'

'Oh, for God's sake, Dad,' I say, fierce but low, so Ma Rothwell won't catch it; 'I just suggest it might be nice to stroll up to the pub and the next thing you know there's an issue made out of it.'

'Nay, lad, nay. We're all willing.'

'Well come on, then. Let's have a change of air.'

The Old Man potters about for another five minutes, changing into his shoes, finding his scarf, feeling to see if he's got any money. Jim and I go out and stroll on ahead.

'Bloody hell fire!' I say, once we're out of the house, and Jim grins. 'Why do people have to get so stupid as they grow older?'

We stand and wait for David and the Old Feller. When they come out we walk on ahead again.

'How's your stock just now?'

Jim shrugs. 'Not bad. She disapproves because I don't come home as much as she'd like me to.'

'She disapproves, full stop.'

'Oh, she's not as bad as all that.'

'No, I suppose not. Nice to know it's not your everyday lot, though.'

Jim's just turned twenty now. He used to be a gangling lad who grew too fast for his strength, but now he's broadening out nicely. A good-looking lad too, though he's a bit sloppy about his appearance.

'You know,' he says in a minute, 'I don't want to be one of these blokes who grows away from his parents, who finds he's got nothing to say to them.'

'I expect you meet a lot like that now.'

'Yes, I do. And you can feel it happening to yourself all the time.'

'Well, I wouldn't go around blaming myself for it. It's their fault as much as yours, if you can call it your fault at all. They're the ones who are hanging behind. It's when they try to hold you back the trouble starts. Not that my mother does it deliberately. She's kind-hearted, means well, and she'd be hurt if anybody told her she was a drag, because she's proud to see you get on. But they don't realize all that it involves. They somehow expect you to get on and stay just like them. There's a whole world outside that she just doesn't begin to understand.'

'Education . . .' Jim says, shaking his head.

'It doesn't need much education, Jim. Intelligence and a bit of perception will do it as well.'

''Course,' he says, 'she's convinced it's a girl who's keeping me away. I mean, she always goes for the obvious solution.'

'And is there a girl?'

Jim laughs. 'As a matter of fact, there is.'

I have to laugh with him. 'Well, I mean, they're not all that daft, Jim. They do know *some*thing about what makes people tick . . . Is it serious?'

'I suppose it is. Oh, she's sweet, though, Jacqueline. You'd like her, Vic. She's got everything. I mean, it's not just a question of bed; I like to be with her all the time.'

And there, if you want one, I think a bit sourly, is an echo of me at his age, only he seems to have hit the jackpot and I wonder if I'm supposed to interpret what he's said in the way I do.

'You mean you have been to bed with her?'

'Well, it's not all that easy to set up, but we do sometimes manage it.'

'You won't go and do what I did, will you?'

'I'm not stupid, Vic.'

'Thanks very much,' I say and he shoots me a quick embarrassed look.

'I'm sorry. I didn't mean it like that. Only we have sense enough to take the usual precautions.'

Usual, I think. It's usual to take your girl friend to bed and when you've got her there you take the usual precautions. And I'm where I am now because I hadn't the nerve to go into a shop and ask for what I wanted. Do the generations change so quickly, I wonder, or is it something wrong with me?

David and the Old Man catch us up outside the Bunch of Grapes and we can't say any more. We go into the best room where there's a fire as good as the one we've left and a fair gathering of men keeping out of the way while their wives cook whatever it is they've got to look forward to. The Old Man insists on buying the first round and asks us what we want.

'D'you mind if I have a whisky, Dad?' David asks.

'I don't mind at all, lad. What about you two?'

'A pint of bitter for me, please,' I tell him, and Jim says, 'Same for me, Dad.'

'Well,' the Old Man says, 'I was going to have a half meself but I'd better make it a pint. Can't let the younger generation show me up.'

Jim and I smile at each other and move over to the fire as David and the Old Feller go to the bar counter.

'Don't say anything to my mother or anybody, will you?' Jim says. He looks at me as I laugh. 'You know, I'll tell 'em myself when I want 'em to know.'

I'm still smiling. 'Sorry, only you sound just like me talking to our Christine.' I see them turning from the bar and I take the last moment to get serious. I'm looking Jim straight in the eye and the laughter's gone from my face as I say to him:

'Only, listen to this, Jim. It's your life. You do what you want to do and don't let any of 'em push you around. Just remember.'

And that's the last chance I get to say anything to him. Which is perhaps just as well. There's not much more I could say without telling him things I don't want him to know; and there's a limit to the advice anybody can take. They've got to experience things for themselves. No two cases are alike and once they begin to find out a bit of what it's all about it's probably too late for them to do much more than start handing out advice to somebody else.

94

We're back home on time so there's nothing my mother can grumble about, though her face doesn't slip as she sets the dinner out and we all gather round to shift it. I wonder sometimes what sort of bloke I'd be if the Old Lady had been a merry, laughing woman.

After dinner the women tackle the washing-up then join the men in the front-room, which is warm now, and we sit round making chit-chat about this and that: young Bobby, my new job and what it's like living in the south; David's new job (which he's got) and what it'll be like living in Leicester (of course, the Old Man knew somebody from Leicester in the first world war and he's played in one or two brass-band concerts there, so he's an expert on it), and a few guarded references to Mrs Rothwell's forth-coming operation.

After a while the Old Man slips off to sleep with his head back and his mouth open and I – always drowsy after beer at lunchtime – shut my eyes, and though it seems to me that I'm hearing voices all the time, I must go under as well because the next thing I know the women are moving about laying the table for tea.

On Boxing Day morning Ingrid and I sleep in, waking to come together in the after-night warmth of the bed in a way that needs no words, nor even conscious signs; only a knowledge of wanting that more often than not matches a similar need.

Brown, the great lover, boosts his ego in the rests in the rhythm of desire:

'Do you miss me?'

'Mmmmm.'

'Do you miss this?'

'You know I do.'

'You're a proper little sex-pot.'

'And aren't you glad.'

'I don't know. I go back with bags under my eyes after a week-end at home.'

'I expect everybody feels sorry for you.'

'Oh, they do, they do. The men think I've left home because I can't cope with it on a full-time basis.'

'I never know when you're kidding and when you're not.'

'Don't you?'

'You don't . . . you don't talk about it, do you?'

'What?'

'I mean this.'

'Not as far as you and I are concerned. Men don't, y'know.'

'Don't they?'

'Only about the subject in general, sometimes.'

'I see . . . You don't think, I mean deep down, that it's not very nice, do you?'

'What isn't nice?'

'Me . . . well, me liking it so much.'

'I don't think it's nice, I think it's bloody marvellous.'

'Do you really, Vic?'

'Well, don't you know?'

'Oh, I know it's all right for you that I do, but I wonder sometimes . . .'

'Look, I don't despise it in a woman, I admire it.'

'Do you?'

'Yes, I do. Proper bloody order.'

'Well, I just – '

'Shut up.'

Her mouth is laughing as I put mine over it. For a second. Then it's serious and responding, taking and giving back, driving us on into that private frenzy where what's said and done is nobody's business but ours, belonging here in the dark and the warmth away from cold sober daylight.

Which always comes . . .

'Are you going back to sleep now?'

'Mmm. It's lovely and warm.'

'What time have you to get away?'

'Two o'clock.'

'That's all right, then. We'll have time for a little chat.'

'What about?'

'Never mind. It'll do after.'

'No, go on, I'm listening.'

'Well . . . you know you once said I could always move in with Mother if it was necessary?'

'Mmm.'

'I think I ought to do that for a while. Till she's had her operation and got back on her feet . . . I mean, we'd keep this place on and live here when you came home.'

I think about it for a minute and can't see any real snags.

'That's all right. I don't mind.'

'You're not busy looking for a place down there, are you?'

'I'm weighing the situation up.'

'But you won't come home some week-end and expect me to pack up and go back with you?'

'There's no hurry yet.'

'No. You might fall out with the job, or something.'

'Oh, I think that'll be all right. You ought to come down and look things over, though.'

'I will, in a while.'

'Well, do what you think's best and we'll talk about it again later on.'

'Righto. I'll tell her. I'm sure she'll be easier in her mind.'

'But you're coming eventually, and on your own.'

'Yes.'

'Don't create any false impressions about that.'

'No . . . What do you want for your breakfast?'

'Better make it dinner and breakfast in one.'

'Eggs, bacon and sausage?'

'And a few chips.'

'Righto.'

'Are you getting up now?'

'Yes . . . Unless you want me to stop for a while.'

'You know what? You're insatiable.'

'So are you.'

'No I'm not. I'm physically incapable of being insatiable.'

'I just want to know you'll be all right for the next fortnight.'

'Oh, one of my second strings'll look after me.'

'Eh?'

'Don't you know? They can see it in my face. They're queuing up for samples.'

'Oh, are they?'

'Good old Yorkshire stamina. It's at a premium down there.'

'Let Conroy demonstrate. He's got nothing better to do.'

'He doesn't seem all that interested.'

'But you are?'

'Oh, all the time.'

'Vic . . .'

'What?'

'I know you're kidding, but . . .'

'What?'

'Oh . . . nothing . . .'

'Then don't be daft.'

10

There's already been enough of winter to cure me of any idea that the move south might bring me into warmer, sunnier climes, and the next few days convince me that as far as weather's concerned I'd have been better off staying at home.

First it turns colder; not bitter cold – grievous cold, and work has to stop on a few of the outside projects. Then it begins to snow, seriously, as if it means it, hour after hour, in heavy swirls of fat dry flakes that settle in a deepening layer on the frozen ground. Then a few more outside jobs stop. With reports of similar conditions all over the country, but especially grim in the west, we realize we're in the middle of one of the worst winters in living memory.

There's a bit of post-Christmas gloom hanging about the office in the couple of days after we get back. It seems to affect everybody. Franklyn, bothered about the effect of the weather on his contracts and preoccupied with finding alternative work for the men concerned, shows a testy side of his personality I've only glimpsed before; which might be one reason why Cynthia's in a deep sulk. Martin's his usual polite but unforthcoming self – no apostle of cheer at the best of times – and I know Jimmy's fed up because I listened to his tale of woe on the train coming down. A conscientious lad, Jimmy, who can't get on with his folks any more and can't bring himself to turn his back on them altogether.

On the Friday afternoon the phone rings. Jimmy answers it then says it's an outside call for me. I wonder as I go over to pick up the receiver who can be ringing me from outside, and I don't recognize the woman's voice on the line straight away.

'Is that Vic Brown?'

'Yes, it is.'

'This is Donna Pennyman.'

'Oh, *hello*!'

'I hope it's all right for me to ring the office.'

'Oh yes, that's okay.'

'I asked for Albert actually, but I understand he isn't in.'

'No, he's out Chelmsford way. He should have been back yesterday but he rang in to say he'd got snowed-up.'

'Yes, hasn't the weather been awful these last few days?'

'It'll get worse before it gets better, as well.'

'Cheerful! Look, I'm ringing to ask if you and Albert are doing anything on New Year's Eve.'

'Well I'm not and I don't think he is.'

'We're having a party at my place after the show. You might like to come if you're not doing anything else.'

'That's very nice of you.'

'It'll be just the people from the theatre, mainly. Bring a bottle, and all that.'

'I'll be glad to come. Can I ask Albert to ring you back and confirm about him?'

'No, there's no need to do that. Just be in the Mitre after the show on Monday and we'll go on from there.'

'We might come to see the show.'

'I shouldn't bother. It's only the Christmas play and it's mainly for children.'

'Haven't you heard that all men are really little boys at heart?' She chuckles over the line.

'Well, just as you like. Only you've been warned.'

'See you Monday, anyway.'

'Good.'

'And thanks again.'

'That's all right. I just thought you might be at a loose end.'

'Tell the truth, I was feeling a bit dreary. Something to look forward to now.'

'It'll only be drinks and a bit of shuffling round to the gramophone, you know.'

'Shuffling's the right word as far as I'm concerned.'

'Don't you dance very well?'

'Not so's you'd notice.'

'Me neither.'

'Perhaps we can have a shuffle together, then.'

I'm aware that I'm grinning as I go back to my board. Jimmy glances at me for a second but says nothing till a minute or two later when I start to whistle.

'Do I detect the intrusion of a note of good cheer?'

'Here's another one,' I tell him, looking at Conroy, who's just coming through the door and glowering round at everything and everybody in sight. 'The original abominable snowman.'

'What a performance!' he announces to the office in general; then walks over to us and tells us the tale of how he was caught in a snowstorm last night, had to abandon the car and walk two miles, then go back and dig it out this morning.

'Talk about Scott of the Antarctic! From now on a shovel's standard equipment in that car. Better still, mebbe I'll get Franklyn to buy a team of huskies and a sledge.'

'It's bad out in the country, then?' Jimmy asks him.

'You're not kidding, mate. There's six-foot drifts across the road in places.'

Cynthia speaks to him across the office without lifting her head: 'Mr Franklyn said he wanted to see you as soon as you got back.'

Conroy turns to her.

'Is he in?'

'No.'

'Where is he, then?'

'I don't know exactly.'

'Well tell me roughly.'

'Somewhere in the works, I expect.'

'What a rare pleasure it is,' Conroy says, 'to return from the brink of death and bask in the radiance of your personality.'

'I'm only telling you what he told me to tell you.'

'Thank you very much.'

'You've come back in a right mood, haven't you?'

100

'I've got good reason for my mood. What's yours? Isn't he being nice enough to you?'

Cynthia flashes a murderous look and the colour rises in her face. Then she's on her feet and slamming out.

Conroy looks at Jimmy and me in turn.

'Oh Christ, I suppose I shouldn't have said that . . . Still, it went straight to the target, didn't it?' He starts to take his coat off. 'I can't bloody stand moody women.'

He walks across to his board, dumps his coat over his stool, then goes down the corridor towards the washroom.

I look at Jimmy. His gaze switches from the door to me. There's a gleam in his eyes.

'What was all that about, then?' I ask him.

'Don't you know?'

'I know she's supposed to be sweet on Franklyn.'

'Did you know Albert used to take Cynthia out a bit at one time?'

'No . . . He did, did he? Well, well. You interest me, James lad. Carry on.'

Jimmy shakes his head.

'That much is fact. Anything else comes under the heading of speculation.'

'Well speculate a bit.'

'You mean is Franklyn knocking her off on the quiet? I don't know. Maybe Albert does, but he doesn't talk about it.'

'Was it serious, then? Between him and Cynthia, I mean.'

'I shouldn't think so. But enough to cause an occasional flash of spite.'

'He's a close devil, isn't he?'

'When he wants to be.'

'Do you know anything about that marriage of his?'

Now it's Jimmy's turn to look gone out.

'You what?'

'You mean you didn't know?'

'I'd no idea. Is he wed now, then?'

'I don't think so. They split up. He told me once when we were at Whittaker's. At the staff party, it was. He'd had a few pints . . . I thought you'd know or I wouldn't have mentioned it.'

'You're right, mate, he is close.'

'I don't think there's anything mysterious about it. He just doesn't talk about it.'

'He certainly doesn't. I never knew.'

'Well for Pete's sake don't let on I told you. He asked me to keep my mouth shut.'

We stop talking as Conroy comes back in. He gives us that same glowering look and growls at us:

'There's still some work to do, isn't there? Don't stand nattering all day.'

Which reminds me that although I live close to Conroy and drink with him, he's still my boss. I remember about the phone call from Donna, think I'll tell him, then decide it'll keep till he's in a better mood. The thought of the party lights a little glow of pleasure in me and sets me whistling softly to myself again, though I hardly realize I'm doing it till Conroy's voice growls up again from behind me:

'Look, Vic, let's keep the musical renditions for later, shall we?'

I stop whistling and don't look round. My mind flashes up a couple of snappy answers but I know that to use them will only rile him more. So I let it go. He'll come round.

The tall bloke in the corner by the gas-cooker gives me a shock for a second. Standing there in sweater and slacks, his back to the room, head bowed and hands somewhere in front of him, he looks for all the world as if he's having a leak; and it's only when I reach down for the half-full bottle of light ale that I've hidden out of the reach of grasping hands that I realize he's got a bird in there with him: a shapely little bit whose head comes up only to his chest. Neither of them takes a blind bit of notice of me and I turn away from the intimate little scene and pour beer into my glass.

The kitchen's quieter now than at any time since we arrived, nearly an hour ago, the draining-board littered with opened bottles of cheap wine and orange squash, and empty light ales. The standard drill for parties like this seems to be that you bring a bottle of wine and drink somebody else's Scotch if you can find where the crafty devils have hidden it. Conroy and I compromised and brought half a dozen pint beers apiece which we've stowed from the gaze of rapacious eyes, of which theatrical companies seem to have plenty. In terms of free booze, I mean. As far as the other thing's concerned I wouldn't presume to judge at this point because apart from the bloke and the bird snogging in the kitchen – and it wouldn't be any kind of party without a bloke and a bird snogging in the kitchen – the whole affair is carrying on on a level a lady lay-preacher could hardly take exception to.

A bird without shoes prissies in, shoots me an automatic smile from big baby-blue eyes, steps on a bottle top and says 'Ooh!' reaches the draining board, tops her glass up from a bottle of Spanish sauterne, sees the couple in the corner (or maybe only the bloke, like I did), says 'Ooh!' again, but with a different inflexion this time, and prissies out. All wrapped up in a tipsy haze.

I wander over and stand in the doorway. There's perhaps a couple of dozen people in the living-room, some standing in corners, others sitting on the sofa, and others with their arms round each other, their eyes looking soulfully into their partner's as they slur their feet quietly over the carpet to the music from the record-player. It's not a bed-sitter but a proper flat with a bedroom and bathroom besides the two rooms I've mentioned, and it's part of a few built into a newish block which has shops on the ground floor. Not cheap for a girl to rent on her own, and it strikes me that if the money in rep. is as bad as Donna makes out she must have some loot coming in from elsewhere.

Somehow I know by a curious instinct that she's not in the room even before my eyes have begun to look for her, and as I'm leaning there against the jamb watching Conroy chatting up the bird who's just been in the kitchen and now gazing at him with a glassy look that he might be taking for rapt attention but which looks to me like she simply can't focus properly, she comes through the doorway on my left, from the hall.

She smiles. 'All right?'

'Yeh. Lovely party.'

'Gosh, it's warm and smoky in here now.'

'It'll get worse before it gets better.'

She laughs. 'So you keep saying.'

'Can I get you something to drink?'

'Not just now, thanks. What's the time?'

'Four minutes to twelve.'

'Good lord, we're going to miss it.'

'What?'

'Letting in the New Year.'

She's up on her toes, scanning the room. 'Where the devil's Paul gone?'

'Who?'

'Paul Merrick. He promised earlier . . .'

'There's a bloke in the kitchen.'

She leans past me, one hand on my arm, the scent of her in my nostrils.

'Yes, that's him. He's dark enough, isn't he?'

'I should say so.'

'I'd better get him out.'

I go with her into the kitchen. She grabs Merrick by the arm. 'Paul.' He twists and grunts at her. 'Come on, Paul, do your duty. Sheila will still be here when you get back.'

'Have you got a lump of coal?' I ask her.

'Not a bit. Should I have?'

'Well, strictly speaking. To do it right.'

'We'll have to manage without.'

'Well give him some bread.'

She opens a cupboard, takes out the remains of a loaf and pushes it into Merrick's hands. We usher him out of the kitchen and into the hall. He stands there, acting stupid.

'What am I supposed to do – eat the bread?'

Donna opens the door.

'You just go out now and come back in when it's struck twelve.'

'I haven't got a watch.'

'Listen for the church bells.'

'With that row going on?'

Donna throws up her hands.

'Oh, my Gawd!'

'I'll go with him,' I say.

'Yes, go on, Vic, there's a love. Only make sure he comes in first.'

'I'm dark, so it won't matter all that much.'

'No, but he said he'd do it and he will. God knows what kind of luck he'll bring me, though.'

We nip out with about half a minute to spare and stand on the landing outside the door, Merrick leaning on the rail with his black shaggy head down and his eyes closed.

'I've been trying to make that Sheila for the last six months,' he announces suddenly without looking up.

'She looked cooperative enough to me,' I say.

'She's got a grasshopper mentality, though,' he says. 'She'll be in a corner with somebody else when I get back. All my good work gone for nothing.'

'You'll manage,' I tell him. Then 'Listen!'

'What?'

'The church clock – striking midnight.'

'You have remarkable powers of hearing, my friend. All I can hear is that bloody gramophone.'

Suddenly the gramophone cuts off in mid-record.

'They've turned it off.' I look at my watch. 'Half a minute past.'

'Is it time for my entrance?'

'It is.'

He straightens up off the rail and starts for the door, checking for a second to look back at me.

'What's the line again?'

'Happy New Year!'

'So it is.'

He throws the door open and charges in clutching the half-loaf. 'Happy New Year! Happy New Year!'

I follow him in as the hubbub of greetings starts on all sides. Merrick has hold of Donna, shouting something about kissing the hostess. She lets him plant one on then wriggles free and pushes him off on to somebody else, turning to laugh at me.

'Thanks, Vic. Happy New Year.'

'A pleasure, love. Happy New Year.'

There must be something in my face because the expression in her eyes changes as I put one arm out to bring her close. Then I have her, both arms holding her, her mouth under mine; and through my mind a chant is going. Not 'Happy New Year' but 'Oh Christ, oh Christ, oh Christ.'

There's a little smile on her lips as soon as we break away, but it's accompanied by a faint flicker of puzzlement in her eyes. I cover as quick as I can, knowing that the moment's got to break and wanting me to do it rather than her. So I plant on a chaser, a quick light stab of my mouth at hers.

'Astonishing good luck, then.'

'All the best to you.'

Her expression is lost to me as she turns her head at somebody's call. The moment's gone and I wonder if the complexities of it weren't just in my mind, and only there. When Conroy moves round my way I'm looking at her standing across the room with her back to me as she chats to a couple who seem to be getting ready to go.

'How're you doing?'

'All right, Albert.'

'Not a bad party, is it? Is there any more booze?'

'Under the draining-board in the kitchen. Behind the waste-bin.'

'Crafty snake.'

I follow him, looking round for my glass as he roots about under the sink and comes up with an unopened pint bottle. There are a few used tumblers about but I can't remember which is mine so I take one and rinse it out under the hot-tap and Albert fills my glass and his. I light a fag and we lean against the sink, quiet for a moment, listening to the sounds of chat and laughter, and the record-player that somebody's turned on again now, in the next room.

'I was a bit short the other day,' Conroy says all at once.

'Eh?'

'Ratty . . . in the office.'

'Oh, that . . . I'd forgotten.'

'It's always a mistake, mixing business with pleasure.'

'I don't get you.'

'Cynthia.'

'Oh . . .'

'I used to take her out a bit at one time.'

'I see. Didn't it work out, then?'

'She's the biggest tease I've ever come across. A professional virgin. Works you up then won't let you get there without raping her.'

'Perhaps that's the way she likes it, as if it's rape.'

'They're no good to anybody, birds like that. They want your cods as souvenirs.'

'I thought you said she was sweet on Franklyn.'

'She is. Just what it amounts to, I don't know. I think he's too canny to let her get her hooks into him.'

'Perhaps he's got too much to lose.'

'Everybody's got too much to lose. There's always a time to retreat in good order.'

'I dunno . . . I . . .'

'What?'

'Well, it just seems a bit cold-blooded, Albert.'

'You've got me wrong, Vic . . . I was married for a while, as you know . . .'

He turns round and tops his glass up while I keep dead quiet, interested in what he's saying and wanting to let him talk if the mood's on him.

'She took a fancy to somebody else . . . She couldn't help that. These things happen. But she had to go away with him. Couldn't live without him. I was the big magnanimous gent. I let her go. Twelve months later she wanted to come back.'

'She made a mistake.'

'Aye, but the trouble was, I didn't want her any more. I wasn't being vindictive about it. I just wasn't interested.' He looks at me. 'The trick is to see the mistake before the damage is done. Before it's too late. You've got to use this . . .' He taps his temple with his finger.

From the way he's standing there looking at me I get the impression that he's doing more than talk for his own sake; that he's trying to tell me something, that he might even have started the conversation off with this in mind. I want to take him up on it while the moment's ripe but I'm stopped by Fleur, who appears in the doorway, somewhat stoned, very flirtatious, and a living hymn to what in effect I've been saying I don't approve of – casual sex.

She pouts at Albert. 'I thought you were getting me a drink.'

'So I was, my sweet. What do you want?'

'A gin and tonic.'

'You'll be lucky!' He pokes about among the bottles on the side of the sink. 'A drop of Spanish sauterne ... no, that's empty. South African sherry. So's that.' He turns to her. 'You'll have to be satisfied with a sip of mine.'

She comes up close to him, pressing her breasts against his chest and gazing up into his eyes as he tilts the glass to her lips. He speaks to me without taking his eyes off her.

'Isn't she just a living doll?' To her he says, 'What can I tell my mother about you?'

She carries on looking at him, dozy-like, without saying anything.

'I want to kiss you all over and then eat you up,' Albert says.

I reckon it's time I left them to it so I go to the doorway, then turn and call to him. 'Albert.' He looks at me and I put my finger to my temple and grin at him. As I go out he's matching his words by cramming the fingers of one of her hands into his mouth and then, a second later, covering her neck and one half-exposed shoulder with kisses while she squirms in his arms in a way that could be either protest or enjoyment.

I squeeze my way round the edge of the room and get a seat on one end of the sofa, a loose-covered piece of furniture which seems to be passing into a comfortable old age with only the odd occasional grumbling twang from the springs. I wonder if Donna carts her own furniture around from place to place or if she chooses furnished flats. One of the few personal things I can see is a painting over the fireplace, an abstract effort: a great ball of orange like the yolk of a fried egg on a pea-green plate seen after a heavy night on the booze. I think of Donna moving about as the jobs come, and all the people here, a lot of them younger than me, who came from somewhere and might end up somewhere else, but now to me don't really exist as people because there's no frame round them. And this is like admitting that I can't see myself without my own frame; that the thing they rely on, that hard core of personality that makes a man what he is wherever he is, is something that in my case doesn't exist outside its context. Context . . . familiar places – a quick easy answer that covers the recognition of a lot of people and the love of a few . . . Lonely people turning to God, the great portable con-

108

text . . . Lonely man sitting on the end of a sofa at the fag-end of a party with people who all know one another but who he doesn't know, thinking dreary depressing thoughts in the early hours of an unspoiled year.

'You're looking sombre.' This from Donna, who perches with her thigh on the arm of the sofa near my shoulder. A long, tender, compassionate thigh that I feel a sudden soft urge to rest my head against. 'Deep and complex thoughts?'

'Dreary and woolly thoughts,' I tell her, answering her smile and covering up with, 'I must suddenly have gone tired.'

'The party's nearly over.'

'They look good for hours yet.'

'Oh, they'll pack up quite suddenly. Except for a few stragglers who'll want to sit about till morning drinking coffee and talking about the meaning of life.'

'I'd better find Albert.'

'I'm not pushing you out.'

'No, love. But he was getting very friendly with Fleur the last time I saw him. If I'm walking home I want to know in good time.'

'I can set your mind at rest about that. Fleur's sleeping here tonight.'

I've got to laugh. I get up.

'Early call tomorrow?'

She shakes her head, smiling. 'Nothing till the show tomorrow night. That's the best of Christmas productions; they go on a nice long time.'

'Well, I'm on at nine o'clock sharp.'

'Sharp?'

'I'm always punctual.'

'Would you like some coffee before you go?'

'You don't want to start that now or you'll be making it for everybody.'

'Oh, I think I could do it discreetly.'

She stands up. 'I'll come with you, anyway. See what Albert and Fleur are doing.'

We find Albert on his own in the kitchen, standing with his glass topped-up again and one hand scraping about in the bottom of a big potato-crisp packet.

'Donna was asking if we'd like some coffee before we go.'

'Oh, are we going?'

'I don't know, Albert. I'm ready when you are.'

'I thought Fleur was in here with you,' Donna says.

'She was. But she went off looking green and saying she didn't feel well.'

Donna says, 'Oh, dear. I don't know why you men can't . . .' Her voice is a touch peevish and colour's come into her face as Conroy chips in:

'Look, don't blame me. I've just been keeping her off it.'

'That's right,' I say, realizing now that he could have given her a drink if he'd wanted to.

'Everybody knows she can't drink, yet they go on giving it to her,' Donna says, as though she hasn't heard him.

'*They* might,' Albert says. '*I* prefer 'em sober then they know what they're doing.'

'Look, I wasn't saying anything about – '

'I don't know what you were saying,' Conroy says. 'I'm just telling you where I stand.'

A sudden sharp little exchange, and me wondering what can have brought it on; the obvious answer being that Fleur's given Albert the brush-off and he's feeling narky about it.

'Oh, I'd better go and see if she's all right,' Donna says and stalks out. She's a fiery little piece, I'm thinking, when she's got her dander up. Plenty of spirit under that calm, gentle outside.

'Are you ready for off?' Albert says to me.

'Any time, Albert. But don't let me drag you away.'

'No, I've had enough.'

He looks at his glass then takes a good swig followed by a rousing belch which he apologizes for, patting his belly.

'Only way to sup bottled beer. Let the gas come out . . .'

He takes another drink that empties his glass, then we go to find our coats. They're in the bedroom and I'm a bit cautious in opening the door in case Fleur's retreated in there. The room's in darkness and Conroy reaches up past me and flicks on the light. It's a small room with cream-painted walls and just enough space for the single bed, wardrobe and the dressing-table, which shows the feminine touch in the frilled skirt round its legs. We get our overcoats out of the duffels, donkey jackets and macs piled on the bed.

'Best two bloody coats here,' Conroy says.

'I suppose we're earning the most money.'

'Aye.' He pulls his coat on. 'There's times when I can't stand bloody actors,' he says, the sourness coming through again.

As we leave the bedroom he says suddenly, 'Hang on a minute.' He goes off into the living-room and I wander after him as far as the doorway. The party's thinned out a bit by now but there's still enough people sprawling about or else hanging on to one another to the noise of the record-player in the dim light and the smoke.

Conroy comes out of the kitchen, stuffing a pint bottle of beer into each overcoat pocket and shoving one at me.

'Here, take that.'

'What for?'

'Because it's ours. We're not leaving it for this scrounging shower.'

As I slip the bottle into my pocket Donna comes out of the bathroom, pulling the door shut behind her.

'She's been sick. She'll be all right now.'

'Get her to bed,' Conroy says. 'That's the best thing.'

'I can't till everybody's gone home.'

'Dump their coats out here in the passage.'

'No, she'll be all right. She's swilling her face with cold water.' She goes off quickly and comes round the same way.'

Conroy opens the door. 'Well, we'll be seeing you.'

'Yes.'

'Thanks for having us,' I say, thinking of the neck of the bottle sticking out of my pocket and how mean it must look if she sees it.

We go down the stairs and out into the cold clear night. I'm feeling just a bit out of sorts with Albert as we walk round the corner and across the thin hard snow of the car park. It's not just that he's spoilt the end of the party, but that I might be associated with his peevishness in Donna's mind.

'Freezing hard,' he says as we approach the car. I say nothing, waiting for him to get in and reach over to unlock my door. The silence gets over to him as he runs the car out on to the road.

'You're not saying much.'

'I've nowt to say, Albert.'

'You mean you don't like saying it.'

'I just thought you were a bit short with Donna, that's all.'

'Did I start it? Am I responsible if Fleur gets too much to drink? I'm not her bloody keeper.'

'It just struck me that the fatal Conroy charm had let you down and you were feeling peevish about it.'

He grunts. 'If you ask me she's as bent as a fiddler's elbow.'

'Eh?'

'I'm not saying she couldn't enjoy it with a man, but she'd as soon have a woman.'

'You *what*!'

'That's what I think.'

'Gerraway!'

'You've heard about it, haven't you?'

'Well, of course I have, but – '

'But you've never come across it in a woman?'

'Oh, I can't – '

'How many men queers were there at the party?'

'None, as far as I know.'

'There were two at least.'

'Well I never saw them.'

'You saw 'em but you didn't spot 'em because they didn't act like pansies. They don't all, y'know.'

'I think your imagination's running riot, mate.'

'The theatre's a gathering ground for 'em, Vic. It goes with artistic leanings, so they say.'

'And what about Fleur?'

'I think she's got a crush on Donna. She's staying the night.'

'Oh, come on, now. You're not trying to say that Donna's bent as well.'

'Probably not. But I've a good idea about Fleur.'

'How do you know?'

'Oh, one or two things she said about Donna and herself.'

'You know, I don't see that a woman has to be queer just because she doesn't want it with you.'

He takes that without rising. 'No, there's more to it than that. I'm sure there is.'

'Oh Christ!'

112

'What's it matter to you if the whole crowd of 'em's bent, anyway?'

'I just hate talk like this.'

'Does the thought of it revolt you?'

'Look, live and let live; but there was nothing queer about the way Donna kissed me tonight.'

'Ah ha!'

'Ah ha what?'

'It upsets you, doesn't it? You like to think you might have a chance.'

'I don't know what you're talking about ... Look, take it easy. There's ice on the roads.'

'It's all right. It clings like a limpet.'

'I felt the back end slide just then.'

'Imagination.'

'Aye, like you with Fleur.'

'All right, Vic, let's drop the subject. But watch it, old lad, just watch it.'

'Again, I don't know what you mean.'

'I know you. I know you better than you think I do. You've got a lot to learn.'

'So it seems.'

Conroy opens the front door with his key and we go up through the dark house – quietly, though the sound of the car being parked in the driveway and the slamming of the doors must have waked anybody ready to be disturbed – and say good night on the first landing outside Conroy's room. Up in my own room I undress and brush my teeth and get into bed without lighting the fire. I wind my alarm clock, check that it's set for eight, then lie with my feet pulled up behind my thighs, waiting for the sheets to get warm, and thinking about what Albert said, and earlier, when Donna wished me a happy new year and I kissed her. That odd fleeting look in her eyes that, if I'm any judge, was an instant of accurate womanly intuition about me. An intuition about a feeling that comes over me again now; foolish, hopeless, with the seeds of all kinds of trouble in it, but with a glimmer at the heart of it, persistent and unmistakable, of something I can only call joy.

11

All I know is that I've got to see her again, and quick. Beyond this is a country of complications where my mind won't travel; probably because the passport to it is a return of feeling by her that I can't imagine either, though it's naturally what I shall come to hope for more and more. It's hard to remember that I once felt this way about Ingrid, watching her walk along an office corridor or sitting on the crowded bottom deck of a bus, without either hope or hopelessness at first, but just curiously happy in the beauty of the feeling itself. But without guilt, either. And that's an ingredient that'll be part of this too soon, whatever happens from now on. I come from a kind of people who see a positive virtue in never having felt temptation.

Well, one advantage to me of her being an actress is that I can see her nearly any time, except that watching her on the stage isn't like actually meeting her, and I can't go so many times to the same show or somebody's going to catch on pretty quick. And there's Conroy. Living on top of each other, like we do, means it's a bit tricky for me to do things on my own without him knowing about it. I've made no friends in the town apart from the theatre crowd and if I say to Albert that I'm off somewhere on my own he's bound to think it a bit funny. It wouldn't matter if I was prepared to be open about it with him, but he's guessed too much already and if I'm going to act like a moonstruck kid I don't want to parade the part for his amusement. Not yet, anyway.

The trouble is that after Donna's party Albert shows no sign of wanting to go to the Mitre and meet them all again. In fact he comes out with the occasional snide remark that sounds like he's gone off them altogether. I take the cracks as being a bit childish, though I can see his point – if she really upset him – why he might not want to seem to be hanging about waiting for crumbs from Fleur's table.

So it's not long before I'm forced to go out on a limb and it happens when I mention going to the Christmas play, which we haven't got to see yet.

'It won't be up to much. Family entertainment, and all that.'

'I thought it might be worth a try. Pass an evening on.'

'Waste of good drinking time if it's a dud.'

'Mmm.'

'You go if you want to.'

'Well, I – '

'Look, Vic, we might be mates but you don't have to live in my pocket. You do what you want to do.'

'What about meeting in the pub afterwards?'

'No. I've got a standing invitation to have supper with some people I know. It's a good chance to take 'em up on it.'

He lets me off the hook with only the faintest flicker of a smile in his eyes, and:

'You don't need me to hold your hand, do you?'

The play's an Arabian piece, a cross between a pantomime and a straight play, based on the *1,001 Nights*, with incidental music from records of Rimsky-Korsakov and Borodin. Fleur's a knockout to look at as the Sultan's daughter and Donna plays Scheherazade, a wily bird, the latest in a series of unfortunate women, who stalls the Sultan (a wasteful old lecher who likes a fresh wife every night) from lopping *her* head off by telling him a string of tales. The thing that's surprised me most on going to the theatre is the colour of it, even in an ordinary play. On this piece, of course, they've been able to let themselves go a bit and there's all the colours you can think of mingling on the stage, in tapestries, hangings, costumes, and skin made up brown where the costumes are on the brief side as they are with the Sultan's slaves and – a treat for the dads – the young houris in transparent trousers and bangles. Remembering the slimness of Donna's wrists and hands and her general air of frailty as Blanche Dubois, I'm surprised to see how firm and well-covered her body is: in the plump hollow of her navel and the fleshing out of her breasts above the gold-coloured bra-like top half of her costume.

I'm sitting down towards the front of the stalls, in the middle of a row, and it takes me some time to get out of the building at the end, crawling up the aisle behind kids in a daze from the combined effects of the show and stopping up later than usual, and parents trying not to get separated from their broods while making sure they haven't left scarves or gloves or coats behind. One nipper of six or seven waits till he's nearly to the foyer before remembering that he slipped his shoes off during the show and he's left them back among the seats. His mother, exploding, turns him round and begins to force a way back against the tide while a chap I take to be the father stands aside and, catching my glance, lifts his eyebrows at me.

'There'll be no dealing with them tomorrow morning.'

'Only once in a while, though.'

'Thank the lord for that,' he says, returning my smile.

I knew it was odds on that they'd be coming over to the Mitre after the show but to make sure of it I've sent a note round to Donna during the first interval, asking her if she'll have a drink with me there. I'm well down my first pint, and not drinking fast, by the time she comes into the pub. I see her first, apparently on her own, as she stands in the doorway to look for me. A wave of the hand takes her eye and she smiles as she makes her way to me.

'Sorry I've been so long but I had to have a bath.'

'You're white again, then, under your clothes?'

'Pink and glowing,' she says, laughing.

'The others still splashing round in the tub?'

'No, an ex-member of the company dropped in and most of them have gone off to another pub.'

'Well look, don't let me keep you if you – '

'No, no,' she shakes her head. 'I see enough of them.'

'What will you have, then?'

'A half of bitter.'

'It'll run to a gin and tonic, you know. Or even two,' I add as she seems to hesitate.

'I don't drink beer because it's cheaper, particularly,' she tells me. 'I like it.'

'Well, be a little devil tonight.'

'In that case I'll have a Scotch and dry ginger.'

'Right you are. Suppose you grab those two seats over there and I'll be with you in a jiffy.'

She goes away and I look after her for a second before emptying my glass and ordering the drinks. She's just a bit taller than Ingrid and put together in the same neat way. Is she prettier? Would you say, seeing the two of them together, that one was more attractive than the other? But there's no point in comparisons of this sort. Detailed item-by-item totting up of physical qualities gets you nowhere when you're judging the power of a woman. Neither does adding personality. Because all these things together can't account for the fact that one man will sell his soul for a woman that another chap will only glance at with casual interest.

And my interest in her is more than casual.

Would I be doing myself a good turn if I had a drink with her then walked out of here and never laid eyes on her again? I might. But all I'm concerned with now is that she's here and on her own, which is a break I never expected. And the knowledge that she's just a few feet away and in a couple of seconds I shall be with her sends surging up through me as I pay for the drinks and take hold of the glasses a wave of happiness, pure and simple.

'Here we are, then. Do you want all the ginger in?'

'Half of it, please.'

I pour half of the Canadian dry into her Scotch and sit down next to her on the bench seat. I don't know whether it's better to be close to her like this or sit opposite so that I can look directly at her. Either way will do. I just wish we had more time. In half an hour they'll be turning us out of here and I don't see how I can set up this situation again without showing too much of my hand. Which wouldn't matter if I wasn't married. Married. That word, after all this time, sounds its old note of clammy doom; and sitting there with Donna next to me, seeing with one part of my vision the fingers round her glass, with the main part the glitter of bottles and glasses behind the bar, the drinkers at the counter, hearing the murmur and clatter of their talk and the soft music coming through off the tape, I wish, I wish like hell, not that I wasn't married exactly, or not in a way that would hurt Ingrid, but that I was free and had choice. And I'm mad as I haven't been mad for a long time with that younger me who fell for a bird, found he didn't love her but still had to have her, and had her in a way that made him twice stupid, turning what should have been a bit of a fling with a willing girl – to be remembered afterwards as an experience and no real harm done on either side – into something that would affect his whole life. I want to thump his stupid head.

'Where's Albert tonight?'

'Visiting some friends . . . It's one reason why I wanted to see you. After the party, I mean. It left a bad taste in my mouth.'

'What did?'

'Well, Albert. I thought he came over a bit childish.'

'I suppose I helped to rub him up the wrong way.'

'I didn't want you to mix me up with it, that's all.'

'I hadn't really thought about it. It's nothing to what *can* happen at parties.'

'I just wanted it straight, for the record.'

'All right.'

She sips her whisky, adds a drop more dry ginger, then opens her bag and feels for cigarettes.

'Here, have one of these. If you smoke 'em with spats on.'

She takes one, smiling. 'I used to advertise these.'

'I beg your pardon.'

'On television. I was the girl who fell into the water trying to throw a stick for the dog. Then my boy friend gave me a cigarette while I sat wrapped in a big towel. "Together – the two of them – and Rolled Gold." Don't you remember?'

'Vaguely.' I can't remember seeing her but I'm very impressed.

'Thank you. Shows what an impact I made. They must have thought so too. I wasn't asked again.'

'Did you like doing a commercial?'

'Oh, I don't think anybody actually *likes* doing them. It's the money that's useful. And they pay well.'

'I thought you must have some sidelines. I mean, you said there wasn't much money in rep. but you have that flat.'

'That's an extravagance, really. I suppose I should share with somebody, but I prefer to be on my own. Besides, I don't keep a place in London like a lot of people in rep. do. This is cheaper than a flat in town – or cheaper than a comparable place, anyway – and I'm near enough to be able to catch anything interesting that comes my way.'

'How long will you be here?'

'Probably for the full season. That's till the summer.'

'And what then?'

'Oh, something will turn up. Perhaps my big break's just round the corner. I thought I was beginning to make headway last year. I had thirteen weeks in "The Matchmakers" on television but then the series folded and the characters with it. That led to small parts in two films. Very small parts. In the second one my one immortal line of dialogue ended up on the cutting-room floor.'

'You've got more guts than I have, being in a business like that.'

'It's an overcrowded profession, but there's always room at the top, as they say. And everybody hopes he'll establish himself a good way up the ladder. I haven't done too badly at all. I work and I live. Though I don't exactly manage to save.'

'How do you manage when there's no work going?'

'You do other things. I've been a waitress, a shop assistant and a cinema usherette in my time. Of course if you're only out for a few weeks you can go on the dole.'

'The dole?' I grin. 'Do actors draw the dole?'

'Of course. They're entitled to it and they all do it now and again. The big fish and the little ones. There's one labour exchange in town, you'd be surprised to see who turns up there from time to time.'

I catch the waiter's eye. 'Same again?'

'Yes, please.'

I order another round and Donna drains her glass and shrugs.

'If things got really bad I suppose I could go home and live off my parents for a while.'

'Where's home?'

'Cornwall. They would have to be bad, though, because it's too far away to keep in touch properly.'

'What do your parents do?'

'Mummy paints and Daddy writes and keeps pigs.'

'An artistic background.'

'Apart from the pigs. They just make it possible.'

'My father's a miner.'

She smiles. 'Genuine Yorkshire working-class stock. It's money in the bank for an actor these days.'

'Why's that?'

'Haven't you noticed? Regional accents are in. It's what's being written.'

'About time too.'

'I'm not complaining. I'll have a go at "Eeh, by gum" along with the anything else.'

'Yes, you would, wouldn't you?' I say. 'You're like everybody else – you think we all walk about in cloth caps looking bloody gormless. Every house with a euphonium in the wardrobe and a whippet in the scullery.'

When I look at her I see she's laughing, her body shaking and her eyes dancing with amusement. I scowl, feeling embarrassed and wondering if she's taking the mickey.

'I'm sorry,' she says in a minute; 'but that was lovely; it really was.'

I have to smile to myself. 'Aye, all right. But it is time we had a few writers.'

'Do you know one called Wilf Cotton?'

'It rings a bell.'

'It should. He's from your part of the world and he's a miner's son, I believe.'

'That's right. He wrote a novel about the pits. *Day after Day*. I read it in paperback.'

'What did you think of it?'

'Bang on. That was the real genuine article.'

'We're doing the première of a new play of his for our next production.'

'Why is he having it done here?'

'I suppose somebody must have approached him. I believe he lives in the south now.'

I smile. 'There was a bird in a pub when I first came down. She said there'd be nobody left in Bradford before long.'

'Yes . . . Have you done any flat- or house-hunting yet?'

'No, not seriously. I have a look in the local rag, see what's going. Prices are up down here.'

'Oh yes, the drift to the south-east is expensive. I wonder sometimes what the attraction is.'

'Well, with me I suppose I'd've stayed at home for the rest of my life; but I had a bit of a setback and when Albert turned up with the offer of this job I thought it'd be a chance for a change.'

'What about your wife?'

'Tell you the truth, Ingrid would stay in her own backyard for ever. But she'll be okay when she gets down here.'

'She isn't a foreign girl?'

'No. Her mother was mad on Ingrid Bergman.'

We share a look and a second's amusement at Ma Rothwell's expense.

'That's really making the grade in the profession,' Donna says.

'Yes, I reckon it is.'

'What about children?'

'No children.'

'That gives you more freedom.'

'Yes . . . Anyway, there's no hurry. I'm still feeling my way around.'

'Do you think you will stay? I mean, do you like it down here?'

'Oh, I like it all right. I like it the more I see of it.'

I feel her steady gaze on me. She's not laughing now and her eyes fall away as I lift mine to her face.

'They're putting the towels on,' she says, nodding towards the bar.

'Yes . . . Time's flown.'

'It has. Thanks for asking me. I've enjoyed it. It's a change from the same old crowd. Even though I seem to have been talking shop most of the time.'

'Blame me for that. My further education.'

'All right.' She begins to gather her things, pulling the thin chiffon scarf close round her neck and buttoning her coat.

'When's the next lesson to be?'

'What?'

'I was thinking we might do it again.'

There's just the slightest hesitation before she says, 'Why not?'

Why not indeed? I'm thinking as we thread our way out. Where's the harm in having a drink with an attractive bird? Freedom, I was thinking about earlier on. At least I've got a bit of it down here. It'd be difficult if not downright impossible at home, with your face familiar to lots of people who might be ready to jump to conclusions and mind somebody else's business. At least here I can explore this thing, have a bit of pleasure without outside interference to throw it all out of joint.

So I think in my happy ignorance. What I don't know just then is that mischief can be made anywhere, if somebody's keen enough to make it.

12

The journey home is getting to be a bit of a bind. Even in daylight it's no feast of scenic splendour. The country in the middle, round Peterborough and Grantham, is pleasant but dull, and the bits at each end, North London and South Yorkshire, are dreary and depressing. But it's better than doing it in the dark as I mostly am now: home Friday night, back Sunday night; once a fortnight, which makes it pricey as well, costing me on average more than fifty bob a week.

But now I'm ready to do it a while longer, long enough to try and get myself sorted out. Before, it was a question of getting settled in at the job, then bringing Ingrid down. Or was it ever as clear cut as that? No; I realize I was content to let things drift for a time, anyway; to let the change work on *me* for a while until I was ready to re-establish the *status quo*. Which I should have done readily enough, and probably before much longer, because I like a tidy, settled life. Now . . . well, let it go. Don't think too much about it. Fine, if it wasn't impossible to stop asking yourself questions . . . What do you want with Donna? You're on the edge of falling in love with her. Suppose when you know her better you go right overboard? You've got no reason to think she could feel anything like that about you, have you? In fact, you've every cause to believe you're out of her league, that she can meet blokes more attractive and more interesting than you any day of the week. So there's a lot of useless agony. But if she did come back with something, what then? An affair? How could you get away with that once Ingrid got down here? And you don't approve of affairs at the bottom of you, do you? You think that messing around like that is wasteful and sad; because you believe in marriage. But it wouldn't be that kind of affair, would it? Not just a chance for a bit on the side. Oh, no. It wouldn't be like that because what you see as marriage is a man and a woman who are everything to each other. Voluntary, with no resentment. And yours isn't like that so maybe you could cheat for a better feeling. And maybe, because your marriage was never like that, you've always left an escape clause there in your mind; at the back, not much thought about, but there all the time. You could leave Ingrid. Who's to stop you? Oh, she loves you; but somebody always gets hurt in situations like this. That's life. And another thing, don't forget you've had this feeling before, mate. You had it with Ingrid and found it was just the old randy urge hidden under a lot of romantic moonshine. Only you couldn't leave it alone. How do you know this isn't the same? And how are you going to find out without doing damage? You don't know. You only know you've been married for nearly four years and you're still bloody lonely. That's the top and bottom of it. She's a good kid; she loves you and you're fond of her in a way and you have some good times together. But she bores you. You've got a growing sense of the world and riches you might reach out and touch; and she doesn't even know why you've stretched your arm out.

There's a nice surprise waiting for me when I get home: a letter from Mr Van Huytens' solicitors saying they've wound up his estate and enclosing a cheque for five hundred pounds, his bequest to me under his will.

'Ey, Ingrid, look at this! Five hundred wonderful smackeroos.'

She glances at the cheque in my hand. A big pink cheque that would be just as big and just as pink if it was for thirty-five bob or thirteen and six.

'I was beginning to wonder if you'd ever get it,' she says.

'Oh, I knew it'd turn up eventually. Lawyers take their time over these things. Pity, in a way, they don't send cash. Five hundred new one-pound notes. You could count them and really feel you'd got something . . . Five hundred quid, though. You'd better see it gets into the bank.'

'They'll be open tomorrow morning; you could put it in yourself.'

'Yeh, I suppose I could. In fact, I will. "I'd, er, just like to deposit this small cheque." Proper distant bastards, some of these bank clerks. Anybody'd think it was all their own money the way they turn their noses up.'

'Are you going to open a new account?'

'No, why?'

'I thought you might want to. You've never had so much money before.'

'It can go into the joint, along with the three pound ten we've already got in.'

'A hundred and four, actually.'

'Have we got so much?'

'Well, I try to put a bit in regularly.'

'Six hundred and four quid. Very nice. Very nice indeed.'

'I just wondered. I thought you might want to keep it separate. I mean, it's not money we've both earned. It was left to you. It's yours.'

'It belongs to both of us, like everything else. And we shall have to watch we don't start dipping into it. We keep it whole for when we need it.'

'You mean for a house?'

'Yeh. When we're ready.'

She says nothing to this but walks away from me and into the kitchen.

You don't live close to somebody for years without being able to sense their moods, and I'm thinking now that Ingrid has been a bit odd in her manner ever since I came in. I follow her and stand in the kitchen doorway, watching as she puts a pan of milk on the stove and gets cups and saucers and plates out for supper.

'Are you all right, Ingrid?'

'Yes.'

'There's nothing wrong, is there?'

'No.'

It's funny how my feeling for Donna makes me more tender towards Ingrid.

'How's your mother?'

'Quite well in herself, really. She's a bit scared about going into hospital, though.'

124

'She'll be all right.'

'It's not a little operation, y'know. It knocks you up.'

'Yeh, I expect it does. Has she heard any more about it?'

'No. She's expecting to hear any day. She spends her time watching for the post. That's what's getting her down.'

She moves about, talking quite naturally, as she does what she has to do. But she's avoiding looking me in the face. There's something wrong and my conscience isn't clear enough for me to press her to tell me what it is. Maybe I've offended her in some way I don't know about. Women are funny like that. Perhaps she's seen my mother and they've had a difference of opinion about something. That's very possible. I go back into the living-room and sit down with the paper, feeling uneasy.

She gives me no reason to throw off the feeling all through Saturday and into evening. It could be my imagination, I think at one point; she's just feeling quiet. But somehow I'm sure there's something else.

Saturday night we go to the pictures in town and when we come out I suggest going for a drink. She's not enthusiastic.

'Oh, do you really want to?'

'Well, just an odd one,' I say. 'Come on, we've just got nice time.'

She lets me take her into a decent pub I know near the cinema. We hardly ever go into pubs together. In fact, I can't remember the last time and I don't even know what she'll want to drink until she hesitates for a second then asks for a lime and lemon.

I try to chivvy her a bit. 'You'll not get going on that.'

'I don't like beer or spirits,' she says.

I get the drinks and she watches me take the top off my pint.

'You were ready for that.'

'Aye. It's a drop of good stuff. Puts hair on your chest and lead in your pencil.'

'You seem to be getting a proper taste for it.'

'Oh, come on, Ingrid. I'm not a soak.'

'But you drink more than you used to, don't you?'

'I suppose I do. There's not much to do down there except go out for a pint.'

'Who do you go with?'

'Oh, Albert mostly. He was always partial to his ale.'

'Haven't you made any other friends?'

'I've met a few people through Albert,' I tell her, thinking: careful now, watch it. 'A few of the local rep., the theatre crowd, come into the pub sometimes. They're a nice lively lot.'

'Isn't that Ken Rawlinson over there, trying to catch your eye?'

I half turn my head, then hold it. 'You're sure he's seen me?'

'He keeps looking over here. I think it's him. He's got a moustache.'

'I'm not surprised. Who's he with?'

'A girl. I don't know her. Why don't you turn round and look?'

'I don't feel like getting involved. I never did care much for him.'

'You can't be rude. He knows I've seen him.'

'Has he acknowledged you?'

'Yes, just now. He nodded and smiled.'

'Ah, well . . .'

I twist my head round and see Rawly sitting on the far side of the room, with a smart-looking fair-haired bit. I don't know if she's the bird he once brought to Whittaker's Staff Dance but she's the same type, Rawly's type: blonde, middle-class, snooty-looking. He sees me looking and we exchange little waves and grimaces that pass for smiles, but there's no compulsion on either side to rush over and start swapping notes. Rawly the culture-vulture, given to superior name-dropping about books and music, when he didn't know the difference between a piano concerto and a sonata for one-string fiddle, or his arse from his elbow, if it came right down to it. I haven't seen him in years. He belongs to the days at Dawson Whittaker's, along with Miller and Hassop, Althorpe, Whymper, young Laisterdyke and the rest. The days when I was free, white and not yet twenty-one; when Ingrid was a tempting little bit in the typing-pool who I could see or leave alone as the fancy took me. The town you were brought up in is full of associations like this; with all your past life lying in wait for you in the streets you walk along and the people you run into.

'I think the moustache suits him,' Ingrid says.

'Do you find him attractive?'

'Well, he's not really my type.'

'I don't see how anybody could really go for him. He's such a bloody phoney I've all on just talking to him.'

'What was it you used to say about him?'

'I've said a few things.'

'Something about him having ten bob each way on himself.'

'Aye. It'll be a quid now, though. The cost of living's gone up.'

We laugh together.

Oh, she's all right, I think. It was just my imagination. If only she'd have a proper drink, that would really relax her.

'What about a sherry or something? That stuff'll chill your insides this weather.'

She shakes her head. 'No, thanks. I'm ready to go when you are. You have another drink, though, if you want one.'

'No. I'm not bothered.'

Going up out of town on the bus I feel this strange gap widen between us again, but I make up my mind not to mention it; to act as though I haven't noticed anything. There's a light on in Chris's and David's window and as we go into the hall I ask Ingrid if she fancies going upstairs to have half an hour with them, but she says no, she'd rather go straight in.

I break the fire up, getting a good blaze going, and take my overcoat off. Then I find the morning paper and look to see what's on television. I'm just going across to the set when Ingrid, who's put her coat over a chair and is standing gazing into the fire, says over her shoulder:

'Don't switch that on just now.'

I stop in my tracks and look at her gone out.

'Why, what's up?'

She says nothing.

'Ingrid . . .' I try a laugh. What the hell *is* up with her? 'Look, there's a programme I want to see.'

'It can wait.' She reaches out for her handbag. 'There's something I want to show you.'

I watch her as she opens her bag and takes an envelope out.

'Here.'

I take it from her and turn it over. It's addressed to Mrs V. Brown, in typewriting, and there's a London postmark.

'What is it?'

'Look at it and see.'

I take the single sheet of notepaper out and unfold it.

Typewritten again, and no sender's address. My guts suddenly contract as a name jumps out at me from the page.

'Dear Mrs Brown, You should keep an eye on your husband. Ask him about a woman called Donna Pennyman he knows in Longford. She is an actress. You do not know me but I thought you should know about this. A friend.'

I just look at it, reading it quickly, over and over again, my guts churning and my heart pounding.

Ingrid's turned to face me, a curious almost defiant glitter in her eyes and two spots of colour on her cheekbones.

'Well?'

'Christ! How can anybody?...'

'What have you got to say about it?'

'The filthy bastard ... or bitch ... Isn't it women who usually write anonymous letters?'

'I'm not bothered about who wrote it just now. I want to know if it's true.'

I don't like her tone – straight, blunt, ready to believe the worst on the strength of this.

'How d'you mean, is it true? If you mean do I know somebody called Donna Pennyman, yes I do.'

'Who is she?'

'She's one of the theatre crowd I was telling you about.'

'How well do you know her?'

'Now just a minute, Ingrid. You can't bloody court martial me on the strength of this mucky thing.'

'I'm not court martialling you and I'm not taking what it says as gospel truth. But I've had three days to think about it while you were two hundred miles away, out of my sight. I just want to know what's made whoever it is write it.'

'Well, malice. Somebody's out to get me – or her.'

'Why should they do that?'

'How the hell should I know?'

'You don't have to shout, Vic. And there's no need to get mad if everything's all right.'

'Look, don't you understand why I'm mad? What if somebody wrote to me about you? How would you feel?'

'Nobody's got any reason to.'

'They don't need reasons, people like this. They could accuse you of anything. Nobody writes a letter like this to be friendly. They're out to cause trouble.'

'You still haven't told me how well you know this woman – or girl, whoever she is.'

'I know her as well as I know two or three other women in the company. They're all in a crowd. Why, they could just as well have picked on one of the others.'

'Why should they pick on her, then?'

'The luck of the draw,' I say, laying the contempt and anger on thick, which isn't hard, because contempt and anger are just what I'm feeling, with a funny underlayer of fear. I find my fags and light one and my hands are trembling.

'Christ!'

She says nothing for a moment, until:

'Vic . . . look at me.'

I force myself to.

'Tell me it's all right.'

'Don't start cross-examining me, Ingrid.'

'I'm not cross-examining you. I just want to know.'

'What do you want to know?'

'You do like this girl, don't you?'

'I like lots of people. If I can't talk to a woman because I'm married, it's coming to something.'

'There's nothing in it, then?'

She's disintegrating now, the defiance gone from her eyes in the face of mine, which I shoot across at her in a furious glare.

'Nobody had any reason to write this.'

'All right.'

She turns away.

'Well, you do believe me, don't you?'

'I've got no choice, have I?'

'Well, that's a bloody fine thing . . .'

'Look, all I know is you're miles away for most of the time and I've no way of knowing what you're doing. And I get a letter like that.'

'From "A Friend".'

'You can be sarcastic.'

'Oh, I can; and bloody mad.'

'You've got to admit, it's not very nice.'

'That's putting it mildly.'

'I've been thinking about it for days.'

'I hadn't been home ten minutes before I knew something was up.'

'I wasn't going to say anything. Then I thought why should I carry it on my own.'

'You did right to tell me. If there's somebody gunning for me I want to know about it.'

'Why should anybody want to do you a bad turn?'

'I don't know. It's something I shall have to think about . . . How did they know your address? That's one thing.'

There's a silence, then she says:

'It's all right, then?'

'I've told you.'

And this is where the tenderness should come in, with my arms round her, reassuring her. But I can't do it. Partly because that would really be barefaced lying and partly because I'm mad that she was so ready to think there was something in it. All right – if wishful thinking is guilt, then I'm partly guilty. But she doesn't know this, and neither does whoever wrote the letter.

'I'm going to bed . . . Are you coming?'

'In a minute. I want to think about this for a bit.'

'Why don't you just burn it?'

'Oh no, it's evidence. I'm hanging on to it.'

'All right . . . What time are you going back tomorrow?'

'The usual time.'

She hangs about for another minute then goes through into the bedroom without saying anything else.

Go after her, you nit, a part of me's saying. Make love to her. No need for words. Get cracking. Sweep her away. Reassure her.

I sit there with the letter in my hands, thinking who? Who? They say that when you're burgled, apart from the loss of your property, there's a strange feeling of shock that someone's actually been inside your house and made free with it. An anonymous letter is from someone who's made free with your private life, who's watched you and planned damage. Because, make no mistake about it, there's nothing 'friendly' about one of these things. It's meant to do harm and the worst thing about it is to try to imagine the feelings of whoever's written it when they're putting it on paper and then slipping it into the letter box, and realize you're the one who's inspired it all. You flinch from the shock of knowing somebody can hate you like that. It's like a spat of pure malice from a complete stranger.

But no stranger wrote this . . .

Who? I think again. Who? There's only one obvious answer and it sickens me even to think of it.

Sunday morning isn't very nice with this thing between us and Ingrid needing big words of undying affection which I'm not able to give her. If I read her right, what she's thinking, it's not so much what's in the letter as the getting of it which has made her stop and take stock. Knowing the way she got me in the first place – that by marrying her I was doing 'the right thing' rather than what I wanted to do – she's been content to jog along, making a marriage that's as good as a lot and better than some, without the big romantic declarations some young couples might well go in for. But what's the state of the nation now? That's what the letter makes her stop and ask. And with every excuse to go out of my way to show her that I've no regrets, maybe even that getting her pregnant was a glorious blessing in disguise, I'm making no move; acting towards her with no more and no less affection than I've always done. And if the four years have worked no miracle beyond habit and custom and a lack of active animosity and resentment, then why shouldn't there just be something in what the letter is suggesting? And where's her power to fight it?

It makes her sad, and it's her sadness that taps some tender feeling I have for her so that I'm moved to lay a soft hand on her shoulder, its touch bringing her round to face me, her eyes searching mine. No words. I bring her close and kiss her, wondering as I do if her reaction to it won't make it a lie. What does she read into it? That there's no truth in the letter? That even if there is she's got nothing to worry about? That I'm simply playing it smart and covering up as best I can? And for me? It's simply an expression of what I feel at this moment. With no strings.

131

But I know as we break and I look at her that it was a right thing to do. And better when I make no move to carry it on to something else; destroy its value by making it a preliminary to a quick session on the couch, which is probably what she'd like as much as I would now, but which I can't make the play for.

We're invited to Chris's for Sunday dinner and that and a walk round to the pub beforehand with David takes care of the rest of the day.

I can see it on her mind again as I shove my gear into my bag prior to going for the train.

'Well, back to the grindstone.'

'Yes . . . I expect you're a bit fed-up of that journey.'

'It is a bit of a bind. Still, it's only once a fortnight.'

'Do you want me to come out to the bus with you?'

'No, you stay inside where it's warm. Will you go round to your mother's when I've gone?'

'In a while, when I've tidied up here. Have you got your scarf? There's a terrible cold wind blowing.'

'Don't worry, I keep well wrapped up. Longford's not the warmest spot I know.'

'I'll see you in a fortnight, then.'

'All being well . . . Look, though, why don't you come down instead? It'll be a change for you and it's really time you had a look.'

'Do you really want me to?'

'Well, yes. We can't really talk about anything till you've been.'

'Could I stay with you?'

'I should think Mrs Witherspoon'd let you share my bed for a couple of nights. It's only a single, but we'd manage.'

'It's Mother, you see. She's liable to be called into hospital any time.'

'Well look, if she hasn't gone in by the week-end after next what about coming?'

'I'll see what I can do. I'll drop you a line nearer the time and let you know.'

'I can meet you at King's Cross. You wouldn't have to find your way out there on your own.'

'No, all right.'

'You'll do your best, then?'

'Yes . . . What have you done with that letter?'

'It's in my pocket.'

'You won't show it to anybody, will you?'

'It's not a thing I'm likely to flash around.'

'What will you do about it?'

'I'll keep my eyes and ears open. Have a think.'

'I wish you weren't going back. I wish you'd never gone. I knew it wasn't the right thing for us.'

'Ingrid . . . You can't let somebody writing anonymous letters rule your life . . . Come on, now, bear up. And don't worry.'

I find myself hoping I can get away before she starts to cry. Don't worry. Glib words of small comfort. I carry away with me the image of her standing there, small and forlorn. I wonder if technically I'll be a bigger bastard if I do what she's half afraid I'm doing already – which I haven't done yet but know I will do if I get the chance – just because she *is* half afraid I'm doing it already . . .

13

Poison-pen letters . . . Well named. They are poisonous, both in the direct harm they do and the way they pollute your mind with foul suspicions about anybody who could possibly be responsible.

There's the sound of music coming from behind Conroy's door as I go up the stairs. I carry straight on up to my room, dump my case, and go back down to him. He waves me in as I tap then look round the door at him lolling back in his chair with one leg up, the foot jerking to the rhythm of Mozart by Beecham. I sit down without speaking and wait for the record to finish, watching him as he lies back with his eyes shut, looking at his bulk, the square hands, his heavy head and low forehead under his hair that used to be a shaggy mop in the old days but's now neatly trimmed in a cut his old back-and-sides merchant wouldn't have thought value for money, working as those boys did on the basis of how near the bone they could get in the neck and over the ears.

Looking at him, my mind turning over, thinking that he's given me a few surprises in his time and wondering if the worst is yet to come. If while I've been growing genuinely fond of him he's been nursing a dislike of me that's been turned into black malice by his lack of progress with Fleur and my interest in Donna. Oh, no . . . Could I sit like that with my eyes closed listening to music in the company of somebody I'd done a thing like that to? Could I, when the music stopped, open my eyes as he's doing now and say as though it was the only thought in my mind:

'Lovely! Smashing!' and look at me and carry on:

'But I keep forgetting, you're not really a Mozart man, are you?' No . . .

'Oh, I can listen to him, but I wouldn't miss him if his music suddenly stopped being played.'

'Aye. You mean you like him better than those nits like Rawly who find easy tunes and profess a liking on the strength of it.'

'I saw Rawly last night.'

'That's a treat. Where was he?'

'In a pub in Cressley. Had a bird with him, the usual Rawly type, blonde, snotty-looking.'

'Aye, Rawly always did go for the white-glove type. "Well, I suppose I shall have to handle the beastly thing."'

He looks at me and we both burst out laughing.

'He's got a tash these days an' all.'

'What had he to say for himself?'

'I managed to avoid talking to him.'

'Pity. You might have found out if he wanted another job.'

'Christ, we'd be landed if we got that bugger down here.'

'Poor old Rawly . . .' Conroy shakes his head. 'He's some mother's pride and joy.'

And I think yes, poor old Rawly. He can't really help it. He doesn't know what he's doing. And he's not a bad-hearted bastard. I don't think he'd ever write an anonymous letter . . .

'Have we time for a pint?' Albert asks.

'Half an hour.'

'Fancy one?'

'Always willing.'

'I can't play any more music or I shall have Madam Witherspoon up on a visit.'

'Let's just pop round the corner, then. It's far enough tonight.'
Conroy reaches for his jacket.

In the saloon bar of the King's Jester, down on the main road, there's a coal fire that's like a prize after the still, breathtaking cold outside. There's going to be some more snow and with Conroy bothered about it and the effect it's going to have on the jobs we talk shop over the first pint. Franklyn's apparently laid off ten men on Friday.

'He had to,' Albert says. 'The job's under four feet of snow with more coming all the time. And there's not enough work for 'em inside. Not that most of them would want it, anyway.'

'It's hard lines for 'em, isn't it?'

Conroy shrugs. 'One of the hazards of the business. They make good money while they are working. It's to be hoped they've put a bit on one side for a rainy day. Or a snowy one, in their case.'

'Look, Albert, how much can the firm stand? I mean, this is one of the worst winters anybody can remember. It's going to knock 'em back a bit.'

'I don't think they'll fold up, if that's what you mean.'

'It's a bit unsettling, that's all. Ingrid's coming down here in a couple of weeks to look round. I don't want to get her all adjusted to the idea of moving and then find myself out of a job.'

'Oh, that won't happen,' Conroy reassures me. 'Don't let that worry you. And if the worst did happen you'd soon get fixed up somewhere else.'

'Aye. Every time you move it costs you money, though.'

'There's only the two of you to think about. No kids. Why worry? Move around a bit if you want to. Get some experience. This isn't the end of the line for me. I shall go when the time's ripe. Pastures new, and all that.'

'It's all right for you.'

'It's all right for *you*. Look, Vic, all due respect to Ingrid, but why should a bloke of your age have to think that every job he takes is going to last him for ever? Time enough to settle in one spot when you've got two or three kids and education to think about. You've made the biggest break – getting out of your hometown and losing all the people who sit on your back and stop you doing what you want to do.'

'I know. I've had all this out with myself.'

'You must have. I'm not saying they *tell* you what to do, but they put pressures on you just by being there. It's harder for you and Ingrid because her mother's a widow and she feels she's deserting her. I know. Suppose you'd stayed on another couple of years, though, and your old feller had cocked his clog. You'd have felt you ought to stick around for your mother's sake. The lucky ones get out while they're still single and have no ties at all. You've made it just in time.'

I take his empty glass out of his hand and go to the bar for refills. When I get back to him I say:

'That's all very well, Albert, but you make it sound as if nobody ought to want to stop at home. I mean, Cressley's no paradise, but Longford isn't either, is it?'

'You can always go back, Vic. People think better of you if you've been around a bit. Even moving away from a firm can do it. If you'd have gone back to Whittaker's when the shop folded you'd have been treated with more respect than if you'd stayed on all the time.'

'Even though it'd've looked as if I'd made a mistake?'

'You got out. You showed you weren't dependent on them. You stay too long in one place and they'll think you breathe by courtesy of them. If you went back now you'd get on better still because you've had some experience elsewhere. But you still wouldn't get the money you're getting here. Remember that one. It's the same with people outside the job. The thing is to have *choice*. Always keep that power of choice. It's one of my golden rules. Don't let other people put pressures on you and tell you how to run your life.'

At which point, with that letter in my inside pocket, a tight little ironic smile wouldn't be out of place. But I keep my face straight, smiles ironic or otherwise having no place in my feeling about that little piece of composition.

'You can't get away from other people, Albert,' I say.

'I'm not saying you've got to kick everybody in the teeth and look after number one. But you're the only one who can live your life. You're saddled with it, mate.'

'It's funny . . . I was giving almost the same advice to our Jim over Christmas. Only that had to do with a bird.'

'It applies,' Conroy says. 'It applies all the way down the line.'

'Ah well,' I say; 'we'll see what Ingrid thinks of it all when she comes down.'

'You've got no plans for her coming to stay yet?'

'No, not yet.'

'I wondered. There's a nice little bungalow development going up out on the Colchester Road. They look to be nice houses. I thought about you when I saw them.'

'I was thinking more in terms of another flat for the time being.'

'It's money gone for ever when you pay rent.'

'Aye, but house prices are up a bit down here.'

'You'd get a mortgage. And don't forget that you buy high but you sell high as well. Higher, if you're lucky. You wouldn't lose money on it.'

He whips back the bottom quarter of his pint as the barman calls for last orders.

'Come on, we can just get another one in.'

'Just a half for me.'

'Sure?'

'Yeh. I've still got half of this left.'

He weaves his way through the crowd to the bar and I watch him go, thinking again, thinking . . . No, it's ridiculous. He's got no reason . . . But who? Is somebody watching me now? I look round the room and have the unlikely idea that Donna might just be there. But of course there's no sign of her and when Conroy comes back with the drinks I'm busy with thoughts of when I can see her again.

'I'll tell you what,' Albert says, tipping the beer from the small glass into my pint with one quick turn of his wrist, 'I don't mind running you and Ingrid round in the car for an hour when she comes down.'

'That's very good of you, mate.'

'No trouble. It'll give her a chance to see more, get an overall picture.'

'Yes, fine.'

'I suppose it'll clip your wings a bit when she gets in residence.'

'How d'you mean?' I say, wary now, watching for signs.

'Well, there won't be as many little sessions like this, for instance.'

'No, I suppose not . . . I'm quite enjoying playing the bachelor as well.'

He grins. 'I know you are, you bugger.'

I'm quick to rise. 'I don't mean I'm – '

He lifts his hand. 'I'm not saying anything. Only that it's nice to be able to chat up an attractive bird without the wife looking over your shoulder.'

I hesitate. Then I say, 'If it isn't the wife it's likely to be somebody else.'

'As long as you're far enough from home.'

'It sometimes doesn't matter how far you are,' I say, keeping my eyes on him and not able to fault his casual puzzlement as he says:

'What d'you mean?'

'This sort of thing, for instance.'

I bring the letter out, slipping the sheet out of the envelope and handing it to him.

He takes it in one hand, his glass in the other hand travelling towards his mouth as he starts to read. He lets it come down again without drinking, then glances quickly behind him for somewhere to stand it. He reads the note properly now, letting his eyes rest on it when he's finished. He says nothing, turning a solemn look on me and holding his hand out. I give him the envelope and he looks at that.

'Hell fire!' he says finally. 'Hell fire!' Soft, just over his breath, and wondering.

'When did this arrive?'

'Middle of last week.'

'Did she take it bad?'

I shrug. 'You know how it is. However much you convince them there's bound to be some doubt left; else why would anybody write the letter?'

'Malice,' Conroy says. 'Why else?'

'That's what I told her. No friend of either hers or mine would write a thing like that.'

'You're right there. Did you get out of it, though? I mean, it's not done any real damage, has it?'

'I don't think so. I admitted I knew Donna, of course. No use denying that. Trouble is, there's just enough truth in what it suggests to make me feel uncomfortable.'

'I can see that. I'll bet it makes you feel creepy as well.'

'Aye. Knowing somebody's been watching me, sizing things up, wanting to do me some harm.'

'Who, though?'

'Aye, who? Who do I know down here outside you and Jimmy and the crowd from the theatre?'

'And how did they know your address?'

'Yeh, that's another thing.'

'You've never seen anybody from home down here, have you?' Conroy asks. 'A rep. maybe.'

I shake my head. 'No, nobody.'

'Have you ever given your address to anybody?'

'No . . . But it's in the office files, I suppose.'

'But who in the office would want to – ?'

'Look Albert, I don't know why *any*body would want to. But it's happened. If you can't think of anybody you begin to suspect everybody. If it comes to that, you're the only one who knows my address and that I like Donna.'

He looks at me, real startled, for a moment.

'You don't mean to say you've been thinking . . . ?'

'I haven't been thinking owt, Albert. I've been wondering.'

He blushes suddenly, the only time I've ever seen it happen to him, a great red flush spreading up from his collar on to his face.

'Well, by bloody hell!'

He turns away from me and picks up his glass, gripping it hard as though wondering whether to let me have it in the face.

'Look, 'course I don't think you did it.'

'Thanks very much.'

'Oh, bloody hell . . . Would I have shown it to you if I'd really suspected you?'

'Confrontation,' Albert says. 'Watch for me to make a slip.'

'Well, if you're going to carry on like this . . .'

I look into my glass, my face set and my own temper rising.

'How the hell do you expect me to behave?'

I snap at him. 'Oh, bollocks.'

We drink together, glasses up and down in unison as though our arms are geared to the same piece of mechanism. He stands there, sideways on to me, looking across the room, his face hard, the colour fading from it now, leaving it, if anything, a shade paler than normal.

'Albert,' I say in a minute. 'Don't be a nit.'

He's a second or two before he speaks and he empties his glass before saying in something like a growl:

'Aye, I suppose you're right. I've never had a letter like that so I can't really know what it's like.'

'No.'

He turns then and looks me straight in the eye, as though he's determined to shift every last shadow of doubt about him out of my mind.

'They certainly do their work, though, don't they?' he says.

In the middle of Monday morning – or climbing up the hill to lunchtime to be more exact – I happen to be nearest to the office phone when it rings, so I pick the receiver up and have the pleasant surprise of hearing Donna's voice at the other end of the line, asking for me.

'Speaking . . . How are you this dreary old Monday morning, then?'

'Oh, you know who it is?'

'I knew your voice straight away. Are you having another party?'

'No, not just yet.'

'We can always think of something if you need an excuse.'

'Yes, I'll bet. Can anybody hear you speaking?'

'Well, there are people in the office but nobody's taking any notice. What's up?'

'Listen, were you planning to come to the Mitre tonight?'

'I was thinking I might well do that.'

'I want to talk to you about something.'

'Well, I'll be there, then.'

'It'd perhaps be better if you weren't. Could you meet me somewhere else after the show?'

'Yes, 'course I can. But this is –'

'Suppose we said the railway station forecourt at twenty past ten? I could get away by that time and pick you up.'

'All right. I must say this is all very mysterious. Shall I wear my wig and false moustache?'

'It might be as well if you did, actually. I'm sorry I can't explain over the phone. I'll tell you all about it tonight. You will be there?'

'With bells on.'

'I'll try not to keep you waiting.'

I'm just opening my mouth to ask her why we can't meet in a warm pub when she rings off and the line goes dead. 'How shall I know you?' I'm thinking. 'I'll be pushing a wheelbarrow containing a full set of the *Encyclopaedia Britannica*.' All very rum. I glance at my watch. And I've got about eleven hours to wait to find out what's going on.

I look round at the people in the office as I go back to my board. Conroy, Jimmy, Martin, Cynthia; a chargehand from the works talking over a job with Conroy, a bird coming in with some papers for Cynthia as Franklyn opens the door of his office and comes out with his sheepskin coat on bound for the shops. Busy. People doing their work and minding their own business. Apparently. Under the feeling of excitement at the prospect of seeing Donna again there's one of niggling unease left by the odd nature of her call and the knowledge that somebody, somewhere – and not far away – is watching me.

The day passes, as even the long ones do. As it happens I don't have to explain anything to Conroy, or act mysterious with him, because during the afternoon he goes off on a trip that will keep him away for one night, if not two. In the evening I decide that the pictures will be the best way of passing a couple of hours. It's a Doris Day comedy; not my usual cup of tea, but enjoyable enough; and I'm out just in time for the ten-minute walk across to the station.

She arrives at twenty-three minutes past, swinging the A40 round on to the cobbled forecourt and opening the passenger door as I step out of the shelter of the station entrance and walk across to her.

'I hope I haven't kept you waiting,' she says over her shoulder, looking behind her for traffic and easing the car back on to the road as soon as I'm in.

'Only a couple of minutes.'

141

'They've gone to the Mitre. You know, the usual crowd. I pleaded a headache and said I wanted an early night.'

We pick up speed, Donna sitting upright and driving expertly, one hand on the gear lever, the other one on the wheel.

I say, 'Look, seeing you again is fine; but I wish you'd tell me what this is all about.'

'I'm sorry I was so mysterious on the phone.'

'And where are we going, anyway?' I say as the car bats on surely up the main street and through the middle of town.

'I thought my place would be best,' she says, and glances sideways at me. 'Do you mind?'

'No, but – '

'Even though it could be more compromising than a pub.'

It's surprising sometimes how long it takes for the penny to drop. Even now I'm not sure I'm on the right lines but just a glimmer of light begins to break through.

'We'll be there in a minute,' she says, and I think, 'Right, I'll say no more.'

Except: 'You know, if our positions were reversed you'd be wondering what you were letting yourself in for and thinking you had a damn' good idea.'

She smiles. 'Yes . . . But I expect you can take care of yourself.'

'Chance is a fine thing,' I say, and she turns her head and looks at me for a fraction longer than's wise when you're driving, but says nothing.

In the flat she switches on the electric fire and we take our coats off.

'Would you like a drink? I think there's still some left from the party.'

I say okay and she goes into the kitchen and fetches a pint bottle of light ale (one that we brought and Albert missed taking away, by the looks of it) and a tumbler, handing both to me along with a bottle-opener.

'You'd better pour your own. I'm not very good at it.'

'Aren't you having any?'

'Not just now. I'll make some coffee in a minute.'

I make with the bottle and glass then lean back on the sofa.

'Right, I'm sitting comfortably. You can begin.'

She smiles. 'Yes. I'm sorry about the mystery; but I thought it was necessary.' She takes a letter off the mantelshelf and passes it to me. 'I thought you ought to see this.'

'Oh, no,' I think. But what the hell . . . ?

The letter, typewritten like the other one, and on the same paper, says:

'Dear Miss Pennyman, you would be well advised to keep away from that Victor Brown. He is a married man and no good. A Friend.'

'Oh God.'

'Somebody round here doesn't like you,' Donna says. 'That's why I acted so mysteriously. So we wouldn't be seen together. I didn't want to phone you but it was the only way to get in touch.'

Oh God, the filth, I'm thinking. The dirty filth, soiling everything.

'I'm sorry, Donna.'

'Oh, you don't have to be sorry on my account. I'm quite used to nasty-minded people who write anonymous letters and make phone calls.'

'What d'you mean?'

'It happens all the time to actresses. You do a couple of television programmes and men ring you up.'

'You mean they ask to meet you?'

'No, that's not so bad. It's the sick ones who ask you if you've got any pants on at the moment and tell you in detail what they'd like to do to your lily-white body.'

'Christ! What do you do about it?'

'Tell the police, have your phone number made ex-directory . . . In this case it looks as though you've got an enemy somewhere and I thought it only fair that you should know about it without letting whoever it is see us together in public again.'

'It's very nice of you to go to so much trouble.'

She slips off her shoes and sits down on the sheepskin rug in front of the fire with her legs curled under her. Her frock is an oatmeal knitted one with a high neck. Again I think, what is it gets me about birds in wool? What is it gets me about this bird in anything?

'It's no trouble,' she says. 'I just wondered what harm they hoped to do writing to me. They'd do better writing to your wife.'

I take the envelope out of my pocket, slip the letter out and hand it to her. She gives me a quick questioning look as I don't speak, then reads the note.

'I see. Now I know why you weren't as surprised as I thought you ought to be. When did this arrive?'

'The middle of last week.'

'Mine came on Saturday morning. It must have been an after-thought. Spread it as far as possible. What did she say?'

'What could she say? She believed me when I said there was no reason for anybody to write it. But there's no smoke without fire, you know.'

'Oh, surely . . .' Donna says, a touch of impatience in her voice.

'I'm not saying she *really* believes there's anything in it. But still, who could have written these things and why? As I said to Albert, there's – '

'Albert knows about the other one, does he?'

'Yes. I told him last night. I even partly suspected him at one point.'

'Surely not Albert . . . '

'No, of course not. It was just that he was the only one I could think of who knew I knew you and had my home address as well.'

'But what could his motive be?'

'Oh, some kind of vague jealousy. You know, that little bit of bad feeling at the party; him having some kind of tiff with Fleur.'

'I don't see what that's got to do with you, though.'

'No, except he could have thought we knew each other better than we do. Or that we might get to be more friendly. Spite.'

She shakes her head. 'I don't see that at all.'

'Neither do I. But there's a kind of vicious madness about these things that's catching. You think all kinds of things.'

Donna sighs. 'Well at least they don't malign me in the other letter. I suppose they think that saying I'm an actress is enough.'

I grunt. 'If it comes to that, saying you're a woman's enough. The actress touch is a nice little refinement. A bit extra to add spice.'

'Yes . . . But all we've done is have drinks together; and always in other people's company until the other night.'

'Oh yes, but that doesn't matter to whoever's written the letters. They just want to do damage and seeing us together has given them a way.'

144

'Your wife must surely understand that.'

'Oh, I told her. Except . . . I didn't tell her about that particular night.'

'Why not?'

'Well, you see . . .' I hesitate, thinking don't be a complete nit, you'll only make yourself look an idiot. But also: here's a perfect chance to give her an idea of how you feel. Find out how she takes it while you're on your own together. Do you think she'll laugh in your face or something?

'The trouble is,' I start again, speaking slowly, 'what the letter . . . well, implies, is partly true. On my side, I mean.'

There's a pause which my heartbeats seem to pound through like a drum. Then she says, her face half-turned from me and looking at the twin bars of the fire:

'I see.' Just that, very quietly. 'I see.'

Nothing else until I crash in again with:

'You can sling me out now if you want to.'

'No,' she says in a moment. 'No . . . I'll make some coffee. Would you like some?'

'Please.'

Mix me some arsenic, if you like, love, I'm thinking. Anything that'll let me stay here a while longer.

She gets up and, slipping into her shoes again, goes into the kitchen without looking at me.

I wonder whether to follow her, then decide against it and light a fag and lean forward on the sofa, my arms on my knees, and glance round the room, remembering the party, how noisy and smoky it was then, how quiet it is now. The electric fire's doing its best to warm things up but the air's still a bit thin, which isn't surprising considering what it's like outside. I get up and stand near the fire, warming myself and drinking my beer, my eyes now on a level with the fried-egg painting which looks from this close range as if it's been done with somebody's thumb, the paint scraped on thick and lumpy. On one side of the fireplace is a three-shelf bookcase with a portable wireless, a travelling-clock, an ashtray and one or two knick-knacks on top and books, mostly paperbacks, on the other shelves. *Anger and After*, by John Russell Taylor, Penguins by Iris Murdoch and Muriel Spark, some Penguin New Dramatists . . .

On the other side, under the standard lamp, a record-player sits on a square table with long-playing records underneath. There are only half a dozen and I pull them out and sit down on the sofa again, looking at the covers as Donna comes in again with a small tray with two cups of coffee, a bowl of sugar and a plate of biscuits.

'I hope I'm not being nosey.'

'Be my guest.'

'Thanks.'

She puts the tray down on the hearthrug.

'It's only instant, I'm afraid.'

'That's my usual tipple.'

'Sugar?'

'One please.'

She sugars the coffee and passes me a cup which I balance on the arm of the sofa.

'Biscuit?'

'Er, no, thanks.'

She sips at her coffee and looks at me.

'Does my small record collection reveal any unsuspected quirks of personality, then?'

'No, it just shows you're interested in music.'

'Doesn't any record collection?'

'No,' I exchange a look with her. 'I used to work in a record shop.'

'Oh?'

'Yes. There's music and what passes for music.'

She says 'Mmm,' and drinks some more coffee while I look at the records. Ella Fitzgerald singing Jerome Kern, *Sinatra's Sinatra*, *Beyond the Fringe*, *My Fair Lady*, soundtrack recording of *West Side Story*, the Francescatti recording of the Tchaikovsky and Mendelssohn Violin Concertos, back to back, the Sibelius Concerto, and the joker in the pack, Rachmaninov's Second Symphony.

I hold that up.

'I don't think I know this.'

'Do you know the piano concertos?'

'Yes.'

'Same Rachmaninov, but a bit more of a piece, if you know what

I mean. It's lovely. I heard it on the wireless one day and ordered the record. Lovely Russian melancholy.'

'What's the passion for fiddle concertos?'

'I used to take lessons. I was never very good.'

'The good old artistic background again, eh?'

'With pigs.'

'Yeh, mustn't forget the pigs.'

'It's true, though, that the arts – music, books, painting – have always been there, part of my life.'

'You were lucky.'

'Was I?'

'Yes. I had to struggle for what I've got. What little I've got, I should say. Culture's a bit of a dirty word where I come from.'

'Oh, it is in a lot of places, you know. It depends an enormous amount on individual families.'

'It was the old man I worked for in the record shop who first led me to music. He took me to concerts, and that. "It's like a wonderful voyage of discovery," he used to say, "with magic over every horizon. There's all the music in the world waiting for you to find it." He was right, too. I've had a bloody marvellous time.'

'Do you take your wife to concerts?'

'No . . . I don't go much nowadays . . . Who did the picture? Your mother?'

'Yes, it's one of hers. What do you think of it?'

'I don't really know.'

'It usually provokes strong reactions.'

'I suppose I'm indifferent.'

'Can you be indifferent to a painting like that?'

'You'd be surprised what I can be indifferent to. I didn't say I could ignore it.'

I drink my coffee and glance at the time.

'I suppose I ought to be off.'

'It'd perhaps be as well.'

I wonder how I ought to take this. Does she mean because of the letter-writer or what I said earlier?

'Do you think I ought to peep between the curtains and see if there's a figure in slouch hat and raincoat lurking across the street?'

'Do you think it is a man?'

'I don't know. I thought it was women who went in for that kind of thing, but God knows who'd want to get at me.'

'You haven't got some woman scorned in your recent past?'

'I've only been down here ten minutes. Give us a chance!'

She stands up as I get my coat and pull it on.

'I'll tell you what, though. Would you let me take the letter?'

'Sure.' She picks it up out of the hearth where she put it aside and hands it to me.

'I'll have a closer look at them both later. I shall have to do something about finding out who's at the bottom of it. I can't make a move without thinking somebody's watching me.'

'Let's hope they're satisfied and don't bother any more.'

'Yes . . . Anyway . . .' I look at her, 'it's not going to stop me doing what I want to do.'

She knows that I mean seeing her. She returns my look and says, 'That's up to you.'

But I resist asking when I will see her again, thinking there's always the Mitre and that there's a way in which the letter to her has done me a good turn, letting me see her alone again and giving me a chance to make a small move. The next move will have to wait its turn.

So I think, not knowing that it's nearly on us, giving us just till we reach the door.

There, a quick 'Well, so long. Thanks again. I'll see you around' would get me out. But her fingers are on the handle and some happy accident of me standing on the wrong side of her in the narrow hall as she opens the door a couple of inches brings us suddenly very close together and for two important seconds we freeze as her eyes stay on me in a deep, grave look. Then I've pushed the door shut again and my arms are round her and her mouth's under mine, mine saying into her hair as we break:

'Donna . . . Oh, Donna, Donna.'

In a moment she holds me off, her look still serious but now with an added element of concern.

'You know, Vic, this can't be good at all for you.'

I shake my head. 'Too late, love.' There's something wild and altogether marvellous exploding inside me.

'It'll get worse before it gets better.'

148

14

If I have a mental picture of her from those early days – the best days – it's of her laughing. They're the best days because although there's better yet to come it seems to arrive in isolated times that are hedged round with a tension and a sense of oppression that the first weeks don't have – in spite of that anonymous watcher who seems to be always behind us and who drives us out of town to places where we're less likely to be seen. There's fun in life and joy in just being with her in the times when she can get away from the theatre. Joy in knowing she wants my company and the certainty that there's a moment soon to come that I've no intention of rushing after, preferring to let it arrive in its own good time and knowing it'll be all the better for the saving.

Sometimes she's laughing at something that's happened at the theatre; sometimes at herself; sometimes at me. It's a good thing to be able to make a person laugh, especially if you love her. There's a streak of the clown in me that comes easily to the top when, as now, I'm happy, in love and, usually, I've had a couple of drinks. But sometimes I find myself feeling a fool, which is different from playing one, and about fifteen years old when all I want to be is the efficient, masterful male.

We're coming back from out of town one Sunday night – the only time Donna can get away for a full evening – when the car gives a sudden lurch and she has to hang on to the wheel to stop us going into the ditch. She slows down and stops.

'Phew, I didn't care much for that, did you?'

'What's happened? A puncture?'

'It felt like it. Better see.'

She gets a torch out of the dashboard compartment and we get out and look at the offside rear wheel.

'That's it, all right. How's your spare?'

'Okay, as far as I know.'

'Let's have it out.'

We get the spare out, along with the tools from the boot, and as

I'm knocking the hub cap off to get at the wheel nuts, Donna's fitting the jack in position and starting to crank.

'If you wait a minute I'll do that for you.'

'I'm capable. I've changed wheels before.'

'Aye,' I say straining against the tightness of the nuts, 'I know you're self-sufficient.'

'I didn't say that. I just meant I can change a wheel.'

'You haven't changed this one recently. The nuts are stuck hard.'

'They'd be tightened with a power tool when I had the new tyres put on.'

'It feels like it.'

'Can you manage?'

'This one's coming.'

Five minutes later, when the job's done, I'm sweating under my overcoat and I want to pay a call. I go to the wall at the side of the road and look down into the field.

'Where are you going?' Donna asks.

'Over this wall.'

'What for?'

'Don't ask silly questions.'

There's a bank of deep snow under the wall and a dark patch of what looks like firm earth. I jump down on to this and it gives under me. I fall backwards, stopping myself from going full length by putting my hand out. It goes up to the elbow in cold snow. When I climb back I'm sure that things aren't what they ought to be. Donna's back in the car and I open the door and ask her for the torch.

'What's wrong?

'I'm not sure, but I think . . .' I shine the beam on my legs and feet and put my hand in the light.

'It's soot!'

'What?'

'It's soot.'

'Soot? It can't be.'

'It is, y'know. I'm covered in the bloody stuff.'

'You'd better get in.'

'But I can't with this stuff all over me.'

'You're not going to walk home, are you?'

'No . . . I suppose not.'

I get in and shut the door.

'Can you beat it! Of all the spots I have to pick that one. What the hell's it doing there anyway? . . . Donna . . .'

She's turned away from me and I can feel her shaking.

'Donna, are you all right?'

She's laughing. She's killing herself over it. She can't speak.

'Would you like me to do it again?'

She shakes her head as the laughter bursts out of her in a sudden whoop. She feels for hankie and wipes her eyes.

'Oh, Vic, you are priceless.'

'You know me, love – owt for a giggle. Headfirst would make a novelty, wouldn't it?'

This only sets her off more. There's something very infectious about her laughter at any time and I feel the sourness going as the funny side of it strikes me.

'Oh God,' she says after a while. 'If you could have heard yourself – how outraged you sounded.'

'Well, I mean . . .'

She starts the engine.

'We'd better get back and clean you up.'

'It's all in my shoes and everything.'

'Shut up,' she says. 'I shan't be able to drive.'

'I suppose I can sneak in without anybody seeing me,' I say as the car moves off.

'Darling, you can't go home like that. You must come back with me and get the worst of it off.'

Which doesn't prove all that easy as we find when we get to the flat and Donna attacks my trousers with a brush in the kitchen while I wash my feet in the bathroom. She comes in with the pants over her arm as I'm standing with one foot up in the washbasin.

'I wish I had a camera.'

'I wish I'd a clean pair of socks.'

'Do you want me to wash those through for you?'

'They'll never be dry in time for me to put them on.'

'Your trousers will do for now, but they'll have to go to the cleaners.'

'What the hell do you suppose it was doing there?'

151

'It was put there for the express purpose of catching Vic Brown, of course.'

I have to laugh. 'All right . . . Have you got any talcum powder?'

'In the cabinet.'

I open the cabinet and look at the bottles and jars. Her things. I think then of her moving about with her record-player, books and picture to wherever the work is, independent, a real person, and I'm suddenly very touched. A great tenderness for her comes over me. When I go into the living-room she's got coffee waiting and a record on the gramophone. We sit together on the sofa.

'You know, this relationship's all the wrong way round,' I tell her.

'Why is that?'

'Well, you've got the interesting career, the car and the flat, and you even put the seductive music on the gramophone.'

'Do you find Frank Sinatra seductive?'

'I'd find *God Save the Queen* seductive if I heard it with you.'

I'm watching a little pulse beat in her throat above the neck of her jumper. I reach out and touch it, then slide my hand round the back of her head and gently pull her nearer. I want her – now. And she knows it. She's not laughing now as she looks at me.

It can't be true. It's not me who's there with her, holding her close, feeling the warm flutter of her breath on my cheek and the sheen of her skin under my hands. No . . .

But it's me a few moments later, spent and sagging before I've hardly touched her, who's apologizing wretchedly, 'Oh, Donna, I'm sorry, I'm sorry.' Her fingers are in the hair in the back of my neck, reassuring in their movement. 'Never mind, never mind.'

'It's just not my night, love.'

'It doesn't matter.'

No, perhaps it doesn't. But we've crossed another bridge and I know that things can never be quite the same again.

Part Three

15

The hotel corridor seems endless, twisting and turning past bogs, bathrooms, linen cupboards and doors marked 'Staff', with the room numbers on plaques which are confusing enough to suggest that the bloke who had put them up didn't start his counting from where I set off; 260 is on the floor below me and, I find eventually, at the very end of the corridor. It occurs to me that I might find a quicker way to it. It doesn't matter now, in the middle of the evening, but I shall feel conspicuous later on. I'm very green at this kind of thing.

At least I know she's here because her name was written three lines above where I signed mine in the register, which stopped me from having to ask for her room number and drawing any more attention to what I'm positive is the general air I'm carrying of being a bloke on what's commonly known as a dirty week-end.

She opens the door to my tap and lets me in. Her hair is all awry as though she's been giving it an intensive brushing but hasn't put it in place yet. She smells warm and sweetly clean under the blue dressing-gown as I give her a hug and a kiss. For a moment we look into each other's eyes and smile with something like quiet glee – like kids who've set up a joke that's just about to come off.

'Did you have a good journey?'

'Yes. I missed the tail end of the rush hour.'

'How long have you been here?'

'About an hour and a half.'

'Eager beaver!'

'Mmm.' She tosses her head in a teasing way.

'I haven't been here long. Just enough to have a wash and change my shirt.'

'You're ready to go out, then?'

'Yep.'

'I shan't be long now. I thought I'd have a bath while I was waiting for you.'

She's across the room now, picking underclothes out of her case. She puts on her suspender belt and briefs under cover of her open dressing-gown with her back to me. Then, still turned away, she slips the gown off and, like all women seem to do, leans into her bra, giving me a leisurely view of her back and, in the dressing-table mirror, a glimpse of her breasts, the shadows in the room with only the bedside light lit, throwing their spacing into dusky relief. I'm revelling in the mixture of modesty and intimacy in the performance while I'm wondering if she realizes the effect it's having on me, and that it's not the best way to get me out for the next hour or two. When she's pulled her frock down over her head and shaken her hair free she asks me to do her up.

'What good is it having a man around and doing up your own zips?' she says, smiling at me through the mirror as I close the back of the dress from waist to neck. I slide my arms round her from behind and snuggle my cheek against hers.

'Is that all this man's good for?'

'At the moment.'

'You shouldn't do these reverse stripteases if you don't want interfering with.'

She laughs. '"Interfered with." I always think that's a marvellous expression.'

'Don't evade the issue.'

She turns to me. 'We are going out, though, aren't we?'

'Yes.'

'I mean, it'll be better later.'

'Yes. We don't want another fiasco.'

'You should forget about that.'

'I can't. It was so bloody humiliating.'

'Never mind.'

'You know, I'm not like that really. I'm actually pretty good, if I do say so myself.'

'Yes, darling, I *know*. You *told* me.'

'It's just that I love you so much I can't believe such a bloody marvellous thing can really happen.'

She shushes me with her forefinger lightly on my lips.

154

'It'll be all right. You'll see.'

She replaces her finger with her mouth for a second, then moves away and starts to put on her stockings.

'Where would you like to eat?'

'Anywhere. You tell me. This is your town.'

'We could go up into Soho.'

'Have you put the car away?'

'Yes, I have, actually. It's in the garage.'

'Well, let's go somewhere within walking distance.'

'There's Earls Court. That's not far and there are one or two decent places there.'

'Okay, Earls Court it is. We'll stroll down, call in the first nice pub we come to for a sneck-lifter –'

She swings round, her mouth open with delighted surprise.

'A what?'

'A sneck-lifter.'

'But what on –'

'You know the old-fashioned iron latches on cottage doors? Well we call them snecks in Yorkshire.'

'And what's a sneck-lifter?'

'I use it for the first drink but I think it really means a couple of bob to get you out of the house.'

'Oh.'

'Well, and then we'll find a restaurant and have a good nosh-up and a bottle of bowjolly, then stroll back.'

'And what then?'

'A nice early night with a good read in bed – you in your small corner and I in mine.'

'It sounds dull, the last part.'

'Oh, we'll probably think of something else as the evening goes on.'

Will I be able to think of *any*thing else, though? I'm wondering. It'll hover over the next few hours like a promise. And Oh God, don't let me balls it up again. How to combine restraint with so much delight. It's unbearable. I help her into her coat and we go out and along the corridor to the lift. The dining-room's busy but the lobby's quiet with the sound of a man laughing in the cocktail bar the only thing that breaks through. We drop our keys on to the desk and go through the heavy glass doors, out of the central heating into the cold of the street. As we step smartly out along the pavement, our heels clicking in the crisp air, I'm suddenly visited by a feeling of the great anonymous mass of London sprawling round us on every side and I'm hit by an enormous happiness that almost takes my breath away. My legs – my whole body, in fact – seem to tingle with the electricity of it, and I know why people dance for joy.

The restaurant we wind up in is a little Italian place with dim lights, soft music coming through off a tape, a corner table for two, and a menu that Donna has to interpret for me. When we've ordered we light cigarettes and exchange little looks and smiles again.

'Here we are, then.'

'Yes.'

'You had no trouble getting away?'

'No. I thought at one time that Fleur was going to wish herself on to me, but I said I was staying with friends. What about you?'

'It's not a week-end when I should have been going home, any-way. Albert has a pretty good idea what's going on but a nod's as good as a wink to him.'

'I suppose he's got to know.'

'Well, we live on top of each other. We established a pattern pretty quickly after I got down here and I can't really ever see you in Longford without him knowing. I mean, in a way he covers up for us with your friends.'

'Somebody there's going to realize before very long. It's inevitable.'

'Will it matter?'

'No, I don't think so. Actors are like old women sometimes, the way they like to gossip. But there are things they keep their own counsel about. Besides, they wouldn't think it a staggering scandal. They've seen it all before.'

'It's different in the theatre.'

She smiles a little. 'I don't mean we spend all our time playing musical beds. There are people who are promiscuous and those who aren't. But it's not a world-shaking act when two people do go to

156

bed with each other. They can do it simply because they're lonely and want to give each other a little warmth.'

Her gaze is down on where she's rolling the lighted end of her cigarette on the rim of the ash-tray.

'And it doesn't make it any less important when you really love somebody.'

I want to think she means me but I've got a sudden intuition that just at this moment her mind's on somebody else from somewhere in her past, a past I hardly know about and can't share. Which doesn't matter. Nor, I tell myself, does the future. It's a great temptation to want now to be a promise for time to come but it would be a mistake to spoil it by thinking of all the complications that lie ahead.

'Shall I tell you something?' I say.

'What?'

'I've never been to bed with somebody I was really in love with.'

She doesn't answer.

'I mean, I've told you about Ingrid and me.'

She nods. 'Yes.'

I wonder what she'd think if I said I'd only ever been to bed with one woman at all, and I think that that's a bit green even for a provincial lad.

'Have there been any more letters?'

'No, just the second one I told you about. "He's still seeing her."'

'Yes.'

'We had a blazing row. It lasted all week-end.'

'You said so.'

'I think she wanted to come down then just to have a look at you, but her mother got the call to go into hospital.'

'Shall I have to meet her sometime?'

'I suppose so. She'll think it's funny if she comes down and doesn't see you.'

'She'll be coming down for good eventually, won't she?'

I shrug. I can't think about that, face what it implies. It's somewhere in the vague future.

'I hate it,' Donna says. 'You going home to suspicion and rows . . .'

'But don't you see, that would have happened anyway. The letters

157

took care of that. We could be completely innocent as far as all that's concerned.'

'Except we're not.'

'No, and I don't care.' I reach across the table and take her hand. 'Donna . . . I said I don't care.'

She nods. 'All right. It's all right.'

A little later the mood seems to pass and we're cheerful together again, happy that we're here alone, away from prying eyes, with tonight and tomorrow and tomorrow night to share. I could wonder, as I have before, what she sees in me to make her be here. She's never said she loves me in so many words. But words like that don't matter. She's here and I love her. I know it later still, when my feeling for her has passed the only test except that of time and we're lying together in the narrow bed in her room, the full silky length of her beside me as she asks:

'Happy, darling?'

'You've no idea.'

She gives a contented little murmur in her throat. A floor board in the corridor creaks and there's the sound of a key scraping into a lock followed by the thump of the door as somebody comes into the next room. In a moment the pipes clunk and gurgle a bit as some water's run. Then everything's quiet again except for the traffic noises from the main road. I expected I'd want to sleep but though my body's relaxed my mind's wide awake . . . So this is it, my mind says. I'm now morally and legally at fault. Well, legally without a doubt, grounds having been well and truly established. But if the law is some kind of reflection of morality, in this case it's a nit. Because I reckon that a marriage that founders on the odd act of adultery has had something rotten happening to it before. And morality? There's a queer old kettle of fish. Go to bed with another woman you love and you're outside the pale; but masturbate into the body of your wife on a Saturday night and you're only exercising your conjugal rights, and everything is nice and respectable and normal. Where can you come to grips with what it's all about? In not using other people for your own ends? Yes, I'll go along with that. In not hurting somebody else? But where does your responsibility to other people cross with responsibility towards yourself? And how far can you sacrifice one for the sake of the other? I've a strong suspicion that goodwill on its own won't do.

Questions, teeming through my mind. But academic; somehow seen clearly but remotely, not touching my contentment now. And not, as might well have happened, rolling in in the wake of the first rush of guilt. Because there is no guilt; nothing like what I felt with Ingrid all that long time ago; when I felt I'd both used her and debased myself. No, nothing like that at all. Donna stirs beside me, resettling her head against my shoulder.

'Hello.'

'Hello.'

'What are you doing here?'

'I'm with a man.'

'Nice feller?'

'Mmmm.'

'What's special about him?'

'Oh, all kinds of things . . . He's gentle and kind and he's got a sort of steadiness and honesty about him . . .'

'That's a laugh.'

'What is?'

'The honesty bit.'

'Why?'

'Because he's a deceitful, lying bastard.'

'Not a bastard. But the other thing . . . it's more complicated than that.'

'Yes . . . When did you first realize I wanted you? It was before the letter, wasn't it?'

'Yes. At the party. The way you looked at me after you'd kissed me. And I knew it meant more to you than a quick kill.'

'And what about me with you?'

'That was later the same night. You were sitting on the sofa, surrounded by people but all on your own. You looked so lonely and I asked you what you were thinking.'

'I remember. I wanted to bury my head in your lap . . . That letter-writer did me a favour. I don't think I'd have dared say anything otherwise.'

'Why not?'

'Oh, you seemed out of my reach; in a world full of men who

159

talked your language and were a lot more interesting than me.'

'Actresses do fall in love outside the profession quite often, you know.'

'I suppose so.'

'In fact, it's better if it happens that way. The other thing can be hell.'

'It seemed impossible, though. It was one night when we were in the Mitre and you were talking to a couple of people. I was watching the way you ran your finger round the bottom of your glass and all of a sudden I felt a fierce ache right through me. Not wanting to take you to bed; just wanting to share a feeling with you, to know I was somebody special as far as you were concerned. The actual sex came later . . . as you know . . .'

'You're scared of sex, aren't you?'

'What makes you say that?'

'You're scared it'll show your feelings to be a sham.'

'Ah . . . It has been known to happen, you know. And anyway, I'm really a very puritanical north-country boy at heart.'

'Yes . . . But lovely . . . and very, very good to be with.'

'Am I?'

'Mmmm. I don't know how to describe it . . . I feel as if I've been stroked all over inside.'

My mouth finds hers and then my fingertips, light as butterfly wings, are exploring the contours of her face that I can't see in the dark. And I'm filled with a wonder and tenderness and gratitude that carry me to the edge of tears.

Guilt, no. Anxiety, yes. I wake up late on the second morning in my own room, with it crawling round my guts like a maggot of doom. Enjoy Now and let the Future alone. Yes, I have done. But the week-end's all but over and where do we go from here? What happens now? There can't be another break like this for some time because of Donna's commitments at the theatre. Can we carry it off in Longford without our anonymous friend keeping Ingrid posted? And with her mother out of hospital now it can't be more than a couple of months or so before Ingrid'll be down here to live. Without the letters I could have taken advantage of Ingrid's reluctance and let her stall as long as she wanted to. But now she smells danger and she'll want to do everything she can to protect what's hers. Me.

All I ask for now is time. Time with opportunity. Time to sort it all out at my pace and not that forced on me by somebody else . . .

'You have seen her again, haven't you?'

'Well of course I have. I'm not going to let a couple of anonymous letters affect me.'

'And there's nothing between you?'

'I've told you.'

'Yes.'

She's confused and distressed, not knowing what to believe; and I'm sorry, I'm sorry, I'm sorry. The letters are right in what they imply. But that's beside the point. She doesn't know this for sure and it would be all the same if I were innocent. Would it? Wouldn't innocence give me the power to reassure her in a convincing way? No, I don't love her enough for that. It's one of the penalties of being married to me. She ought to know it by now and not ask for more than I can give. It's the dormant things in our marriage that the letters have agitated; and there's their real foulness, what can never make them well-intentioned and right. There's no way for the writer to know the balance of the relationship he's interfering with, what kind of fuses his words are lighting and what kind of charges they're connected to.

'I suppose it's no good me asking you to give that job up and come back here?'

'What, and let her rule our lives?'

'Her?'

'Well him, then. Or it. I don't know.'

'I think it's her.'

'Who?'

'This girl.'

'*What*!'

'I think she's writing them.'

'But what in hell's name for?'

'To get you away from me.'

'Oh, for Christ's sake! She's had one herself.'

'That could be a blind. To stop you suspecting.'

'Look, don't make me think you're more stupid than you are.'

'I suppose she's bright and intelligent. I suppose you can talk to her about all the things I don't understand.'

'Look, for Christ's sake will you shut up about her! Will you just shut up!'

My watch says ten-fifteen. There's a tap at the door. I shout come in, thinking it's the chambermaid, but when there's no sound of a key going into the lock I get out of bed and open the door to find Donna.

'Did I wake you?'

She brushes by me in a wave of scent and freshness, looking at me in my crumpled pyjamas, unwashed, unshaved, my hair tousled, and at the still warm unmade bed. There's a gleam of amusement in her eyes.

'You know you've missed breakfast?'

'I'm not bothered.'

'I've had fruit juice and cornflakes, egg, bacon and sausages, and toast and marmalade.'

'Sadist. It sounds horrible. I'll have a kiss now and a cup of coffee later.'

She backs away after the first kiss.

'That's your ration for now.'

'I suppose I don't look much like God's gift to women just at the moment.'

'I don't mind. But the maids are on the landing.'

'We don't want a queue, do we?'

She laughs.

'I'll get dressed, then. Shan't be long.'

'Shall I wait downstairs?'

'No, don't go.'

'What about the maids?'

'Oh, bugger the maids. You don't think one of 'em's our anonymous friend in disguise, do you?'

'No, but – '

'Anyway, they'd see you come in, so you won't be compromised.'

'You're getting bold, aren't you?'

'I'm just getting fed-up with being pushed around by somebody I don't even know.'

I run water into the basin and strip off my pyjama jacket. I *want*

162

her to watch me wash and shave. I want to bring the intimacy of the little ordinary things into our relationship. There's no morning after with her. It's as valuable in its way as midnight.

'What's the plan for today?'

'We shall have to be out of here by twelve, I suppose.'

'Yes. Do you want to be back at any particular time?'

'No. I've been thinking. I'll skip the train and go back with you in the car.'

'Is that wise?'

'Oh, to hell with wisdom. We can spend the afternoon here and arrive back after dark. You could drop me off at the station. It's going to be tricky enough, so let's make the most of this while we can.'

'All right.'

Slopping water over myself at the basin I turn my head and look at her.

'As long as you haven't had too much of me.'

She shakes her head. 'No.'

'Would you mind passing me the toilet bag out of my case.'

She finds it and brings it across, reaching round me and at the same time placing one hand flat in the middle of my back. I'm suddenly overcome. I feel as if she's touched my bowels and I close my eyes for a moment as a wave of black, black despair rushes over me.

16

It doesn't last, of course, while we're together; but it visits me again in a diluted form that's a kind of defeatist feeling about the hopelessness of the whole thing after she's dropped me off outside Longford station and I'm walking home through a sudden thaw along the dark wet streets. When we're together we're very, very close; the moment we part a whole hostile world comes between us; and by Monday morning the week-end has begun to seem like an impossible dream.

The new play opens on the Monday night. 'World Première,'

163

the notices say, 'of *Jack told my Father*, a play by Wilf Cotton, author of *Day after Day*.' Donna says there'll be critics from the national dailies there as well as representatives of West End managements. It's a big night for the Palace and Conroy and I, sitting in the circle before the curtain goes up, look at the faces of the people in the front two rows to see if there's anybody famous we can recognize.

It's a kind of north-country family piece, as authentic as fish and chips, but with a curious offbeat way of looking at some things that brings you up short with a jolt every now and again. The Jack in the title is a brother who's gone away and made good and he represents something different to each of the family at home, who are all failures in some way. Until finally he comes back and it turns out that what Jack represents is Jack and they'll all have to stand on their own feet. Donna plays the younger brother's girl friend who Jack tries to make and who's the prime mover in blowing the gaff on the whole illusion.

The V.I.P.s have drinks in the producer's office afterwards and Albert and I repair to the Mitre to sink one or two on our own before going to Donna's where there's a later get-together. We go up the stairs carrying a few bottles of ale each and ring the bell. When nobody answers we walk in, dump our coats in the passage, and go into the crowded living-room. There's music coming from the record-player but it's background stuff and nobody's dancing. This is evidently a talking party and we edge past one or two groups standing nearest the door and make for the kitchen. We meet Donna coming out. Her face is flushed, as though she's too hot, been drinking too much, or had a difference of opinion with somebody.

'Oh, there you are. Get yourselves something to drink in the kitchen and come and circulate.'

I'm hoping for some small special look from her but I get nothing. There's a tall good-looking bloke in the kitchen as we go in, wearing a fawn sweater and a bow-tie. He's got brown wavy hair and clean-cut features. A smoothie, if ever I saw one. A split-second impression because he eyes us both casually and goes out straight away, carrying a glass of what looks like whisky. We stand our bottles on the draining-board and look round for something to drink out of. There are no glasses about so we get a couple of cups out of the cupboard and use them; and I'm just expounding on the deficiencies of bottled beer after draught and feeling myself in for a session of quiet burps with the gas when Donna comes back with a lean dark-haired bloke, a year or two older than me maybe, in a suède jacket with leather patches on the elbows and a charcoal-grey wool sports shirt under it.

'Look, you two . . .' Donna's saying as she comes in. She sees the cups. 'Is that all you can find to drink from?'

'We're all right,' Albert says.

'You're sure?'

'Well what are you going to do about it if we're not?' I say, conscious more than anything else of wanting to put my arms round her because I haven't seen her for twenty-four hours.

'True enough,' she says. 'Look, though, I wanted Wilf to meet you two. You're all from the same part of the world. Tykes, isn't it?'

'If you like,' Albert says. He's looking at the other feller. 'This'll be the author, I gather.'

'Yes . . .' Donna performs the introductions. 'Can I leave you for a minute while I go and see to my duties?'

'Tykes . . .' Wilf Cotton murmurs, lifting his eyebrows. 'What part do you come from?'

We tell him, Cressley, and he nods.

'I know the area. I came from Bronhill originally. That's a mining village between Barnsley and Sheffield.'

'My old man's a miner.'

'Oh?' He looks at me, smiling slightly. 'Your credentials are in good order, then.'

'Yeh. Donna was telling me it's like blue blood in the theatre.'

'It is as long as the right stuff's being written. The trouble now is, the tide's on the turn. People won't take north-country working-class stuff for its novelty value any more. It's got to be good in its own right.'

'Is that why you're living down here?'

'What? No. No, that doesn't matter. I still write about the same things.'

'I thought writers were tending to stay put now,' Conroy says, 'what with the provinces opening up a bit.'

Cotton shrugs. 'Some do, some don't. Some like to stick close to their material and others benefit from shaking the provinces off their backs for a bit and seeing the thing in perspective. My idea is to try London for a while and then think of going back later. I've got mixed feelings about it but Marguerite – that's my wife – she loves London. Are either of you married?'

I tell him I am.

'You know what I mean, then. You've got somebody else to consider.'

He's holding an empty tumbler and I ask him what he's drinking.

'Beer, if there is any.'

I fill him up from one of our bottles as Conroy says:

'What about this play? Will it go on anywhere else?'

'That's in the lap of the gods; the critics and managers who came out to see it. The idea in putting it on here was to see if it held together. If they do us proud tomorrow it could do something else.'

'West End?' Conroy asks.

'I daren't think about it.' Cotton pulls a face. 'A long run in London, two hundred pounds a week while I'm writing my next book. I'd be set up.'

'I'll say!' I'm suddenly busy with thoughts of two hundred quid a week rolling in and Wilf, seeing this, laughs.

'It doesn't happen every day, mate.'

'No, but . . .'

'The possibilities are there,' Conroy says. 'You do make a living by writing, don't you?'

'In a manner of speaking.'

'You must have done something before, though,' I say.

'Oh, yes. I was a wages clerk in a pit office at first. Then I worked in a shirt factory for a bit. Nobody starts out being a full-time writer.'

'I don't know how they do it at all. I wouldn't know where to begin.'

'Good,' Cotton says.

'What d'you mean?'

'You're honest. I get sick and tired of stupid arrogant bastards who are going to write a book when they find the time. We can all do it, you know. It's just a matter of getting down to it. I tell

166

them to get cracking. No capital needed. Buy a ream of paper and a tanner ballpoint and you're in business.'

'Are you better off with plays or books?' Albert asks. 'I mean, if you don't mind us quizzing you.'

He shakes his head, the little smile there again. 'No, that's all right. But you can't really measure it like that. It depends what you want to write. I suppose you could say that in a roughly equivalent play and a novel – whatever that might mean – you'd make more money out of the play. At least everybody pays to see it, but the trouble with novels is that not many people buy them. They tell you they're fifteenth on the list at the public library in a way that suggests you ought to pin a medal on them for being so keen.'

Having said one right thing I now drop a clanger, blurting out without thinking:

'Surely you must have made a packet out of that paperback of yours. It was all over the bookstalls at one time.'

He looks at me. 'Oh, I'm half-way to being a millionaire; anybody can tell you that. Ten thousand in hardbacks, a hundred thousand in paperbacks, magazine serialization and a film right option that nobody looks like taking up. Say four and a half thousand, less income tax and expenses. It's not a fortune, is it?'

'It's not as much as I'd've thought, but still . . .'

'Still it sounds nice, doesn't it? And if you could do a book a year like that you'd be comfortable. Except you can't. You strike lucky with only one now and again.'

'You've got to do other things?' Conroy says.

'Yes. Like sending the wife out to work. Haven't I, love?' he says, turning to the good-looking girl with a haughty way of holding her head who's appeared in the doorway.

She's only been there a second and Cotton was standing with his back to the door. I'm wondering how he sensed her presence as she comes forward and slips her arm through his.

'What was that?'

'I was telling Albert and Vic how you keep the domestic ship afloat.'

'Don't exaggerate,' she tells him. 'I came to see if you were thinking about going. You know we said we wouldn't be late.

You've got to be up and out in good time in the morning.'

'I know, and we'll go in a few minutes.'

He kisses her on the tip of her nose and Conroy shoots me an amused look. This kind of thing between two people when others are there can be irritating but I find the effect now rather touching. And suddenly, seeing the two of them like that, obviously batty about each other, Wilf Cotton as Yorkshire as I am and his wife a rather frosty Standard English type, it seems more possible somehow for Donna and me. Except that he's Somebody and I'm just a common or garden draughtsman. But still . . . It's as though I've suddenly opened my mind to the feasibility of a future for us; a notion that doesn't seem as ridiculous and beyond thinking about as it somehow did before. Little things . . .

The tall feller in the bow-tie comes in looking for somebody who turns out to be Wilf Cotton.

'Look, Wilf, what do you think. Don't you think she's absolutely right for it?'

'I think she'd be great, Clive. But she doesn't seem exactly sold on the idea.'

'Have you talked to her?'

'Yes, I told her the story-line and a bit about the character, but I detected a noticeable lack of enthusiasm.'

'Oh, don't worry. I can handle Donna. Leave it to me. Where is she?'

He darts out into the living-room and Cotton and his wife exchange a look which ends with him giving a silent shrug.

This Clive's back in a minute, pulling Donna behind him. Almost literally pulling, with his hand round hers in a grip she can't get free of.

'Here she is. Now you tell Wilf. Put him out of his misery.'

'Really, Clive. I can't just – '

'Look, ducky, he's completely sold on you, wild with enthusiasm.'

Cotton looks at them both, saying nothing.

'But I haven't even read the script.'

'There'll be one in the post Wednesday morning. But he's written it and I'm going to direct, so you can take our word for its not being rubbish. In fact, it's the best woman's part I've seen in six months.'

'I really don't think this is either the time or the place to – '

'Oh, stop stalling, Donna. Don't you want to get out of that flea-pit and do something big?'

A very forceful bloke, this Clive. I wonder if anybody else besides me can see that he's still holding Donna where she's standing by brute force, his fingers round hers in a way that must be twisting and crushing them something painful. It's there in her eyes, though she's saying nothing. I reach out and take his arm.

'Steady on, mate.'

He twists his head to me, an irrelevant interruption.

'What?'

'You're hurting her.'

'Oh, rubbish.' He turns away. 'Now look –'

But I keep hold of his arm, tightening my grip until he's forced to take notice of me again.

'Mate.'

'Look, what's the matter with – ?'

'Let go of her hand. You're hurting her.'

All eyes are on us now.

'Who the hell are you?' Matey says and a great spasm of anger and hatred for him shakes me. I don't want to shout so I say low and hard through my teeth:

'Let go of her bloody hand, and quick.'

He lets go and a cross between a sneer and a smile comes to his face. My heart's beating fast. I hate scenes in public but he's not getting away with that kind of thing. Donna rubs her fingers. They're white where he's had hold of them. I wonder why she hasn't slapped him down. She's got the spirit for it.

'Aren't you the forceful north-country boy?' this Clive says.

'I just don't like blokes who manhandle women,' I tell him.

'Brings out all the chivalrous instincts in you, does it? Is he a friend of yours, Donna?'

'Yes, I am a friend of hers but that's beside the point.'

'I've got the picture,' he says. 'Mustn't spoil a beautiful friendship. Got to give our friend a chance to play the protector.'

Cotton moves to break it up. 'Come on, Clive. You let yourself get carried away.'

'He'll get carried out, if he doesn't watch it,' I tell him.

This Clive's half a head taller than me but we're about even in weight and I'm mad enough to make up for any disadvantages I don't know about.

'Our friend seems set on a brawl,' he says as Wilf takes his arm.

'Never mind that,' Cotton says. 'It's time we were off, and you've got to drive us back.'

'Such a pity to disappoint him,' Clive calls over his shoulder as Wilf ushers him out, turning his head for a second to wink at me.

Marguerite hangs back for a minute to speak to Donna.

'Are you all right?'

'Yes, of course I am. I don't know why there had to be such a fuss. I'll come and see you out.'

'Don't bother; we can manage.'

'I'll come with you to the door.'

'Bastard,' I say to Conroy as they go out. 'Did you see how he'd got hold of her hand?'

'No, not till you mentioned it.'

'He was nearly breaking her fingers and she was standing there saying nowt.'

Albert pours himself some more beer.

'I thought you were going to drop him one on.'

'Another word and I should have done. What was it all about, anyway?'

'I think they were talking about a TV play.'

'And who the bloody hell does Mister Clive What's-his-name think he is? God Almighty?'

'Carter, they call him. Here, have some more beer.'

My heart's only now beginning to stop thumping. I put my hand inside my jacket and feel it as Albert passes the bottle over.

'I wouldn't make a fuss about it to Donna, if I were you.'

'What d'you mean?'

'I gather they used to know each other before.'

'What the hell's that got to do with it? He doesn't bloody own her, does he?'

'No, and neither do you.'

'Look, Albert, he was crushing her hand – hurting her. I had to go for him.'

'Yes. And now you've made your gesture. I'd let it drop and mind my own business.'

'Well, for Christ's sake, Albert – '

He cuts me short, taking my arm.

'Come on, let's circulate and find Fleur.'

The Christmas show was Fleur's last with the company and this party is partly a farewell do for her as she's going back to live in London. We've timed it nicely because as we go into the living-room the producer, a chap called Sanderson, is on his feet on the hearth, calling for attention.

'Listen, everybody . . .'

'Order, please,' somebody shouts in a deep voice.

'While we're all here . . .'

'Let's not get personal.'

'Order, please,' the voice shouts again.

'Thank you, Geoff,' Sanderson says.

'Order, *please*!'

'Yes, Geoff. *Thank* you . . . I was saying . . .'

'Will you kindly give order!'

'Sit on him, somebody.'

'Thank you . . . Now, while we're all here, I've got to remind you that one of our number is leaving us. I don't have to tell you how Fleur has graced the old Palace boards . . .' There's a few wolf whistles and calls of 'Good old Fleur.' ' . . . But now she's done her last production with the company and she's off to try her luck in the big city. I'd like you to join me in drinking to her and wishing her all good fortune in the future. To Fleur!'

The toast is taken up all round the room and a cove standing at one end of the sofa turns round and falls gracefully backwards across the knees of the people sitting there, ending up with his feet on one arm and his head in Fleur's lap. He looks soulfully up at her.

'Say it's not to be for ever, dearest.'

The three of them push at once, rolling him off so that he falls on his face on the carpet at their feet. He stays there, looking as if he's gone to sleep.

I look at Albert.

'What now, then?'

He grins. 'I've got her new address, mate; don't you worry.'

I hang on as the party starts folding up, hoping to be able to see Donna alone; but finally I find myself going down the stairs with the last leavers. Once at the car, though, as the others are going off, I tell Albert I'm going back.

'To Donna's?'

'Aye, I want to talk to her.'

'Well, if you don't mind walking home, mate.'

I nip smartly back up the stairs and give the bell a short jab. She opens the door.

'Oh. Have you forgotten something?'

'No.' I step inside. 'I wanted to talk to you.'

She leads the way into the living-room. Her face looks pale and drawn with tiredness. I suppose a first night is a big strain anyway, without other things on top of it.

'Look, I just wanted to say I'm sorry about tonight. About making a scene, I mean.'

'Oh. that's all right.'

'I had to do it. I mean, any decent bloke would've cut up.'

She nods. 'Yes. He's all right. A bit . . . well, impetuous and full of himself.'

'You knew him before, didn't you?'

'Yes, I know him from some time back.'

She shivers a little as though somebody's walked over her grave and looks round at the dirty glasses and overflowing ash-trays.

'The trouble with parties is they're so sordid afterwards.'

'Like casual sex.'

She musters a tiny smile. 'Yes.'

'I'll help you to clear up. It won't take long.'

'No, I'll do it in the morning. I'll just make some coffee and go to bed. Do you want some?'

'Please.'

She starts towards the kitchen and I look round for a minute then begin to collect the glasses up. When I take all I can carry into the kitchen she's got the milk on and is standing at the table measuring Nescafé into the cups. I put the glasses down and go to her and put my arms round her from behind, sliding my hands up to cup her breasts; not in anything like lust, but just with a yearning to comfort her in some way, because somehow I know this is what she's in need of.

172

My touch seems to melt her. The next thing I know she's in tears.

'Donna . . . Donna, love.' I turn her round and she rests her face on my chest. 'What's wrong?'

'Oh, I shall be nothing but trouble for you. You'd be better off never having met me.'

'A bit of trouble, that's to be expected. But don't you know how happy you've made me? Don`t you?'

'How long will it be before you start hating me, though?'

'You're talking silly now. The milk . . .'

I reach past her and lift the pan as the milk comes to the boil.

'Look, you go and sit down in there and I'll see to the coffee. Off you go. I'll be with you in a minute.'

She goes away and I make the coffee and add sugar, then half-fill the pan with water from the tap and put it in the sink before carrying the cups into the other room. Donna's standing looking down at the electric fire and I put both cups on the low narrow mantelshelf and stand beside her, one arm round her shoulders.

'Do you want an aspirin or something?'

'No, thanks. I'll be all right after a good night's sleep.'

'Can you sleep in tomorrow?'

'Yes. I'll stay as long as I want to.'

'It'd be nice if I could come round and take you out to lunch.'

'You couldn't, though, could you?'

'No, there isn't the time. But I like you in daylight as well as at night.'

She lifts her hand and presses mine where it rests lightly on her shoulder. Our days and nights are both numbered. Time running out. Unless . . .

'You'd better sit down and drink your coffee.'

'Yes.'

She does as I say and curls up with her feet under her at one end of the sofa.

'Did you think it went well tonight?'

'I don't know. It was a bit stiff. And with the place crawling with managers and critics we were all a bit keyed up. Did you like it?'

'Very much.'

'It'll settle down later in the week. It's a pity they all have to come on the first night.'

'Did any of them drop any hints about how they liked it?'

'Oh no, they're too discreet for that. They go and phone their notices in then drink with you and smile and make pleasant conversation. By the time you see it in print it's too late to argue. Not that that would do any good anyway.'

'This other thing that Carter and Wilf Cotton want you to do; is it a television play?'

'Yes. They want me for the lead.'

'Don't you want to do it?'

'I don't know. I haven't seen the script yet.'

'It could be a big break for you, couldn't it?'

'Yes. But all kinds of things come into it ...' She puts her hand to her forehead. 'Oh, I don't know; I can't think about it tonight.'

'No, you've had enough. I'll clear off and let you get to bed.'

I put my cup down and go and sit beside her for a moment, kissing her lightly on the cheek.

'I'd like to undress you and carry you in and tuck you up like a little girl.'

'Except I'm not a little girl. I haven't been for a thousand years.'

'It's very convenient, all things considered.'

She turns her head and looks directly at me with something like the grave intensity of that first night when I kissed her in the hall. Only a few short weeks ago. So little time ago, so little time to come ... Only now her eyes are searching mine as though she's looking for something she wants from me but which I for some reason can't give her. And I'm out of my depth, suddenly shaken to the core by a feeling of both helplessness and fear.

17

It's my week-end at home so I go to the Palace again on Thursday, by myself, partly to have another look at the play, but mostly because I just want to see Donna. Watching her perform on the stage gives me a terrific thrill. She's very good and I'm tremendously proud of her.

There's only one interval and during it I slip out to the stalls bar and run into Wilf Cotton.

'Now then. You here again?'

He laughs. 'I can't keep away.'

'I thought I'd have another look at it myself. It's settling down a bit, don't you think?'

'Yes, it's amazing the difference a couple of nights can make.'

'How were the reviews?'

'Mixed. Some quite good, some indifferent.'

'But none really bad?'

'No.'

'Well, that's something. D'you think anybody's going to take it up?'

'Well they're not biting one another's hands off, let's admit it.' He shrugs. 'There's always a chance but I'm not very hopeful now. The trouble is the best reviews were in the wrong papers.'

'You can't win, can you?'

He laughs again. 'No, it's a hard life.'

We're standing drinking beer near the door, watching people come in and fight for their drinks. One or two, noticing him and remembering his picture on the programme, throw discreet little looks his way, wondering if he really is the author.

'You get some interesting free opinions just mingling with the audience,' he says, refusing with a shake of his head as I offer him a cigarette. 'I've just heard somebody say it's not as good as *Look Back in Anger* and somebody else who thinks it's streets ahead of *A Taste of Honey*.'

'Not a bad middle position.'

'No, I suppose not. Here, let me . . .'

He takes my glass as I fumble one-handed with matches and holds it while I light my fag.

'Thanks. By the way, I'm sorry about that little bit of unpleasantness the other night.'

'With Clive Carter, you mean? Forget about it.'

'I seem to be spending my time apologizing for it. And he was in the wrong.'

'Of course he was. Marguerite didn't half give him the treatment on the way home. She can be very cool and cutting when she wants to be.'

'Isn't she with you tonight?'

'No, she had something else on.'

'I just thought he was an objectionable bastard. I'm sorry if he's a friend of yours.'

'Oh no, he's not my type, mate. But he's one of the best television directors in the business and I'm lucky to get him for my play. He came out both to see *Jack* and look at Donna. To see if time had been kind to her was his typical way of putting it. He'd an idea she'd be good casting for one of the parts.'

'They've worked together before, I believe.'

'They used to live together. That's the trouble with the dramatic world. You never know when you're putting your foot down just what private corns you're treading on.'

Too true, mate, I'm thinking. And the actors aren't all in the profession, either. Some ordinary people are occasionally good at it. Like me, just now. Those heavy reactions you get in films and plays, they don't always happen in real life. You get a thump and your face stays straight and you just go on talking.

'Is she going to do the play?'

'I really couldn't say. They've got it between them. I'd like her to. She'd be good in it and it's a good part, even if I do say so as wrote it.' He smiles. 'And having been wrong before.'

The bell rings and people start drifting back into the auditorium.

'Well, back to the fight.'

He looks round for somewhere to put his glass and I take it and put it with mine on a narrow shelf that I can see now.

'All the best with it, if I don't see you again.'

He waves as he goes off. 'Thanks. Been nice seeing you.'

I go straight round to the flat after the show. Donna's lent me a key and I switch the fire on, put the Rachmaninov on the record-player and sit down and think while I'm waiting for her. I'm conscious all the time now of screws tightening, of pressures bearing down on me, of decisions that ought to be made. Were there ever any ideal conditions for an affair, when you could sail along on an even keel with no more strain than's involved in a bit of discreet covering-up? But I never wanted that kind of affair. I knew, at bottom, that if I got involved then decisions would come into it. The trouble is they've come into it a bit too soon and if I don't make them now circumstances will pretty soon do it for me.

Can I leave Ingrid? Is that the question? Or wouldn't it be better to ask myself if I can bear losing Donna? It's all happened so quickly. If only we could let time bring the answers up gradually. Put them on the agenda for six months from now. But we can't. What about her? What does she want from me? Is she ready for any kind of permanent arrangement? How would it work out with her career? I could never expect her to settle down to being just a housewife, could I?

What with the music belling out and me in a brown study, I don't hear her come in till she's right in the room.

'You're looking very serious, darling.'

'I was thinking.'

'That much was obvious.'

'I was thinking about us.'

She puts her bag and short coat on a chair and comes and bends over and kisses me, then looks into my face from a distance of six inches.

'You looked the picture of gloom.'

'I'm a bit of a melancholy type. Didn't you know?'

'Yes. If you haven't got any problems you'll invent some.'

'Oh, my problems are real enough.'

'Are they the same old ones or a fresh batch?'

'The old ones are good enough to be going on with. Anyway, I don't have to think about them now you're here.'

She lifts her hand. 'Do you like this?' Meaning the music.

'Mmm. Lovely.'

'I thought you would. But I'm not going to let you indulge yourself. I'm putting something more cheerful on.'

I watch her as she goes to the player and takes the record off in mid-movement. She seems to have got rid of her mood of Monday night. She's quite gay. Whether it's genuine or a pose, I can't tell. She puts the *My Fair Lady* recording on.

'Why didn't you give yourself a drink?'

'I thought I'd wait for you. And anyway, I don't like to go poking about too much in other people's homes.'

She pulls a face. 'Am I "other people"?'

'No – you're "the other woman".'

'In letters of flaming scarlet.'

'Luring me into nights of vice and debauchery.'

'To the accompaniment of Rachmaninov.'

'A typical stroke of subtle corruption. Did you see Wilf Cotton tonight?'

'No. Was he there?'

'Yes. I had a drink with him at the interval.'

'I'll get you one. What do you want?'

'Albert and I left some beer, I think.'

I get up and wander after her as far as the kitchen doorway as Rex Harrison begins to sing *I've grown accustomed to her face*. I don't know which goes more with my mood, this or the Rachmaninov. At least that's abstract and doesn't put it directly into words.

'What had Wilf to say for himself?'

'He was eavesdropping on audience reaction.'

'Was it good?'

'The bits he quoted to me were.'

'I like him, don't you?'

'Yes, he seems to be a good lad.'

She hands over my beer, having found some red wine for herself, and we go back into the other room and sit on the couch.

'I like his work, too, I must say. His new television play's very good.'

'You've read it now, have you?'

'Yes, the script came yesterday.'

'He keeps his promises.'

'Who?'

'Clive Carter.'

'Some of them.'

I shoot her a quick look but there's nothing in her face that I can read.

'Are you going to do it, then?'

'I think I am.'

'You haven't definitely made your mind up?'

'It's a lovely part.'

'Well, what are you waiting for?'

'Oh, there are other considerations involved.'

'Like Carter, you mean?'

It's her turn to give me a quick look now.

'Why did you say that?'

'Something Wilf Cotton said tonight.'

'About me?'

'You and Carter.'

'Gossip?'

'No, just something he let drop in conversation. I don't think he can know about us or he probably wouldn't have said it.'

'What was it he said?'

'That you used to live together.'

'Was that all?'

'Wasn't it enough?'

She twists on the couch, looking straight at me.

'Oh God . . .' Her eyes rove about my face. 'You're not going to act as though you're hurt, are you?'

'Have I said anything?'

'Enough. God, but it's funny how the puritanical provincialism always comes to the top.'

'Look, I – '

'You're shocked. No, I can tell you are. You can have an affair but when you find out I lived with somebody else for a while your small-town mentality comes straight through.'

'Look, will you stop jumping on me. I am *not* shocked. But I had to find out. I'd rather you'd told me yourself.'

'You only met the man on Monday night. I've hardly had time to tell you.'

'You could have told me then.'

'You didn't think you were the first man I'd ever been to bed with, did you?'

'Look, you're getting me all wrong.'

'Am I?'

'Yes, you are. It was obvious he was influencing whether or not you'd do this play. I just thought you might have been a bit more open and discussed it with me.'

'Vic, Clive Carter is somebody I knew before I met you. He's got nothing to do with you.'

'But when he influences what you're going to do now he has. Or hasn't he?'

'I'm not your personal property, Vic.'

'No.'

'Oh God, why do you have to be hurt about it?'

'I suppose it's mainly because I don't like the bloke.'

'Look, darling, I'm twenty-four years old. I've known a lot of people and done a lot of things before I met you. Nothing I'm particularly ashamed of, as it happens. But do I have to run over it all for your approval now?'

'Donna . . . do you love me?'

'Darling, it's one of the most stupid and misleading words in the language.'

'Not for me it isn't.'

'Vic, let's stop this, shall we?'

'What do you want from me? I mean, what do you expect?'

'What kind of a question is that?'

Yes. Just so. What can she say till I put my own cards on the table?

'What happened with this Carter feller?'

'Well we lived together, like the man said.'

'Why didn't you get married?'

'We might have done if it had lasted. But it didn't. It went on for nearly a year and then we split up.'

'Why was that?'

'Temperament, I suppose. Incompatibility, the lawyers call it. Only we didn't need lawyers. We just walked out on each other and called it quits. That was a couple of years ago. I hadn't seen him for over a year when he turned up this week. It was a complete surprise. I wasn't expecting him.'

She stops and gives me a little smile. 'Was that what you were brooding about when I came in?'

'No, as a matter of fact it wasn't. Just the situation in general.'

180

'Well you can stop it for a while now I'm here.'

'Yes.'

'Are you going home tomorrow?'

'Yes.'

'Will you make love to your wife this week-end?'

'What?'

'You see, that's the sort of question I could ask you. Wives are supposed to abhor the thought of their husband having another woman, but mistresses have to put up with it. Have you never thought of that?'

'No. But mistresses are depraved creatures anyway.'

She smiles. 'That must be the answer.'

The smile fades into an expression I've seen on her face before, the eyelids half down as she looks at me. She puts her head on my shoulder.

'If you're going away tomorrow would you like to stay for a while tonight?'

'Can I?'

'If you think you can risk it. Will it be all right?'

'Might as well be hung for a sheep as a lamb.'

'Not a very tactful way of putting it.'

'I must have left my tact in my other suit tonight.'

'Mmmm. Do you want another drink?'

'No.'

'Shall we go now, then?'

'No time like the present.'

It's cold in the bedroom but when Donna turns the sheets back I say:

'What's this? An electric blanket?'

'Yes. I switch it on every night before I leave for the theatre. What's wrong, don't you approve?'

'Well, yes, it's fine.'

'Would it make you feel easier if you sinned in discomfort?'

'It'd be easier if you stopped needling me.'

Her eyes are laughing at me. I love her and sin is a word invented for somebody else.

And when I'm holding her I've got an awareness of how we are together that's keener and more piercing than anything I've known before: an agony of both sadness and joy, and so near to heart-break you'd think I had some way of knowing it's for the last time.

18

I go home all tensed up, expecting a week-end of rows or at best frosty silences and a general attitude of keep your distance; but instead I find Ingrid calm and loving and neither Donna nor the letters is mentioned. She could be doing the smart thing; boxing clever; but in any event it's such a relief that I feel myself winding down a bit and seeing things in a better light. When we get round to the subject of finding somewhere to live and her coming down, I begin to box a bit crafty myself, playing for time. The weather's on my side. It's as bad as ever, with sleet and snow and ice, and we don't propose to begin looking round seriously till it lets up a bit. And there's something else, I tell her. With this bad weather I'm just a bit doubtful about the firm. I'd like to hang on a bit longer and make sure they won't start making economies such as cutting back in the number of staff to offset a bit of what the winter has lost them in working hours. No, it's not likely, but if the worst did happen I might want to come back here and it wouldn't do to burn our boats. As me coming back is what Ingrid would like more than anything else she can't help but see the sense in this.

Early the next week Donna goes up to town to see her agent and the casting director of the television company and comes back with the part. Rehearsals start in a few days, as soon as she's finished with the play at the theatre, and she'll be away for a fortnight, staying with Fleur. On the Sunday night before she leaves we drive out into the country and have a meal at a pub Donna knows, a real genuine old place with roaring fires, oak beams and settles. After we've eaten we stand at the bar for a while and Donna, mentioning some old pub she knows in Cornwall, gets the landlord started on about the history of the place. What he's talking about is interesting enough but I'm only half listening most of the time because I've got a growing nagging feeling that there are things I ought to be saying to Donna, that she might be expecting me to say;

but it's not until we're going back in the car that we have a real chance to talk.

I put my hand in her lap as she drives.

'I'm going to miss you, love.'

'I shall miss you.'

'I was wondering if we couldn't manage something next week-end.'

'Won't you be going home?'

'I could make some excuse and not go.'

'No, if things have calmed down a bit you don't want to go stirring them all up again.'

'Maybe it's about time they were really stirred up. Brought out into the open.'

'Darling, you – '

'She doesn't own me, does she? I mean, I'm still a person in my own right and I don't *have* to put up with a situation I don't like.'

'Vic,' she says, 'don't go thrashing around causing trouble.'

'I'm talking about getting rid of trouble; throwing it all off.'

'Is it as easy as that?'

'It can be if you make up your mind what you want and go straight for it.'

She says something else, very short, that's lost in the noise of the engine. And then I ask her, straight out:

'Would you marry me if I were free?'

There's a pause before she answers.

'I'd live with you.'

I snort. 'Live with me . . . Is it all you can think of – living with people? Don't you ever commit yourself?'

'You believe a lot in marriage, don't you, Vic?'

'I suppose I do.'

'Well, so do I. Enough to want it just once and for good.'

'But not with me?'

'Oh, Vic, you're not free and you can't act as though you are. There's somebody else involved.'

'I'm talking about getting free.'

There's a long silence. The car presses on through the dark, but not too fast because the roads are winding and the surface isn't to be trusted. Once, coming out of a bend, the back wheels slip on a patch of ice but Donna corrects the slide with a quick twist of the wheel.

'I wish you hadn't brought this up,' she says at last. 'It's not the right time.'

'Time is something we just haven't got. That's the point.'

'The fullness of time.'

'What?'

'Nothing. It's a lovely phrase, though, isn't it?'

I grunt and she drops her left hand, finding and squeezing mine.

'I'd marry you tomorrow if I could,' I tell her. 'That's my position in a nutshell.'

'Darling . . .' She turns her head and looks at me for a moment. 'Life and feelings . . . they're so complicated . . . Promise me you won't go off the deep end and do anything rash.'

And what, I ask you, can you say to that?

I miss her like hell the next two weeks. I can't stop thinking about her. She's not out of my mind for two consecutive minutes. Even when I'm talking to people she's hovering there waiting to take over the moment I've no need to make any response.

Franklyn calls me in one day and I try to concentrate on what he's saying, which will be more than the friendly chat he starts the conversation with. He asks me how I'm settling down with the job and when I say okay he says he's glad, because he's happy with the way I'm shaping and he hopes I'll stay with them.

'Have you done anything about bringing your wife down?'

'No. Her mother's just had a serious operation and Ingrid doesn't want to leave her yet. She's a widow, you see.'

'Ah. Well, it's not the best weather for house-hunting. You'll perhaps be as well leaving it for a couple of months . . . Anyway . . .' He gets his fags out and we light up before he pulls a rolled print towards him and opens it out on his desk, weighting the corners with ash-trays and books. 'I've got a job here that I think will interest you. It's a bit tricky, so you'll have to keep your eyes open, but I think you'll cope with it all right.'

It's a design for a new-type seaside chalet-cum-bungalow based on a metal structure. The structure is what we're interested in and what Franklyn wants to quote for. The quotation, he tells me, has to be done in three ways, in quantities up to a thousand off. So it's worth having, and if it caught on it could be a nice steady line for years to come, with the jigs and templates paid for in the first order. The costing department will get the price out but before they can do that I shall have to sort out the structure from the rest of the assembly; and that's where the tricky bit comes in because it's all contained in one general assembly drawing with figures all over the place and the print we've got is a very bad one with some of the dimensions so near to unreadable that they'll have to be guessed at.

'We want eyesight money for this one,' I say, and Franklyn laughs.

'Yes, you'd think they could at least send us a decent print. I can write and ask them for another one, but there's a deadline on the job and I'd like you to push on as best you can in the meantime.'

'I think we can manage.'

'I'm sure you can. Have a word with Albert if there are any real snags. I'd have given it to him but he's got enough on his plate at the moment. And anyway, it's time you had something interesting to do.'

He flashes me a quick on-off smile and I leave him, taking the print with me.

I've got it spread out on my board when Jimmy passes by.

'You've got a right 'un there.'

'It's a beauty, isn't it?'

'You want a magnifying glass.'

I say aye, and laugh, thinking he's kidding, but he goes away to his own place and comes back in a minute.

'Here you are, then.'

He reckons to pore over the print with the glass, making little clucks and grunts in his throat.

'Yes, yes, Watson. It's quite obvious that this print was made by a left-handed Chinaman with dandruff who lives in Wapping.'

'But that's astonishing, Holmes. How do you know?'

'Elementary, my dear Watson. He's my brother-in-law.'

I'd forgotten that Jimmy was always fond of gadgets, like patent pencil-sharpeners, three-colour ballpens and circular slide rules.

'I can have your fingerprint outfit and false moustache if I need 'em, eh?'

'Any time.' He holds up the glass. 'With this in your hand a fascinating new world of flaws and imperfections is yours. Nothing is as it seems. Look at that line of typing on that material schedule. It looks perfect to you but I'll bet it isn't.'

He looks at it through the glass.

'No. The letter "s" throws a little to the right and above the line. Happens every time. Which shows that it was typed by a squint-eyed Portuguese from Hitchin, using the toes of his left foot.'

'Aye, I know,' I say, taking the glass from him and looking myself. 'He's your mother's cousin . . . You're right, though, it is out of line.'

'The magic glass reveals all.'

'Aye, well piss off then and I'll get it to reveal some of the dimensions on this print.'

'There's politeness,' he says, going away. 'Just return the glass when you've finished with it. No need to grovel in gratitude.'

I run the glass over the most blurred of the figures on the drawing and see that I can make them out now without much trouble. Then I sit back and light a fag, thinking of the best way of setting about the job. I pull the material schedule over. There'll be one of these to do when I've got all the bits and pieces sorted out. Then the costing boys will work out a price based on the amount of steel needed and the labour and jigs involved in cutting, drilling, welding, etc. Jimmy's aroused my curiosity about the typing and, knowing what way my mind's moving, I wonder, no more than casually, if all typewriters write with similar faults. There's a memo on my place, typed on Cynthia's machine, and I take that and examine it through the magnifying glass. No. There might be characteristics an expert could see, but nothing I can spot. I glance round to see that everybody's working then take out one of the anonymous letters – the first one, as it happens – and apply the glass. The shock I get then makes my heart give a little lurch. The letter 's' is slightly out of alignment to the right and above the line.

I let the first shock fade and then, finding I can't sit still, let alone concentrate on the job I ought to be doing, I go out and down the corridor to the bog, taking the magnifying glass with me. There, locked in a cubicle, I examine all three letters. I flush the lavatory as a cover, let myself out, and walk back, glancing into the general office as I pass. A little doll called Wendy Bamforth with hair like pink candy floss is sitting at the typewriter with the long carriage that's used for material schedules and anything else that's too wide for the other machines. I wonder who's been in there when nobody else was about and used it for typing anonymous notes.

'It's lovely for examining young women's nipples in naughty books,' Jimmy leers across at me as I go back into the office.

'What a filthy-minded beast you are, Slade,' I say.

19

There's no Donna at the end of the fortnight, when she should be back. The expected phone call on the Monday doesn't come through and late in the evening I go to the Mitre in the faint hope that she'll be there and then round to her flat where I get no reply to my ringing. I think of asking Conroy for Fleur's phone number and ringing up to find out what's happened, but decide that this might bring Fleur in on the act and the fewer people who know about me and Donna the better.

It's nearly the end of the week when I get a letter to tell me she's down with the 'flu: 'I did the final recording with a raging temperature then flopped straight into bed where I've been ever since until today when I've got up for just a little while. I'm glad I managed to finish the job, though. It was a very exciting part to do and my agent has rung since to say that everyone seems terribly thrilled with it and it looks like bringing me some more work.'

She can't say when she'll be back in circulation again but she hopes to see me soon. I send her a note in reply, telling her to take good care of herself and not to go out in the cold until she feels properly fit. Then I compose myself to wait for her in patience.

Another week passes by before I get the second letter, which tells me she's not coming back at all.

'My agent has got two more parts for me now, another one pending and next week I'm to read for a new B B C series. He says the management at the Palace are being very cooperative in releasing me from my contract, which has a little while left to run. Fleur's got this flat, which is ruinously expensive for one person, and wants me to share, so all in all it's best for me to stay in town now.

'Those are the professional and economic considerations. The other thing is us. Is it more immoral to have an affair with a man without trying to take him from his wife? Knowing something of the way your mind works I can imagine you probably arriving at this conclusion and becoming indignant at the way I've trifled with your affections. Dear Vic . . . Things are never as easy and clean cut as that. If I say that I don't want you to leave your wife for me you'll think that I never have had any real feeling for you, which isn't true. It would never work for us. Mistakes are terrible when you make them for yourself; they're doubly so when other people are involved.

'I'm writing this instead of seeing you and telling you because I don't want to argue with you and I don't want to quarrel, which we've been near to doing a couple of times. I want you to have time to work it out for yourself. If you decide you'd like to come and see me here I'll be glad. If you don't I'll miss you terribly, but understand.'

'Miss you terribly . . . understand . . . real affection . . .' Words. Words, words, words. And all I know is feelings: how much I want her. I feel as though my fingertips have brushed eternal joy and it's been snatched away from me. Of course I know there's no such thing. You just make the best possible bid for it, and this was mine. Perhaps the only chance I'll ever get.

I don't reply, thinking I'll at least see her when she moves her gear from the flat. But when four or five days go by without sight or sound of her I walk round there one night and let myself in with the key she lent me and I never gave her back. Most of the furniture is still there but Donna has gone. No record-player, records or books, an empty wall over the fireplace where the fried-egg picture hung, nothing in the kitchen cupboards and a collection of empty bottles under the sink, including half a dozen pint light ales.

It's the sight of these that really sets the melancholy flowing. The times here and at the Mitre seem like legendary days of happiness, never properly appreciated while they were here, and gone now for ever. The sadness is mixed with some anger and bitterness at the knowledge that she could come and go without telling me or wanting to see me. It hurts, and I'm standing there feeling very sorry for myself when I hear a noise behind me and look round to see a middle-aged man in a grey smock in the doorway.

'What are you doing here?'

'I'm a friend of Miss Pennyman's.'

'She's gone. She doesn't live here any more.'

'I know. I was just looking to see if she'd left anything behind.' He's watching me as if he thinks he ought to call the police.

'How did you get in?'

I hold up the key. 'With this. It's one of hers. Who are you, anyway, might I ask?'

'I live down below. I look after these flats. I saw the light from the street.'

'You'd better have this, then,' I say, walking towards him and holding out the key.

He takes it from me, standing aside to let me by. I walk out while he's still weighing it up, probably having dark thoughts about actresses and strange men with keys.

I live off wounded pride for some time after this. She shouldn't have done that, treating me like a child who can't be told the truth to his face and be expected to take it reasonably. Why should I run after her to London? What's in it for me? It's the full-scale banquet I want, not the crumbs from her table. Conroy lends a sympathetic ear when I pour most of it out over a pint one night and doesn't offer me useless advice or say I told you so. It helps a bit, I think, and we don't talk about it any more after that.

When Ingrid suggests coming down again I let her. She comes on the Friday night and I meet her at King's Cross and take her out to Longford, managing to drop into the conversation on the way the fact that she won't be meeting Donna because she's gone. She doesn't react openly to this but it must be welcome news and she can only be pleased. Conroy's as good as his word, running us round the town on Saturday morning. We have a look at a couple of new developments, the prices on the signboards making Ingrid gasp.

'Four and a half thousand for these poky little places! Honestly, Vic, it's daylight robbery.'

'That's the way it is down here. And like Albert says, you buy and sell in the same price range, so it doesn't make much difference in the end.'

When we're ready for lunch Conroy suggests running out of town and of all places he has to take us to the Coach and Horses, where Donna and I spent our last evening together. I don't know where we're going till we're nearly there and it's too late to get out of it. Conroy hasn't seen Ingrid for years and she never cared much for him when we all worked at Whittaker's. Now they've taken to each other straight away. Albert seems to be able to tune straight in on Ingrid's wavelength in a way I never could and she responds with a spirit I haven't seen in her for a long time. There's no doubt she's looking as attractive as she ever did and there'd be many who'd say I'm a lucky bloke to have her. I sit at the table, letting them talk, answering when I have to, but most of the time keeping quiet and missing Donna in a way that's almost like mourning for her.

Two days later I try to telephone but get Fleur who tells me that Donna's away for a few days. We have a bit of inconsequential chat and she asks after Albert who she hasn't apparently seen for some time. I tell Conroy this.

'I thought you'd be hopping into town at every available opportunity.'

He grunts. 'I haven't bothered. It was funny, but once she'd gone I somehow didn't care any more. A case of out of sight, out of mind.'

Just like that. Easy. And there are no other considerations stopping him. It gets me on thinking how wanton attraction is; how the world, which is short of love, is full of people loving in the wrong places at the wrong time. The great life force striking indiscriminately through all the barriers and restrictions, and causing as much misery as hate.

I try phoning again a week later and get no reply. If only I could snap my fingers and erase her from my memory. If I could treat it like a sickness and take a course of pills. Is hypnotism any good? Will time do the trick if I hang on long enough? Time does in fact begin to have some effect because during the next few weeks the pattern of wanting her changes gradually from a continuous almost unbearable longing to a consistent mild depression that goes off the deep end every day or two and plunges me into bouts of misery so bottomless and black I feel sure I'm on the edge of cracking up. It's in one of these attacks that I give in and admit I'm beaten. I've got to see her. It doesn't matter if it's not very often. It doesn't matter if I can't make love to her even. Just seeing her, talking to her, holding her hand in a pub, maybe; I'll settle for that. And when Ingrid comes down for good, well, I'll think of something. I'll find a way.

I set off straight after work one night, armed with an A to Z street guide, catching a train to Liverpool Street and transferring to the Underground there. It's a station I'm sick of the sight of; that and King's Cross. Which is quicker: change at Tottenham Court Road for Belsize Park or Oxford Circus for Finchley Road? I settle for Finchley Road. Just let me get there quick. It's nearly two months since I've seen her. I have to concentrate to see her face clearly in my mind.

Once off the main road at the other end I'm in a maze of curving avenues of big houses that I'd be hopelessly lost in without the guide. There are cars parked along practically every foot of the kerbs. Gascoigne Gardens. Here. It's beginning to rain. Number fifteen. Three bells. Royd on top, Lister below, Dunham in between. Press and wait. I'm here, Donna. I love you and all is forgiven.

In a moment there's a shadow looming behind the glass. The door opens. It's Fleur.

'Hello, Fleur.'

'Vic . . . Come in.'

I step into the hall and she shuts the door.

'Is it raining?'

'It's just starting. Is Donna in?'

'You'd better come up.'

I follow her shapely behind in tight tan trousers up the stairs and into the living-room that's sparsely furnished with a square of carpet and a few pieces of furniture. The fried-egg picture hangs on one wall.

'Did you ring up earlier?'

'No.'

'I wondered. I came in as the phone was ringing but it stopped before I could get to it.'

'Isn't Donna in?'

She's got a queer look on her face now but it's hidden as she bends to pick up cigarettes, the mane of red hair falling over one eye. We both take cigarettes and go through the business of lighting up.

'I'm afraid you've missed her.'

'Oh hell, what a shame. Will she be late back, do you know?'

'She's gone home.'

'What, to Cornwall, you mean?'

'Yes.'

'When's she coming back?'

'I don't know.'

'Well, she is coming back, isn't she?'

'Not for some time, I don't think.'

'Is there something wrong with her or something?'

Fleur gives a queer little shrug and pushes back her hair with one hand. Suddenly her eyes are closely watching my face.

'She thinks she's pregnant.'

I'm speechless. My mouth must look as if it's saying 'But . . . but . . .' only no sound comes out. They talk about history repeating itself, but this is ridiculous. I look behind me for a chair and sit down. Then I finally manage to say 'Oh Christ.'

The next one is one I should see coming but don't. First the feint with the left and then the right jab, rock hard and brutal, straight to the heart.

'I don't think she's told him yet.'

'Who?'

'Who? Carter. Who else?' Her eyes are still on me. 'Didn't you know about them?'

'I . . . I knew that . . . before . . .'

'I thought that was why you weren't seeing her any more.'

'You knew about us?'

'Yes, of course I did. You hadn't a price, Vic. She couldn't promise you anything with him around. She's been mad about him for years. When he came out to Longford it stirred it all up again.'

'That was why she couldn't make her mind up about the play.'

'Yes. And then the swine has to go and make her pregnant. I told her to get rid of it and make him pay. A friend of mine knows a place. A private nursing home. Clean and safe. A hundred guineas and no comeback. But she wouldn't listen. Said she'd go home and have the baby, if there was one, and try to sort herself out.'

'She isn't sure?'

'She's practically certain. I must say it looks like it to me.'

'Oh God, what a mess. I mean, what about her career and every-thing? All those parts . . .'

'She's just recorded another play. The other things fell through.'

I can't think straight. My mind's numb with shock.

'Will they get married, do you think?'

'I don't know.' She shrugs again and sits down across the room from me, smoking in short nervous puffs. 'It didn't work out when they were together before so I don't see what difference a wedding ring will make.'

'But the baby . . . and Donna's parents.'

'Donna's people aren't Victorian tyrants. They won't turn her out of the house.'

'God, what a mess,' is all I can think of to say again.

'It's all happened before, and it'll happen again.'

'You're right there.'

She uncurls herself and gets up.

'Would you like a drink? I expect you feel like one.' She crosses to a corner cupboard-cum-bookcase. 'I can't offer you any beer but there's some gin and some tonic to go with it. Oh, and a drop of sherry.'

'Gin and tonic, please.'

It's not my favourite tipple but it'll do for now.

'What about you, then? What are you doing now?'

'Oh, I'm all right. I'm doing commercials for bath soap.' She poses with one hand lifting her hair at the back. 'I sit around dressed in bubbles all day and get well paid for it. It's much easier than acting.'

She pours the drinks and hands me mine.

'Drink it down . . . It's not the end of the world, is it?'

'It feels bloody near, Fleur.'

'But you hadn't known her long.'

'It doesn't take long, love.'

She's having his baby, carrying it. I wish, I wish to God it was mine. A spasm of jealousy seizes me, so ferocious that I actually tremble and the glass shakes in my hand.

'You hadn't a chance, you know,' Fleur says.

'I didn't try hard enough,' I tell her.

I gulp at my drink. It tastes sour and strange, setting my teeth on edge and making me shudder.

'I'd better go,' I say in a minute. 'You'll probably be wanting to go out.'

She shakes her head, the thick glossy hair catching the light.

'No, I had a date but it fell through. I was going to have a quiet evening watching the telly, but you can take me out for a drink if you want company.'

'Some other time, Fleur. Thanks all the same.'

'Is that a promise?'

I look at her, feeling dim surprise. 'Well . . . yes.' I don't know if I mean it or not.

She comes downstairs with me. The flats open straight off the landings, the bottom one directly off the hall. There's a wireless playing very loud in one of the downstairs rooms, a man's voice booming at an audience who respond with laughter and applause.

'Anyway, don't let it cut you up,' Fleur says. 'There's plenty more pebbles on the beach.'

'Like my wife, for instance.'

It's a terrible thing to say, but what does she think all this is about?

We stand for a moment in the hall. She's got her hand on the knob but she doesn't open the door.

'Give me a ring when you're coming up again and we'll arrange something.'

'Okay, thanks.'

She moves slightly forward and to one side, looking directly at me. It's only a tiny movement, more a settling of her stance than anything else; but it tells me as plain as words that she wants me to kiss her. I take one step forward and pull her in, jamming my mouth down on hers with a force that presses her lips hard against her teeth.

'I always did like you better than Albert,' she says as we part. Poor old Conroy, I think. Is there no bloody justice in this world?

The rain falls steadily on me as I walk back to the station. Brown, the demon with women. Have I been carrying some charm about with me all these years that I didn't know about? I've asked myself before what it would be like to have that gorgeous body and now I know I could find out. Not tonight, perhaps, but another time, with a bit of application. And do I want it? Oh yes, I do. I remember the press of her thighs and the firmness of her breasts under the thin wool and it rages up through me as I walk along: animal longing, pure and simple. I'm almost tempted to go back, nursing some idea of purging my feeling for Donna through outrage.

I just miss a train and I'm by myself on the platform for a time. I stand near the edge and look down at the rails, the live one proud of the others. They usually wait till the train's rushing in, don't they? Then one step forward and out. Easy, but public, and more obviously violent than say a gun. They win hands down. The mood brings on the inclination to toy with the weapon, try it in the death-dealing position. Then the simple pressure of one finger. In private, at leisure. Pick your own moment. Messy for somebody, but not for you; you're finished with all messes. You're out of it. Out of the rotten cheat that runs through the middle of everything.

On the tube train I mull over the notion of getting out in the West End and walking about among the bright lights for a while, perhaps having a drink. I ought to eat as well. But I'm not hungry and it's a big, lonely town, too frightening for me.

God I hate railway stations. There was a time when they seemed romantic places, the entrances to holidays and exciting journeys. Now all I seem to see on them is derelicts and weirdies; like one chap standing very still watching the place names click over on one of the indicator boards. He's stocky and muckily dressed in a long overcoat over trousers with wide ragged bottoms that slop over his boots and touch the floor; a red ugly face and this awful round flat depression in his skull that looks for all the world as if somebody's clouted him with the business end of a hammer. I stand beside him for a moment to check what time the next train for Longford leaves.

On that train, with forty minutes in front of me and nothing to read except the postal information in my diary, I try cursing Donna, thinking about her hopping out of bed with me and in with Carter. What if I'd gone to London straight away? Would she have slept with both of us? The cheap tart, the rotten little bitch. But it's not true. I don't mean it. I love her and I'm calling her to relieve my feelings and it doesn't work.

A pint. Drain off some of the tension. I go into the first pub I find after leaving the station, entering by the first door I come to. I sink a quarter of the first pint in one go then put my change away, open a new packet of fags, light one and try to take stock. I'm a nit; I ought to be back there in town chatting Fleur up instead of moping here on my own. I'm flattered. I didn't know I had the physical magnetism to attract a bird like Fleur. She must have plenty of offers. She's not without choice. Perhaps it would work on other women as well. Maybe I ought to put it to the test. Have every one that's willing. Have 'em and heave 'em. Spit on women in my career as a ram. To prove what?

She wouldn't have gone with Carter if I'd followed her straight away instead of nursing my pride. She didn't hear from me, thought I'd done with her. I could have gone to her and played for time enough to make her see things my way, persuaded her that I needed her and it *could* work for us. I just didn't try hard enough.

There's another room behind the partition, a bigger, posher place, and the mirror behind the bar lets me see into it. Among the flash and colour of bottles and glasses I catch a reflection of pinkish candy-floss hair. A second later a chap blocking my view moves aside and I can see that it's Wendy Bamforth. Sitting with her, in a black suit, white shirt and narrow scarlet tie, his hair slicked up with grease, is Wally Chisholm, a smirk on his face as he talks to her and she listens, her eyes fixed on him in an expression that tells him he's Rock Hudson's measure any day of the week.

I'm so surprised I nearly drop my glass. I step back out of their view and lean on the partition, thinking now about something that's suddenly as plain as the nose on your face.

I wait half an hour for them to move, drinking another two pints and keeping an eye on them as best I can without letting them spot me. When they both stand up together I empty my glass and follow them out, giving them a start before stepping out of the doorway and walking after them. They take their time, strolling along with their arms round each other in a touching picture of young love, and I have to keep stopping and looking in shop windows, hoping neither of them will turn round and see me in the light. Once they leave the main road, though, it's tricky in another way: there's less chance of them recognizing me now but more of them realizing they're being followed; especially as they don't step up the pace at all.

But I manage to trail them without arousing their suspicions and they lead me into a council estate on the edge of the town. They stop for a moment at a gate then open it and go through. I'm thinking that if he's got his feet under the table I'll be in for a long wait. But no, they walk into the shadows along the side of the house. I can hear them talking in low voices as I pass by, and make out the shape of them as they snuggle together for a good night snogging session.

I cross the road and walk back on the other side. I'm about ten yards past the house going back the way we came when Wally comes up the path and I hear the gate-latch click. I let him draw level with me than start to cross over, calling to him:

'Chisholm. Hey, Chisholm.'

He checks for a moment, looking round.

'Who is it?'

'I want to talk to you, Chisholm.'

He begins to run. He goes fast but he hasn't got much of a start and though I'm not as sound in wind and limb as I once was I don't have any bother keeping close behind him. Instead of making for the lighted main streets where I can't get him he turns off down a side road. At the far end there's a group of half-built houses with piles of bricks and timber and rubble round them. He makes into these and for a minute I think I've lost him. Then I hear the clatter of his feet on a plank as he crosses a trench and a second later he falls full length over a wheelbarrow. I follow the sounds, stepping as carefully as I can among all the hazards there in the dark, and come on him as he's picking himself up, swearing.

'Now then.'

'What's wrong?' he says. 'What do you want?'

'Don't tell me you don't know, Wally boy.'

He looks at me, pretending to recognize me for the first time.

'I didn't know it was you.'

'Who did you think it was?'

'There's some blokes. They've got it in for me. There was some trouble in a pub one night.'

'What have you been doing to 'em? Sending letters to their wives?'

'I don't know what you mean.'

I manoeuvre him so he's got his back to the wall of a contractor's shed and I'm blocking his way out. He looks at me all innocent.

'I don't know what you mean, honest.'

'You're a nasty malicious little tick, Chisholm. You want stamping on. Just because I once showed you up in front of your old feller you have to get your revenge. Well he was the one to blame. Why don't you send letters about him to your mam?'

'Look, I don't know what you're on about and I'm not standin' here talking all night. I've got to get home.'

'You'll go when I'm ready to let you go, lad. I'm interested in the way your warped little mind works. Wendy Bamforth knows already.'

'What's she been saying about me?'

'She's your girl friend isn't she? What would she say? You wrote some anonymous letters to my missis and Wendy's so bloody overseen in you she typed 'em up and got my address out of the office file.'

'You're barmy, mate.'

'Am I, then? Would you like me to take it to Franklyn? He'll soon have the truth out of her.'

He sneers. 'You wouldn't dare do that. You wouldn't dare.'

'Oh? How's that, then?'

He's given himself away and he covers as quick as he can.

'If she's been saying things like that she's –'

'She's what? Suppose I tell you I worked it all out for myself?'

He's losing his front. He can't carry it off.

'You daren't tell Franklyn. You'd have to tell him you'd –'

He stops again.

'Tell him what, Wally? What wouldn't I like him to know?'

'You know.'

'What, Wally?' I get hold of his lapels and pull him close. 'You tell me.'

'About that bird at the theatre.'

'Why, you vicious little get!'

I slap him twice across the face, once with the front of my hand and once with the back, on the return stroke. It rouses him. He swings at me. He's no waster, Wally, and there's some weight behind his fist. But when I dodge that same weight carries him forward off balance so that I can land him one that slams him back against the side of the hut.

'I'll bloody teach you to interfere with me.'

There's all the rows and worry about the letters plus the loss of Donna packed into the next one. It buries itself in his guts, punching the wind out of him in a grunting gasp and sending him down. He groans and one arm comes up to cover his face.

'Leave me alone.'

He must be expecting the boot going in, which is probably what he'd do to me in his position. But I've finished.

'Just remember, mate, I'm watching you from now on, and if you step out o' line just once I'll really get you.'

I walk away from him. My heart's pounding and my hands tremble. Violence upsets me. I always hold that it's hardly ever an answer to anything. But by God, there's pleasure in it sometimes. In a minute or two a strange kind of exhilaration seems to take hold of me. I feel that I'm walking tall, my legs and spine stretched, and lightly, on the balls of my feet, my heels not touching the ground. I've got an urge to do something wild. I'd like to smash something, indulge myself in some enormous act of destruction.

Conroy's car is standing in the drive when I get to the house. I halt and look at it. I passed a test once so that I could drive Mr Van Huyten about; but then he stopped going out much and finally sold the car. My licence must still be in order but it's twelve months since I've been behind a wheel. But I'd like to drive like hell down winding country lanes, not caring about bends or other traffic; just hurling the car on through the night. To somewhere . . .

I try the door. It's locked. I go into the house and up the stairs to bed, thinking it's perhaps just as well.

20

So now I'm going home to hurt a good woman who loves me. I shall put the knife in and watch it stab her to the heart. But a swift clean wound that will heal. Not the steadily festering sore that would be our life together from now on. This is for me and for her as well. Because it's right for both of us in the end and before it's too late. I can turn away her love that wants to keep me now, not knowing what's to come, and see that it'll pass and there'll be a new life, a better life, for her as well as for me. The loneliness will be bad for both of us and it would be easy now for me to settle for the comfort of what I know, and what I know I shall miss. Until she learns to hate me for not being what she wanted and has every right to expect and what she'll find with somebody else if she's lucky.

The obvious thing is the easiest to do. And the one that would keep me popular. What I'm doing is hard. Being a hero in the front circle of the pictures with everybody approving is one thing; the real-life hero with nobody looking on to tell him he's brave is another. And so is doing what you know is right when you're dead certain everybody will think you're a bastard for it.

So do I expect a medal for it? What has what 'they' think got to do with my life? They'll think what they like whatever you do and some might be right and some might be wrong. But they can't know because nobody lives inside your skin but you. Not sometimes now and again, but always, waking and sleeping, twenty-four hours a day, from the day you were born till the day you die. How to mend a fuse, fill up a form, buy a house: that's advice anybody can give and take. How to live your life depends on knowing who you are, and who you hope to be. And it's hard enough to sort out for yourself without bringing somebody else in on the act. In the last resort you're on your own. Nobody knows but you. It's you who makes the decisions and lives with them.

So am I expecting approval for what I'm going to do? Do I send a memo round explaining, so I won't be misjudged? And if I do and manage to get it all down accurately, will they understand then?

Because after all of it I could be wrong. But that's for me to find out, and you can only take one step at a time, doing the right thing as you see it – the right thing for *you*. Which isn't selfish. It means that having done what's right for you, you're a better person in relation to everybody round you. Except the ones who think you're a bastard and will be hurt for ever because you haven't done the right thing as they see it.

You can't win. But nobody's totting up a score and there aren't any prizes at the end of the line. You just plod on regardless.

You can tell I'm no hero because I think of all these things.

Scene One is the living-room, Saturday night; nearly twenty-four hours have passed by while I waited for the right moment to speak and realized that there is no right moment to say what I have to say; that you've got to make the moment and you badly need the services of one of these drawing-room scriptwriters who'll set it up in one of those scenes where stiff upper lip manages to say in cut-glass accent: 'Felicia, I want you to give me a divorce.' All very cool and calm and civilized, emotions kept firmly under control . . .

'It's that girl, isn't it?'

'No.'

'You're going with her. Those letters were right all the time.'

'No. I'm not going with her. She's gone away.'

'Where has she gone?'

'Home, to Cornwall. She's . . . she's having a baby.'

'Not yours?'

I'm staggered at her calmness, but then I realize it's like the stillness of a coiled spring and I wonder what will press the catch and unleash it.

'No, not mine.'

'Could it have been yours?'

'I haven't seen her for months.'

'That's not what I meant.'

Her control is amazing considering the questions she's asking and the answers I have to give her.

'Yes, then.'

A long shuddering sigh passes through her.

'I knew it. I knew it all the time.'

'Those letters were pure malice, Ingrid.'

'I'm not bothered about the letters now.'

'Ingrid, I . . .'

I can't get over the way she's taking it, as though it's something she's prepared herself for and is going to see through as bravely as possible. And it's almost to me as though I really love her. I'm nearer to it now than I've ever been since the very beginning. Tenderness even. I want to put my arms round her and comfort her and say, 'Oh, love, love, love. I'm sorry, but it's got to be this way.'

And would that make it any easier for her to take? Perhaps I should make her hate me, so that she'll be glad to see me go. I feel like a priest in the Spanish Inquisition comforting some poor sod they're going to roast alive. 'Ah, my son, my son, the flames will purify you and bring you into the everlasting radiance of God's grace.' 'Stuff God's grace. Let me out of here!'

'There's that money Mr Van Huyten left me . . . half of it's yours. You've got your job; you'll be all right.'

'Oh, Vic, I don't understand all this. I don't know what you want, what you mean. Why do you want to break things up, all this, nearly four years of marriage? We're all right, aren't we?'

'Yes, we're all right. As all right as thousands of couples, I'd say. And we might go on being all right in the same way. Eventually we'd have kids and we'd squabble and bicker a bit and watch 'em grow up. And then they'd leave us and we'd be on our own, glad of a bit of peace and quiet after it all. And we might grow together and find it's what we've waited all our lives for – or we might find we've nothing to say to each other. D'you think I don't know how warm and cosy it is in here? It's cold outside, but I've got to go out and find what there is there for me. And I'm going to do it while there's till time for both of us.'

'But I've got what I want. I don't want anything else. Oh, I know we fight sometimes and we don't see eye to eye on a lot of things, but it's what I want.'

'You deserve something better. You deserve a chap who'll love you as you ought to be loved, who'll marry you because he wants to spend the rest of his life with you. Really wants to – and nothing and nobody twisting his arm. There's still time for you to find him. It's not too late yet, but it will be. Every year that passes it'll get more and more too late. It'll close in on us and fasten us a bit tighter.'

'Isn't that what all marriages are like?'

The tears are there now, plain to see; and suddenly I'm scared I'll get too sorry for her till I can't do what I have to do.

'It's a sham,' I shout. 'It's phoney from start to finish. It's got nothing to do with anything that's of any value at all. There's a whole world out there that I know next to nothing about and I want to see it and hear it and taste it. I want to *live* in it, and I just don't think I can do it with you.'

'But you could have with her?' Ingrid's voice is still quiet, but under it there's all the jealousy in the world and the hate one woman feels for another woman who's touched something of hers.

'Yes.' I turn away. All at once I can hardly get the words through my clogged throat. 'Yes, I could have with her.'

'And I suppose you found all this out when she got down on her back and opened her legs for you!'

Here's the venom now, the words spat out, each one a bullet of vicious contempt.

'That had nothing to do with it.'

'I don't believe you. I know you and I don't believe you.'

'It's not a question of not believing. You can't understand.'

'A misunderstood husband. That's original!'

'You can't understand because sex is the only thing you've ever given me that we could share.'

'Oh God. Oh, you rotten bugger. You rotten bugger to say a thing like that to me when she's off carrying another man's baby.'

'Look, I'm sorry, I didn't mean it like that.'

'What makes her better than me, except you're the only man I've ever slept with? Is that something to hold against me? How do I compete with a cheap bitch like that? Do I have to go out and find a few more men to sleep with and get a bit of experience?'

'Will you keep her out of this? She's gone, I tell you, she's gone.'

'But it's her all the same. Do you think it doesn't hurt to know you've had her? That you've touched me while you've been having her? Well, I'd have forgiven you that . . .'

'Thank you very much.'

'Yes, I'd have forgiven you that. But you cared for her. You cared!'

'And that's what you can't stand?'

'Yes. It's what I can't stand.'

'I believe you'd rather I'd gone with a tart off the streets than had a genuine feeling for another woman.'

'I'd rather you'd *killed* somebody!'

She spits it at me, eyes scorching my face, before slamming out, leaving me shaken and shocked, shocked to the very core.

I light a cigarette, wondering how I imagined it could end in anything but hate. And I thought that writing a letter was cowardly, that I ought to have it out face to face. Now I know why people who are away just stay away, and those who are here slip off leaving a note. So that there won't be the terrible scars of the knives people ram into each other. No hate to kill all the fondness there's ever been.

I hear the water running in the bathroom and wonder what she's doing. I'm suddenly scared she'll harm herself and I go through and try the door. It's locked. I tap on it.

'Ingrid.'

There's no reply and I say her name again.

'What do you want?'

'What are you doing?'

'I'm having a bath.'

'Are you all right?'

'What difference does it make to you?'

Perhaps she's cutting her wrists this very second, I think, all sorts of visions running wild through my mind along with newspaper headlines like 'Jilted wife found dead in bathroom ... Husband admits quarrel ... I was leaving her, he said ...'

I want to go now, walk out before there's any more of it. But I'm scared. Unreasonably scared stiff. But still scared. And shaken. I finish my cigarette, holding it with a hand that trembles like somebody with palsy. In the morning, I think. We'll talk about it then. Calmer. In the morning.

Scene Two starts with weeping in the night which develops into hysterics in the living-room when I leave the bed and take refuge there in the cold light beside the dead ashes of the fire.

'Don't you walk out when I'm talking to you.'

'I thought you were just crying.'

'I was saying something.'

'I've heard enough. I don't want to hear any more.'

She takes a running kick at me, the hard sole of her slipper catching me a painful clout on the shin.

'You'll bloody listen when I talk.'

'And I'll break your bloody neck if you do that again.'

I rub my shin, thinking how near it all is to farce. All it needs is a slight shift in tone and it would send an audience wild.

She draws herself up in her dressing-gown.

'You can go when you're ready.'

'That wasn't what you were saying before.'

'It's what I'm saying now.'

'Righto, then.'

I go into the bedroom. I've dressed and got my grip packed in less than five minutes.

'I'll write to you about the arrangements.'

'What arrangements?'

'Things'll have to be sorted out, won't they?'

'I don't want anything of yours.'

'Half of it's yours.'

She says nothing. I get my overcoat.

'So long, then.'

'Are you going now?'

'Yes.'

'There aren't any trains running at this time, are there?'

'I'll find something.'

'You can't go to your Christine's, can you?' she says. 'She's heard it before.'

'I should never have come back that time.'

'You should never have married me.'

'I thought I was doing the right thing.'

'You think you are now, don't you?'

'Yes.'

'There's nothing else I can say, then, is there?'

'No, not really. Only, I'd like to think we could part as . . . as friends.'

She's standing with her back to me, looking into the cold grey ashes of the fire, but I hear quite clearly what she says.

'I hate you for what you've done to me.'

Scene Three finds me an hour and a half later, dropping from the cab of a lorry at the Ferrybridge roundabout on the A1. The driver leans out and gives me a friendly farewell.

'Hope you get there okay, chum. I'd stand the other side of the roundabout if I were you. There'll be plenty of 'em going south. You'll get fixed up.'

Nice bloke. I think he'd have liked company all the way to Grimsby. I shout good night and thanks as he goes on his way, pulling the big wagon across the intersection.

I feel very much on my own as his tail-lights disappear over the hill and the noise of his engine dies. Quiet. I walk round and stand on the southbound lane, wondering how long it'll be before another Good Samaritan takes pity on me, but not daring to start walking on because that'll take me on to the clearway where they're less likely to stop.

There's a high, almost cloudless sky with plenty of stars and it's quite light when you've been out a bit. But cold.

It's over with. There'll be some music to face from the others later on: my mother and father, Chris, Mrs Rothwell ('I always told you so.') and maybe even young Jim. But the deed's done. I'm free. You say something and a matter of hours later it's all over; nearly four years gone.

And God! Oh God! what a terrible thing. I'm thinking of her, small and scared and lonely in that flat and me, small and scared and lonely here. And Donna . . . Is it dark and cold in Cornwall as well? Ah, Donna, Donna, I'm standing here on the roadside in the middle of the night. Going where, and to what?

Headlights suddenly rake the sky. I watch them approach and sweep round the big island. I wait for them to hit me and light me up before stepping forward and raising my arm.

Going forward, I'm thinking as I wonder if he'll stop. It's all you can do. Going in fear and trembling, maybe, but forward, knowing the best and hoping against hope that it'll come to you; and just refusing to notice, just simply trying not to acknowledge, how cold and dark it is outside.

More About Penguins

Penguin Book News, an attractively illustrated magazine which appears every month, contains details of all the new books issued by Penguins as they are published. Every four months it is supplemented by *Penguins in Print*, which is a complete list of all books published by Penguins which are still available. (There are well over two thousand of these.)

A specimen copy of *Penguin Book News* can be sent to you free on request, and you can become a regular subscriber at 3s. for twelve issues (with the complete lists). Just write to Dept EP, Penguin Books Ltd, Harmondsworth, Middlesex, enclosing a cheque or postal order, and your name will be added to the mailing list.

Some other Penguins by Stan Barstow are described overleaf.

Note: *Penguin Book News* and *Penguins in Print* are not available in the U.S.A. or Canada.

Also by Stan Barstow

A Kind of Loving

The magnificent forerunner of *The Watchers on the Shore*.
A young man is physically infatuated with a girl he
doesn't love. Inevitably he gets caught, for miracles only
happen in fairy tales. His struggles to find a solution
to a classic problem are told by Stan Barstow with a
realism and honesty that put his first novel into a
class of its own.

Ask Me Tomorrow

With a first novel in his typewriter and two women
on his hands Wilf Cotton finds life away from home
a lot freer – and more complicated –
than he expected . . .

The Desperadoes and Other Storie

A group of young tearaways on a night out that begins
with horse-play and ends in tragedy; the loneliness
of a drunken miner's wife; a war-shocked ex-sailor
forced beyond endurance – these are some of the stories
included in this collection.

Not for sale in the U.S.A.